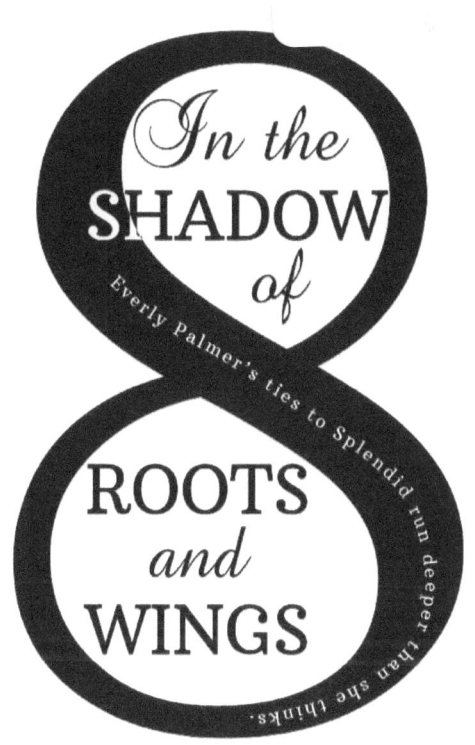

In the SHADOW of ROOTS and WINGS

Everly Palmer's ties to Splendid run deeper than she thinks.

A.D. BRAZEAU

In the Shadow of Roots and Wings
Copyright © 2025 AD Brazeau
All rights reserved.

ISBN: (ebook) 978-1-964636-49-8
(print) 978-1-964636-50-4

Inkspell Publishing
207 Moonglow Circle #101
Murrells Inlet, SC 29576

Edited By Yezanira Venecia
Cover art By Emily's World By Design

DEDICATION

For the seekers. Never stop asking questions.

AD BRAZEAU

PART ONE
Repetition

AD BRAZEAU

CHAPTER ONE

The hero was dead.

Even though she hadn't spoken to Nathan Stratton in ages, Everly wasn't sure how her story would continue without him living in the world. She'd thought there was time, time to reconnect, time to apologize. But the realization that she was wrong, that time—her time—was finite, had shaken her to her core.

Everly stepped out of her rental car, golden leaves skating across the blacktop in the fresh mountain breeze. Mid-October was still hot in Splendid, Colorado, the temperature in the seventies, the sun bright and full overhead.

The Octobers of her childhood had not been this warm. By this time of year, her mom would light the fireplace in the evenings before making cocoa, and Everly would decide which coat would look best over her Halloween costume. With the weather this warm, Mom probably still had the A/C on full blast.

Everly peeled off the black blazer she wore over a boring black shift dress, not wanting to sweat from the heat, even though nervous perspiration dampened her underarms and the small of her back.

She'd flown through a blizzard to get there, white-knuckling the arm of her seat as the plane's tail swished in the wind, thick snow pummeling the windows like balls zinging around a pinball machine. The entire southern part of the state was a blanket of white, but of course, the second the plane broke through Splendid airspace, all was calm and quiet.

Tardy by design, Everly scanned the parking lot. The inevitable social situation would be far less awkward if she slipped in late. She planned to hover near the back of the crowd, mix in with Nathan's acquaintances and work friends. There was a possibility *they* wouldn't even see her, those friends who'd once been her whole world. If she remained hidden, she could pay her respects to Nathan and leave without ever having to perform the usual niceties with a fake smile plastered across her face.

Everwood Cemetery hadn't changed much in the almost thirty years since Everly had been there last. There was a new section off to the north with smaller, more modern markers, but thick oak trees—over two hundred years old— still shaded almost the entire sprawling property as deer lounged among tombstones as old as the trees. They used to come here in high school, she and her friends. They would come at night, never during the day, to tell ghost stories and investigate whispers of hauntings for her *Haunted Happenings* column in the school paper.

The group would nestle themselves between the tombs of their ancestors, basking in their shared camaraderie, the unique and safe perspective that living in Splendid provided. She would have done anything for them. They had not felt the same.

Everly shook off the memory. None of them had spoken to her in twenty-nine years, what felt like a lifetime. Those people were no longer her friends.

The gravesite was near the oldest section of the

cemetery. Nathan's family was an old one in Splendid, among the first to settle in the area. Not the very first, like hers, but close. His family crypt stood tall, proud, and Greek, with intricate Corinthian columns and expensive marble encasing the entire structure. On the large expanse of green grass off to the right was where the service would occur, long rows of white chairs already occupied by somber-looking, well-dressed people. This was fine with Everly. There was no way she'd stay long enough to get comfortable.

She took up the rear, standing back, out of the way.

Many of the women wore hats to shade themselves from the bright sun. Smart. All Everly could do was shade her already shiny forehead with her hand as she squinted toward the front of the crowd.

An older man she didn't recognize stood at a podium, the minister, she assumed, alongside a table holding an urn, some flowers, and a large portrait of Nathan Stratton. His smile beamed from the frame, his face as cheerful as it always was, eyes bright and warm. He had aged, but aged well. She wasn't sure how old he was when the picture had been taken, but he was far older than the last time she'd seen him when they'd been teenagers in their final year of high school.

Nathan had become her confidant, her sounding board after the others had begun to freeze her out. He had continued to check in on her, calling her every other night to listen to her latest conspiracy. At least for a while. After a time, even Nathan had had his fill. Still, he'd never been unkind to her, and at graduation, the last time she'd seen him, he handed her a single yellow rose with words of congratulations. They'd hugged one final time.

Everly's throat tightened. She bit down on the inside of her lip to keep the tears welling in her eyes from falling. Nathan had been too young. Whatever had happened, he'd been too young.

Her gaze scanned the first few rows of white chairs.

There were the friends of her past, sitting all together in a row, directly behind Nathan's mom and sister.

There was no misrecognizing Rose. The most gorgeous, brilliant woman to ever live. Every girl who met Rose was instantly jealous, but at least in high school, Rose didn't care about beauty. Which, Everly supposed, made Rose even more annoying. Her lightened hair was long, much longer than it had been in school, hanging in loose waves over the back of her chair. When she turned her face to talk to Fletcher, the sun glinted off the bronzed skin of her perfect cheekbones. From this vantage point, she didn't appear to have aged a day. Not that Everly was surprised. These days, Rose was a multi-millionaire, bestselling author of young adult fiction. She had the money to spend on keeping the years at bay.

Fletcher, from what she could tell, had aged but not poorly. His salt and pepper hair was cut short, and his dark skin creased around his eyes, but only slightly and in a way that can be attractive on men as they age.

Everly squinted. She couldn't tell if the woman who sat on the other side of Fletcher was Leigh. Everly knew that Fletcher and Leigh had married halfway through their time at Yale, but this lady couldn't be Leigh. From what Everly could tell, the woman was gaunt, sunken almost. What was once porcelain skin now appeared sallow. She wore a scarf around her head, and she didn't seem to have any hair, which made Everly wonder if she was ill.

Everly's gut pinched. She hoped it wasn't Leigh. Not that she'd wish illness on anyone, but Leigh ... she had been the heart of them all. And they had kids, two that Everly knew of. Stalking social media was her hobby when the nights grew long.

The knots in her stomach released by a few degrees. Jonathan wasn't there. Recognizing him would have been easy, since Everly hadn't been able to get him and her regrets out of her head since the day she left. Seeing the others was bad enough, but being face-to-face with

Jonathan would have been a nightmare.

"Thank you all for coming." The loud, deep voice of the minister startled Everly out of her thoughts. "Let us begin."

The service had been longer than Everly had anticipated, but Nathan was accomplished, so there'd been a lot of ground to cover. The minister spoke for at least forty-five minutes before asking if anyone would like to say a few words.

Please let this be brief.

Everly's feet were getting sore inside the brand-new pumps she'd bought at the airport, the sun at her back scorching her bare shoulders.

The first person to leap to their feet was Rose. No surprise there. In a moment of terror, Everly realized that if Rose were to speak, she would be directly in Rose's line of sight. There was nothing to do except take the full assault of Rose's stare of death. In high school, Rose had been known for this stare, so coined by Fletcher, because she could make a person want to lie down and die simply by glaring at them.

Everly breathed through the butterflies in her stomach. She wanted to turn and flee, but bit the inside of her lip instead as she tried to remind herself that she was a grown-up and she no longer cared what they thought.

Rose swept to the podium, her black lace dress fishtailing out behind her. She pushed her hair back over a shoulder, staring at the stand before her. Then, after a few seconds, she took a deep breath and looked up at the friends and loved ones gathered to celebrate Nathan's life. She looked more beautiful than ever.

A breath caught in the back of Everly's throat before Rose began to speak. "This is a sad day for us all. Jenny, Abby, Charlie." She looked toward Nathan's mom and sister, and a younger-looking man sitting next to them. Everly hadn't noticed him before. Keeping up with Nathan's life had been harder without a social media presence. "We share in your grief. For the three of us—myself, Fletcher, and Leigh—we feel we've lost a part of ourselves. We will forever be incomplete. Nathan was—" Rose stopped.

Everly had been staring at the back of Leigh's head. *Shit, that is her.* When Rose paused so abruptly, Everly's stomach dropped to her toes. Everly looked up to see Rose staring right at her, or more likely, trying to stare a hole straight through her.

Everly sucked in a breath, passing a hand over her belly. She refused to let Rose see her shake, although she was quaking inside.

Fletcher and Leigh turned in their chairs, along with everyone else. Everly felt like she was inside a fishbowl. But, instead of retreating, which she wanted to do with all she was, she dug her heels into the grass and smiled. She smiled at everyone, teeth out, at a funeral, like the freak she was.

Fletcher's face was unreadable. Leigh smiled back, just for a second, before turning back around.

"Nathan was the best of us," Rose continued, not looking away from Everly. The sea of bodies turned back to face Rose. "The smartest of us, the kindest. As the city's chief historian, his passion was for preserving Splendid's rich history. He wrote three books about our town, one of which earned him an invitation to the White House to meet with other historians from all over the nation. That was only six months ago. Nathan was giddy when he returned, talking about some new archival techniques he learned while there and how he couldn't wait to use these techniques at the museum. That was Nathan, always thinking about how best he could serve the history of Splendid. He served us, as well, as the sweetest friend we could have ever asked for. Thank you, Nathan, for blessing us with your life." Rose's voice broke on the last word, and she finally looked away from Everly.

Rose resumed her seat on shaky legs. Fletcher reached his arm around her. The young, good-looking man named

Charlie rose to speak, but Everly couldn't bear to stand there any longer. Her feet and back were killing her, her heart as broken as her body felt.

The cemetery's old and grand trees shaded her as she walked away from the mess of her former life. She'd done what she came to do. She said goodbye to Nathan.

The cemetery was different during the day. She'd only ever been there at night when she and her friends would break in long after the caretaker had gone to bed in his brick cottage at the back of the property. Once inside, they'd find a gravestone, always a different one, sit around it, and light a candle or flick on a small flashlight. Then, they'd tell each other spooky stories or discuss a new case for the *Haunted Happenings* column.

Haunted Happenings was Everly's brainchild, a way for her to explore some of the stranger stories the locals whispered about. She and her friends had worked on the school newspaper together. The five of them did everything together until that final semester of school. Everly had her column, and Nathan had his *Historical Hotspot*. Leigh and Rose wrote the harder-hitting pieces, articles on teacher pay, and sexual harassment. Fletcher was the photographer, constantly snapping pictures for the paper or just for fun. Rose called him the paparazzi but squealed with delight anytime he turned his camera on her.

Strolling through the cemetery in the daylight was a new experience. Less scary and more calming. The hot sun filtered through the leaves and branches, dappling the green grass with specks of gold. These were the colors of Splendid, deep, earthy greens of grass, leaves, and pine needles, and bright yellow golds of aspen leaves and sunlight. If your gaze traveled further west, you'd be greeted by other colors, such as the deep blues and purples of the Rocky Mountains, but Splendid was all greens and yellows.

Everly strode toward the back of the cemetery, to the section she knew was the oldest. The markers here were more prominent, some tall obelisks, some giant slabs of granite or marble. Most were so old that the names and epitaphs were faded, barely legible in some places. She'd never been that far in, but something propelled her away from the funeral, in the direction opposite her car. The farther she walked, the quieter it was.

A tall gravestone, the likes of which she'd never seen, caught her eye. She moved toward what appeared to be a cylindrical column. As she drew closer, she realized the column was a tree trunk.

"Wow." She ran her hand over what felt like plaster, spread on the piece in a way that made it look like real bark. A few branches jutted off at various angles, adding to the naturalistic effect. A symbol was etched below the epitaph.

She pulled her reading glasses out of her vintage handbag, then knelt on the ground. She'd seen Mason's symbols on graves many times, but never had she seen anything like this. This was a figure eight, the symbol for infinity, lying on its side. Inside one loop was a wing, and inside the other was a tree with exposed roots. She ran her finger over and around the loops. There was something familiar about the symbol, but she couldn't say what.

Unusual, for sure.

She stood, pulling out her phone to snap a photo of the grave. If anything, this may be fun to investigate, to give her something to do while she was in Splendid. Standing back to line up her picture, she spied another tree trunk-like grave not far off.

"What in the world?"

She captured her picture, then took off for the second grave.

"Everly." The deep, smoky voice that called out was unmistakable.

I should have gone to my car. Why hadn't she done that?

Everly turned her heel in the grass. "Hi, Rose."

There was a glare behind Rose. The sun streaming through tree limbs framed her in goddess-like light. She stood before Everly in her designer dress, her sky-high heels in one hand. They were probably too expensive to get dirty.

Everly was right about one thing: Rose hadn't aged a day. Even up close, she'd barely changed. Matured, maybe, her face a little slimmer in the cheeks, but all in all, she looked the same.

Rose wasn't alone. Fletcher and Leigh, hand in hand as always, walked up behind her.

Rose glanced over her shoulder at them momentarily, then directed her attention back at Everly. "We were surprised to see you here. Pleasantly surprised."

The sentiment took Everly a little aback. She needed a second to compose her thoughts and make sure she didn't say anything stupid, but then matched Rose's honesty with her own. "I surprised myself. Mom told me what happened last week, but I didn't decide to come until this morning. A last-minute plane ticket meant a back-row seat."

"Sitting by the bathrooms is the worst." Rose looked Everly up and down. "You look great, Ever. You've hardly changed."

Everly blinked in surprise. Not only had Rose been friendly so far, but she'd used the nickname she'd given her in preschool. Before Everly could respond, Leigh moved up alongside Rose.

"Hardly a wrinkle," Leigh said. "And the same chestnut hair I always envied. Now, I'd take *some* hair. Any kind." Leigh touched the edge of her blue head scarf. Her once bright blue eyes were dull and bloodshot, the skin around them sunken and dark.

Discomfort edged around Everly's gut as her mind scrambled for something to say. She ran a hand through her hair, then felt like maybe that was showing off. She wanted to throw up. Social interactions had never been her strong suit. "It's dyed these days. There are so many grays, I'm considering letting it go."

How do you ask a former best friend about her apparent illness? Was it rude to ask, or was it rude not to ask? If only someone would speak and save her from this moment.

Everly glanced over at Fletcher, who was staring off into space. He looked like his dad had when they were in school, except Fletcher was more fit. His hair was more gray than black, his face smooth, except for two deep parentheses lines on either side of his mouth, and the crinkles around his eyes.

Rose cleared her throat. "Well, how long are you staying?"

Everly shrugged, grateful that the spell of awkwardness had been broken. She shifted her feet. God, they hurt. "Not sure. I don't have a return flight, so I might stay for a few days. I haven't seen my mom in years."

"Of course you haven't." Leave it to Rose to get in one good shot.

"Yeah, well, I'll see you guys around." Everly took off toward the parking lot. Drawing this out any longer was pointless. She heard Leigh say something behind her, but Everly was already twenty feet away, and there was no way she was turning around.

She flung off the too-tight pumps as she marched through the grass, past tombstone after tombstone, not bothering to retrieve them. They didn't fit anyway, kind of like her.

CHAPTER TWO

This new insanity felt a lot like déjà vu.

Rose watched through narrowed eyes as Ever ran off like she always did. To say *had* was better. Ever *had* run off. The day after graduation, she'd split town, leaving behind everyone and everything. Ever had no qualms about ghosting them all, and Rose still felt the acid taste of what that day felt like in the back of her throat.

That day, Rose had gone to Ever's house intending to smooth things over. She'd missed her best friend, their gatherings at the cemetery, and their meetings in the snug crow's nest on the third floor of Ever's house. There was a lot to miss. She and Ever had been inseparable since they were tiny. She'd had things to apologize for, but so had Ever. So, imagine her shock to find Everly Palmer had packed up her little Toyota and left town.

"Well, that was strange." Fletcher had his arm around Leigh. They, too, had turned to watch Ever run off through the graveyard.

"Did she fling her shoes off?" Leigh looked at Rose, her sunken eyes wide.

"Yeah, the faster to get away from us." Rose rubbed a

17

hand over her heart. She wasn't sure why, but there was a faint pain there, a phantom reminder of memories dead and buried.

The day was beautiful, and she preferred to focus on the fresh breeze, the warm sun, and the comfort of being with her friends. Her final friends. The thought sent a shiver through her despite the warm temperature. Although Ever wasn't dead, she'd been as good as to them for a long time, and now Nathan was gone. Five attached-at-the-hip friends down to three.

Leigh pulled out of Fletcher's protective grasp, her hands in the pockets of her loose black pants. She wandered onto the gravel path, looking around. "I don't think I've been here since we were kids. Didn't we stop coming after Everly stopped talking to us?"

"I think so," Rose said, doing her best to reel in her thoughts.

Fletcher kicked at the ground. "Did Everly stop talking to us, or did we stop talking to her? The last two months of school were a blur with graduation and getting ready for college. I just remember Everly going nuclear over thinking she was being stalked or something."

"I remember you kissing her, so that probably had something to do with our falling out." Leigh turned in the gravel, a rare smile on her face. That smile was a playful challenge, and it warmed Rose to her core.

Rose was glad to see some mirth from her friend. Leigh was at the end of her treatments for breast cancer, and her latest scans were clear. Now all she needed to do was regain her strength. The surgery and chemo had been rough on her small frame.

"Oh god." Fletcher dropped his head, his chin almost resting on his chest. "Thanks for reminding me, Leigh. Don't forget that you and I had broken up because we thought we'd go to different schools. Both Everly and I immediately regretted it. I think she said something about how weird it was to French her brother."

"I know. I'm sort of kidding. We were all kids, but it did hurt my feelings. I think that made it easier for me to pull away from her when she became obsessed with the whole *'There's something wrong with Splendid'* thing." Leigh gazed off into the distance.

Rose didn't care for reminiscing. She didn't see much point to it. They'd all made their choices in life. Ever had made her own choice by leaving for destinations unknown, skipping out on a full-ride scholarship to Stanford to study medicine. To Rose, that had been more unforgivable than anything else. They'd all had such big plans for their lives, Ever included, but instead of becoming a doctor as she'd always dreamed, she flushed her future down the toilet because of her obsessions. With the advent of social media, Rose had been able to check up on Ever, which she did now and again. Rose knew, as did everyone else, that Ever was now a self-styled paranormal investigator who lived in New Orleans. What that meant and what Ever did for money wasn't clear to Rose, but Ever had written a couple of booklets about New Orleans hauntings for a local tourist company, and she'd recently been on a pretty popular podcast talking about the Casket Girls of New Orleans.

"There's nothing wrong with Splendid. Ever was going through something," Rose said.

"Speaking of going through something." Fletcher's eyes softened as he shifted from defensive to concerned. "Rose, do you know what happened? How the hell did Nathan die? We'd all just had dinner, and he was as fit as ever."

Fletcher had the same concern Rose did. She'd also been at that dinner with Jonathan, Fletcher, Leigh, Nathan, and Charlie. Everyone was happy and healthy. They were celebrating the end of Leigh's treatment with expensive champagne. Nathan talked about the new archival technique he'd learned in D.C. and mentioned a notebook he'd uncovered in the museum's archives. He was excited about studying the contents, and Fletcher was right, Nathan had been fit, glowing even in his love for Charlie as the two smiled and teased each other.

The next day, their friend was dead. Dead at forty-seven.

"I only know what everyone else knows. The girl who interns at the museum, Melody or something, knocked on Nathan's office door because she was going on a coffee run. He didn't answer, so she opened the door and found him unconscious on the floor. The paramedics said it was a heart attack." Rose stared off after Ever, who was now a speck darting between tree trunks and gravestones.

"That's some crazy shit." Fletcher raked his hair with his hands. "I mean, no one was a bigger health nut than Nathan. Charlie had gotten him on a vegan diet, and he ran about five miles every morning. So, what's the point of this healthy bullshit if we're going to drop dead anyway?"

"Fletcher, stop." Leigh crossed her arms.

She didn't like that kind of talk. She was too sweet for it, but Rose could commiserate. What *was* the point? Fletcher was right again. Nathan had been the poster boy for middle-aged health. Not that they were middle-aged. Rose didn't feel close to that old.

"What happened to Nathan is scary, for sure, but all we can do now is carry on. Right?" Rose looked at Leigh and Fletcher in turn. Leigh nodded. Fletcher raised his eyebrows. "Anyway, it doesn't do Nathan any good to speculate. Let's get out of here. Charlie was going to meet us at the bar. I don't know about you two, but I could use a stiff afternoon drink."

The bar was the same place they'd been going to since they were eighteen. When they were home for any sort of break, they would converge on The Peak like it was their job. They didn't have fake IDs, and they didn't need them. Murphy, the owner of The Peak for decades, never cared to check.

The new owner, Murphy's son and their longtime friend Jonathan, was much stricter, but the three were far beyond their carding years.

The Peak sat on a busy corner of downtown Splendid, across from the park with the shade trees, the benches, and the million-dollar fountain that many residents had balked at. The fountain's mosaic globe with water spurting out at timed intervals sat right in sight from The Peak's front windows.

Downtown Splendid was always busy with both pedestrians and cars. As a result, parking was sometimes hard to come by, but the adventure of finding a spot was always worth the effort. Once parked, locals were rewarded with the best boutiques, bookstores, and cafés around, the blue-green of the Rocky Mountains, the perfect backdrop to the linear streets lined with old brick buildings.

Fletcher led the way inside, pulling open one side of the enormous double glass doors. The bar was relatively quiet in the middle of the afternoon, something for which Rose was grateful. The odor of wood polish cut through that sour alcohol smell most bars can't seem to do without, creating a scent unique to The Peak.

Charlie, early thirties, brown-eyed and gorgeous, waved from a four-seater high top in the middle of the room.

As Rose drew closer, she could tell he'd been crying, his eyes bloodshot and red-rimmed. They'd all been crying. Rose had cried from the funeral to the bar but had touched up her makeup after parking on Main Street. The grief she felt for Nathan was almost overwhelming, and seeing Ever had also affected her in a way that had surprised her. Rose would have had difficulty explaining if asked to describe how she felt. Confused was the best word she could use to express the emotions stirred up by Ever's visit.

"Hey." She put her arms around Charlie, feeling his warm breath on her neck. "How are you holding up?"

"Not great." Charlie barely managed to get out the words before the tears started falling.

"Of course you're not." Rose slid onto the seat next to him while Fletcher and Leigh gathered around.

Fletcher waved over the waitress, a young woman Rose

didn't recognize. "Two ciders, please, whatever you have on tap, and …" He trailed off, looking toward Rose.

"Whiskey, neat."

Charlie was nursing what looked and smelled like a gin and tonic.

Leigh leaned over the tabletop, reaching out a hand to Charlie. "I thought the service was lovely. Everything was perfect."

He smiled through his tears. "It was. Thanks to Rose, and thank the heavens it didn't rain."

"No," Fletcher scoffed. "You know Splendid, the weather's never bad on important days."

The four of them laughed.

The young waitress, whose name tag read Marty, dropped off their drinks, then turned to another table.

"Oh, excuse me, Marty," Rose called.

Marty turned back around, a slight roll of her eyes. "Yeah?"

"Is Jonathan here today?"

The slight eye roll turned into a full one. "No, he'll be here later tonight."

"Why are you asking about Jonathan?" Leigh's voice was low, so Marty couldn't hear her as she walked away.

"I'm wondering if he was at the funeral. Did anyone see him?"

Everyone at the table shook their head *no.*

"Not surprised. Jonathan's a super reserved guy, but he would have seen Ever if he had been there. I wonder if he even knows she's in town." Rose shrugged a single shoulder as she sipped at her whiskey.

"Do you think they still talk?" Leigh had leaned forward again in a way that spoke of shared secrets.

"No. Ever barely even speaks to her mom. I seriously doubt she's kept in touch with Jonathan."

Fletcher dropped his face into his hands. "I can verify they have not kept in touch, and why do we keep talking about Everly?"

Charlie, staring at them like this was a soap opera, asked, "Who the hell is Everly?"

Rose shot him a look. "Nathan never spoke of her?"

Charlie's brows knit together in thought. "I don't think so. The name isn't familiar." He gasped. "Is she the one you all were staring at for a full five minutes while Rose was speaking?"

"She's the one." Fletcher took several gulps of cider.

"Okay, wait. Yeah, Everly is the girl you guys were friends with in high school who bailed, right? I think Nathan showed me some of your school newspapers when we first met, and he talked about each of you. I remember a brief mention of the girl who ran a column about ghosts or some shit. She's pretty."

"I thought it was nice of her to come." Leigh pulled lip balm from her pocket, slathering it over her dry lips. "She didn't have to. That tells me she still thinks about us, still cares."

Rose stared into the deep amber of her whiskey. There were other things to worry about than Ever and what she was or wasn't thinking. Ever was a mystery that would never be solved. She turned her attention back to Charlie. "Is there anything you need, Charlie? We're here to help."

Nathan's family had been far too distraught to put the arrangements together, so Rose took over. Helping made her feel more in control when Nathan's death made her feel like she was in a runaway car. Leigh, too, had been helping by taking casseroles to Charlie and Nathan's family. Probably far more than they could eat.

Charlie took a deep breath, his hand spinning his glass on the wooden tabletop. "I would love to get into his office at the museum. I'd like to have a couple of personal items, but they won't let me in."

"Why won't they let you in?" Rose turned on her stool until she was face to face with him. "If this is because Nathan was gay, so help me god, I will sue the shit out of that place."

Charlie held up a hand. "No, that isn't the problem. The intern, Melody, the one who found his …" Charlie's voice cracked. He cleared his throat. "She said the lock to his office has been changed so the room can be properly cleaned, which she seemed confused about. But she said she'd make sure that I get his things as soon as possible."

"Why was she confused?" Fletcher asked before polishing off his cider.

"Because, according to her, there was nothing to clean up. She thought it odd and said as much."

"That is weird, but maybe this is a museum procedure. I'll get his things for you. It would be best if you didn't worry about that," Rose said.

"I think I'm going to invite Everly to dinner tonight," Leigh blurted.

"What?" Fletcher looked at her like she was crazy.

"I'm doing it. That's what I'm doing." Leigh seemed like she was convincing herself. "This is right. We should catch up. Rose, Charlie, you're both invited."

Rose was momentarily taken aback. She thought she'd seen the last of Ever, but now there was a real possibility she'd have to sit across from her at a dinner table and make conversation. The thought gave her heartburn, or maybe it was the whiskey.

She shrugged. "You know life can never be too strange for me," she said, then knocked back the rest of her drink.

CHAPTER THREE

Houses in Splendid were often generational, passed down through families like a wedding ring or a set of delicate china. Her mom still lived in the same house they'd both grown up in.

Splendid never changed, and except for the trim color, neither had her childhood home. The house was still white, but the red shutters and trim had been repainted a soft sage.

Everly leaned against her rental car, parked along the sidewalk, as she gazed at the house that had been her home for so long. The Queen Anne-style house was built around 1900 and sat smack in the middle of the best neighborhood in town. There was a gable, an expansive front porch with trim that resembled lace, and a crow's nest on the tippy top of the house that was like a lighthouse lookout. That crow's nest had been *the* hangout spot for her and her friends. If they weren't at school, they were up there, listening to vinyl and lounging on bean bags.

Everly grabbed her suitcase and backpack from the trunk, took a deep breath, and turned up the brick-paved walk.

A breeze swirled leaves at her feet, which she crunched

as she ambled. She glanced down at the walkway and stopped in her tracks. That's why the symbol on the tree trunk-like grave was so familiar. She remembered now. The same character was etched on a brick in the walkway to her front steps. It had been so many years since she'd been home that it'd been easy to forget.

Strange, but then there was no shortage of the bizarre in Splendid. Maybe it was a manufacturer's mark. She didn't have long to think about this when she was struck by something else as her gaze traveled back toward the house. A ramp. She hadn't seen it at first because it was off to the side. Who in the house needed a ramp?

She went up the stairs, past orange and white pumpkins nestled casually on each step, then opened the darkly stained front door without knocking. An empty jack-o-lantern bowl sat on the bench of the Victorian hall tree, ready to be filled with candy come Halloween night.

"Mom," she called out, setting her bags down. The familiar scent of pine floor cleaner rose to greet her, every surface gleaming, as always.

The interior was cool, with air conditioning blowing through the vents, and everything was just as beautiful as Everly remembered. Wainscoting, stained dark, wrapped half the walls of the foyer, green and blue botanical wallpaper covering the rest. Above her head, the art deco chandelier swayed gently, crystal drops catching the light from the transom window over the front door. A landscape painted by her ancestor, Eli Palmer, hung on the long hallway wall.

The giant staircase to the right also had a new accessory. Everly was shocked to see that an electric chair lift had been installed along the wall.

"What is going on?" she asked the empty room.

"In here, Everly." Her mom's voice hadn't changed. The high, almost childlike voice made Everly feel like a kid again. Like all the years of estrangement hadn't happened, like she hadn't left home right after high school, angry at everyone, angry at the world.

She'd spoken to her mom here and there over the years in short telephone conversations, never initiated by her. Her mom even visited her in New Orleans twice for long weekends, the last time being about six years ago. Everly didn't have a dad. Mom was artificially inseminated, or at least, that's the story she always maintained. Everly had doubts, but her mom never wanted to talk about it.

The voice came from the kitchen, so that's where she headed.

When Everly rounded the corner, concealing her shock took all her self-composure.

"Mom, what's going on?" She realized as soon as she asked the question that there was probably a better way. Not knowing how to act in uncomfortable situations was the bane of Everly's existence—one reason why she generally kept to herself.

Her mom smiled from her wheelchair. Everything else about her looked the same as it had six years ago. Mom had let her hair go gray, but it was in that chic way that so many women are doing now, styled in a choppy bob. She had gained a few wrinkles, mostly around her eyes, but they still glittered with her always bright smile. "It's not a big deal. I thought I told you during our last visit." She wheeled herself around the modified kitchen. The island had been removed to allow for space, and the counters had been lowered.

"What?" Everly tried to remember that last visit to New Orleans. They'd spent three days walking the city, popping into French Quarter shops and marveling at every Garden District home. Her mom had been slower, but she'd recently celebrated her seventieth birthday. "Mom, tell me what?"

"I have MS, honey. It's okay." Mom smiled again as she wheeled over to the fridge. "Do you want some lemonade?"

"No, Mom, I don't want lemonade." Everly had to brace a hand against the wall behind her. "Please explain this to me a little more. Like, do you need me to move home and help?" Confusion sliced through Everly's brain. How could her mom not have told her this?

Her mom pulled out a pitcher of lemonade anyway. "I do not need help. I'm still doing fine on my own. I have a housekeeper who comes on Fridays and a nurse who comes in the morning to help me bathe and do my exercises. I'd had symptoms for years and years, but I chalked it up to getting older and tired. I had recently been diagnosed when I came to see you the last time, but I'd had it for a while. I could have sworn I told you, but maybe I wasn't ready to talk about it yet." She set the pitcher on the counter.

That seemed more like her mom. Neither of them was big on talking. Not when it came to anything even remotely serious.

What Everly couldn't understand was why her mom had this illness in the first place. People didn't generally get sick in Splendid. Illness was almost as rare as criminal activity, and now that she thought about it, Leigh was also ill, which was odd. Two people sick in Splendid with a serious illness? Everly didn't voice these thoughts out loud.

"You didn't tell me." Everly lurched away from the wall. "Let me get the glasses." She opened the cabinet over the stove. It was empty.

"They're down here now." Mom pulled two glasses from a lower cabinet. "See, I have everything I need within reach. How was the funeral?"

"Fine. Weird."

Everly took the pitcher to pour out the lemonade. Lemonade was something she was not getting out of, even though her stomach hurt. The back of her throat felt tight, and she had to bite the inside of her lip to keep from crying. That spot was starting to get sore. What was going on around here? First, Nathan, then Leigh, and now her mom? There had been far too much to process in such a short time. Everly sipped her lemonade rather than talk. She couldn't speak. Thinking of something to say was impossible. Her mom felt so alienated from her that she didn't feel like she could talk to Everly about her illness. This was why her mom hadn't gone to the funeral, but Everly could have helped her had she known.

"Audrey is coming over for cards any minute. Would you like to play with us? You remember Audrey, don't you?"

Everly remembered Audrey, their neighbor, a lady the same age as her mom. Audrey wore 1950s-styled wigs and way too much red lipstick. That lipstick bled into the wrinkles around her mouth in a way that frightened Everly as a child and made her think of bleeding wounds.

"No, thanks. I'm tired from the flight. I'll go upstairs and take a nap, and then I'll take you out to dinner."

Mom made a *hmmm* sound, then said, "I have dinner plans at the club, but you're welcome to join."

Everly did everything in her power not to roll her eyes. Her mom was talking about Red Manor, a place for the old denizens of Splendid. She'd always hated Red Manor. She and Rose broke into the mysterious building one night for kicks during senior year, back when the club was for men only. It seemed they'd now deigned to allow women into their ranks.

There was a brief moment of hurt when Everly realized her mom was not rearranging her life just because she was in town. Everly also couldn't blame her. Why would her mom drop everything to accommodate a daughter who hadn't even known she was sick?

She shook her head. "I think I'll skulk around town tonight. Check out a few old haunts."

"Sounds fun." Mom put her glass in the sink before wheeling around. "Let me know if you change your mind." And with that, she was off to the drawing room.

Everly waited for her mom to be out of sight before she bent over the sink and turned the tap on. She splashed her face with the coldest water possible. Maybe she could get on a flight back to New Orleans tomorrow. She didn't belong in Splendid; she had never belonged there. Her fight or flight had kicked in, and not shockingly, she was in flight.

She pulled out her phone, leaning against the frigid porcelain of the sink. The airline app showed nothing for the next three days. Every single flight was sold out. Of course, she could always take another airline, but she had miles to use and was not exactly flush with cash these days.

Standing in the kitchen, she booked the earliest flight, three days from then. Again, she was in the dreaded last row, but at least she could get the hell out of Splendid.

There were too many memories and reminders of what she'd left behind. None of it had been her fault. Not really. Her friends had grown tired of her scheming and her theories, and her mom had just grown tired. Life in New Orleans was great. Better than great. Everly had everything she needed. A sometimes-decent job, a lovely little studio overlooking St. Charles Avenue, and so much free entertainment that it was impossible to be bored. Her neighbor, whose name she didn't know, even had a tabby cat who came over occasionally for scratches and tuna. She didn't need Splendid, she never had.

CHAPTER FOUR

After the day she'd had, Rose didn't know what to do with herself. Leigh and Fletcher had gone home after their drink. Leigh needed her late-afternoon nap, and Charlie had an appointment for a massage. If Rose had been smart, she would have also gone home for some self-care, but she was too jittery. Two glasses of whiskey had done nothing to soothe her, succeeding only in increasing her annoyance with the world.

Life had been perfect and tranquil only a week before for all of them. Now, Nathan was gone, and Ever was back in town. If Rose went home before the sun went down, she'd do nothing but stew until dinner time. She'd accepted Leigh's invite and would only ruminate on everything she wanted to say to Ever for the next few hours. Finally, she decided in her warm, inebriated state that the best thing to do was to go to the museum. Charlie shouldn't have to wait to collect Nathan's things. He should have those personal items to sort through at his leisure. The museum was wrong to keep them from him, and Rose would make sure they knew how wrong. Charlie had been through enough.

The Museum of the Founders, Splendid's local history

museum, was housed in the old courthouse, a spectacular granite building reflective of the classical style of architecture that was popular in the early 1900s. The building's domed clock tower loomed over the busy downtown corner where the museum had sat for over a hundred and fifty years.

There was something about the building that always felt cold to Rose, which was evident by the shiver that ran up her arms every time she entered the massive marble lobby, but Nathan loved the place. He spent more time there than he needed to, often working late into the night, perfecting exhibits and working in the archives. She'd found him more than once huddled over some ancient manuscript well after he was supposed to meet them for dinner.

Rose tipped up her chin as she opened the heavy glass door of the museum, her Jimmy Choo heels clicking over the hard floor as she strode to the welcome desk. Her cheeks were a bit warm, her ankles a bit wobbly from the whiskey, so she tried to keep her head high, her arms casual, like nothing was amiss. She still wore her black lace dress from the funeral, and more than one casually dressed tourist side-eyed her as she walked by.

Melody raised her head, sliding her phone underneath a stack of brochures like she might get in trouble for scrolling while staffing the desk.

"Oh, hi, Rose." She waved, the sleeve of her too-large suit jacket ballooning out as she did so. "We just reopened. So sad about Dr. Stratton."

"I didn't realize the museum had closed for the funeral." Rose braced a hand on the edge of the desk. She'd seen Melody there and a few other people in the identical navy blue suits Nathan wore all the time, but she hadn't thought they would close. Then she realized Nathan had been the head of the museum, so, of course, it made sense.

"Yeah." Melody nodded.

"How are you holding up, Melody?" The intern didn't look quite as peppy as she usually did. Rose had to remind herself that Melody had found Nathan's body, an event that would be hard for anyone, whether you knew the individual or not.

Melody smiled, but the gesture didn't reach her eyes. "I'm okay. Last week was super hard. My therapist says to move forward; I have to give myself time."

"That's good advice. Maybe I should start seeing your therapist, mine is a joke." Rose tried to force a laugh but wasn't in the mood. "Anyway, I need to get Nathan's personal effects for Charlie. As you can imagine, he's going through it. Having Nathan's things from his office would be one less stress for him to deal with."

Melody made a cringe face, her gaze darting to the side. Rose looked in the same direction, seeing no one.

"I'm sorry, Rose, but I can't." Melody dropped her voice so low that Rose had to lean forward. "Like I told Charlie, the locks on the office were changed. I couldn't get in there if I wanted to. I was told by the mayor that the room had to be cleaned per city ordinance because this is a public building, and that he would personally pack up Nathan's things."

Rose tried to make sense of what she was hearing and came up blank. "What? What do you mean, city ordinance? And the mayor is handling this himself?"

Melody shrugged with another glance to the side. "I know as much as you do. I'm sorry, Rose. Charlie will get Dr. Stratton's things, I just don't know when."

Rose dropped her shoulder, leaning on the desk in a way she hoped Melody would find alluring. She'd been prepared for a no. "I completely understand, Melody, and I would never want to get you in trouble. So why don't you take a coffee break? Or go outside for some air? I may not look the type, but believe me, I've never met a lock I couldn't pick."

"Excuse me?" Melody's eyes went wide, her face registering shock at what Rose suggested.

There was a moment of slight discomfort as Rose

realized she was confessing criminal activity to a young woman she barely knew. Still, the whiskey coursing through her veins, sloshing around her empty stomach, had emboldened her. Besides, she was Rose Hibbard, a local celebrity. She'd been on national television many times promoting her wildly popular novels. Her books regularly sat on the *NY Times* bestseller list. So, if there was anyone who could talk an intern into turning her back, it was Rose.

Rose winked. "Oh, come on, Melody. How ridiculous is it that the mayor wants the room disinfected? It's not like Nathan had tuberculosis or something. He had a heart attack. There's no reason for the dramatics. You and I both know it." Rose leaned ever closer, hoping to draw Melody into her scheme.

Melody's gaze flicked up to the ceiling. "I can't," she whispered, looking back at Rose. She took a step back, crossing her arms across her chest. "Thank you for stopping by, Ms. Hibbard. We'll inform Mr. Fields when Dr. Stratton's effects are ready to be picked up."

Well, that was that. Even Rose knew when she'd lost.

"Fine." She pushed herself back from the desk with a roll of her eyes. "I'll go to the mayor's office then."

"Good luck."

Rose couldn't tell if Melody was being facetious or genuine. Still, she pursed her lips, a thought gnawing at the back of her mind. "I need to use the restroom before I leave. If that's allowed." The parting shot was unnecessary. Rose often had to have the last word, especially when she felt she'd been backed into a corner. Melody was only doing her job, a job that, as an intern, was probably tenuous at best.

Melody didn't respond as Rose slunk away toward the restrooms at the far end of the museum. There were closer restrooms, but Rose had a thought. She wanted a glimpse of Nathan's office, which she would have to pass on the way.

The click of her heels echoed throughout the main lobby. Wanting the whole world to know she was there, she may have slammed her feet down a little harder than was necessary as she walked. Melody might be afraid of losing her position at the museum, but Rose had nothing to fear, not from the museum, the mayor, or anyone else.

She wasn't blowing smoke when she'd said she'd go to the mayor. She would tomorrow. The mayor, Richard Hart, was her former high school principal. He wasn't much older than her, maybe ten years or so. He'd been the youngest principal Splendid High School had ever seen. Much had been made of it at the time, and she and her friends had thought he was so cool, which he was. He listened to the same music as them, watched the same movies, and said things like *awesome* and *rad*. Richard Hart walked the hallways like he was one of them. If anyone would get her into Nathan's office, it was Richard.

The door to the office was closed. There was no tape across the entry or any other sign that something ominous had occurred within. Rose stopped, peering in the small, glazed window above the nameplate that still read *Nathan Stratton, Ph.D., Museum Director.*

If anyone watched her, she didn't care. No one came by to tell her to move along. Not surprising since there was nothing to see. Rose squinted, moving her head left and right, but the glaze on the window was impossible to see through. All appeared dark inside. She couldn't even make out the shapes of the furniture.

She gave the knob a good shake. Locked tight. She grumbled, annoyed that this was becoming such a thing. She'd hoped to triumphantly hand Charlie a box packed to the brim with Nathan's belongings at dinner. Now she'd have to ambush Richard and demand to know the problem, and that thought felt exhausting.

Rose rested her head against the cool glass. Enduring Nathan's funeral had been soul-ripping. That event should have signaled the end of her day, but there was still dinner. Dinner that would be eaten as she sat across from Ever. She should have declined the invitation. Why had she not done that? Curiosity? A morbid fascination with Ever and what she was up to these days? No, the reason she wanted to sit across from Ever had nothing to do with those things. Rose wanted to look into Ever's eyes and ask her point-blank what the hell her problem had been. That's what she wanted. Maybe it was the whisky making her feel confrontative, but Rose thought they … no, *she* deserved some explanation. And if she made dinner uncomfortable, if Ever left in a huff, then so be it. That's what she expected. She expected Ever to turn tail and run—again. Maybe it's what Rose wanted—to be rid of Ever and her drama once and for all.

CHAPTER FIVE

The crow's nest hadn't changed. Not one bit. The place was like a time capsule.

Everly closed the door behind her, taking in the space she occupied with her friends and herself for all those years. The crow's nest, the small, raised room on the very top of her home, was better than any playground could have ever been. She'd let her imagination go wild up in the air, surrounded by trees and the tops of the neighborhood houses. Maybe a little too wild.

Everly had always been sensitive to what people might call spirits, and there was something off about the house, something that called to the side of her that frequented haunted places. This was a haunted house, even the little girl she'd been had known that. The presence in her childhood home differed from the one that had been with her since that night at Red Manor. Whatever that presence was, it had been stuck to her since she saw it on the staircase, always there, always cold on her right side. The presence in her home was softer, more muted. It never scared her as the other one did.

All was silence in the room as Everly looked around. The

crow's nest was so separated from the rest of the house that noise had never been a problem. They could be as loud as they wanted and play their records at full volume, and her mom never complained.

Everly ran a finger through the dust on the record player's plastic cover. Decades of debris sat on every surface, while cobwebs clustered in the corners of the windows like blobs of cotton candy.

The 1970s yellow couch sent up a puff of musty air as she flopped, records piled on the floor at her feet. She picked up a few and flipped through them. Pixies, Nirvana, Echo & the Bunnymen, and Depeche Mode. The music of high school.

She caressed the couch's fabric as she imagined all the times she and Jonathan had sex there. The first time had been so nerve-wracking, but he'd made it wonderful, always sweet, always gentle. On her phone were several pictures of the two of them, digital copies made from Polaroids taken mostly by Rose, one taken by Fletcher, and the big camera he used for the school newspaper. It was strange to keep them, these reminiscences of a past relationship, but she'd never been able to let them go. They'd been so in love then, unable to keep their hands and lips off of each other. Leaving him behind had been the hardest of all.

Everly lived in the past; she always had. Living in the present was something she was still working on. Her therapist didn't think Everly had ever, not once in her life, lived in the present. To dwell on the past puts stress on the mind and body, her therapist had said, shocked that Everly didn't look eighty. But how did one move on from the past when there was so much that didn't make sense? When there were memories that didn't feel quite right?

Her high school journal sat on the crate they'd used as a coffee table. The wooden box was stained with incense ash and coffee rings. She picked up the journal, a child's diary, pink, with a lock. The key for the lock was probably long lost, so she cracked it open by slamming the cheap plastic on the edge of the crate. The pages fell open. Everly flipped to the middle. The entry was from the summer before junior year.

July 1993,

Rose was caught kissing Mia in her backyard. Her mom slapped her in front of Mia, who was in Splendid visiting her grandma. Mia left, and Rose ran all the way here barefoot. I washed and bandaged her heel, which she cut on a sharp rock. I hate her mom. Rose is sleeping on the couch. I wish my mom could adopt her.

Rose. It had been Everly and Rose against the world for so long. Losing her friends had left a gaping hole inside Everly's heart, but losing Rose had torn her soul in two. How had it all gone so wrong? Her friends started to hate her shortly after she and Rose broke into Red Manor, which her mom called *the club.* Everly had started seeing things, the nightmares she'd always had reaching a fever pitch until she had to get out of Splendid. There was no other way. Breathing there, existing there had become impossible. She'd kept it mostly together for several months, even going so far as to take on the *Haunted Happenings* column at the school paper. Doing so felt like the only way to learn more about what she was experiencing. But it didn't last long before she'd broken down entirely, and they could no longer stand to be around her.

What a shitty day.

She gazed at the faded denim bean bag under the south-facing window. An object in a crease on the top of the bean bag glinted in the sunlight. Everly dropped the journal. Two small, golden butterfly hairpins were nestled in the crease. They were Rose's, of course, straight from 1994. Everly picked up the pins, clutching them tight in the palm of her hand. She sank into the stiff bag, beans snapping as she settled herself.

The window she now looked out of faced Nathan's childhood home. Through her online detective work, she'd discovered that he still owned the house but hadn't lived there since his dad died. His mom moved in with her daughter right after the car crash that claimed her husband's life, and Nathan had bought it from her. His current address was that of his boyfriend, Charles, probably the man at the funeral, a condo in a historic building that ran alongside Seven Mile River. This was the extent of the information she'd gleaned without a social media presence.

As Everly gazed at the window, she saw Nathan as a child, signing from his bedroom across the expanse of lawns separating their homes. Nathan's sister was hearing impaired, so they'd both learned ASL in elementary school.

The longer she stared at the window, the more it came into focus. What looked like a piece of paper was taped to the corner. Another mode of communication that she and Nathan had used many times.

Everly had to squint; her eyes weren't what they used to be, and her glasses were downstairs. She moved closer to her window, squinting and concentrating. A piece of paper *was* there, and something was written on it.

"Everly."

A voice behind her startled her into the glass. She whacked her forehead, rubbing it as she turned her head. That felt familiar. Their other longtime neighbor, Audrey, stood in the doorway, one hand on the knob, one on her hip. Audrey's red lips were even more garish than Everly remembered. The lady's pasty white face appeared pulled back unnaturally, making her look even worse.

"Hi," she said stupidly.

Audrey eyed her with disdain. "Hello. There's a call for you. Your mom can't get up here, you know."

"Yes, ma'am, I know." Everly dug herself out of the bean bag, Audrey watching her every move. She kept the hairpins held tight in one hand. Who in the world would be calling her at her mom's house? "Do you know who's on the phone?"

"How would I know?" And with that, Audrey was gone,

hobbling back down the stairs.

"Hi, Everly." The sweet voice on the other end of the line belonged to Leigh.

Everly's stomach did a weird flip.

"Hey, Leigh. Everything okay?" Everly was the worst phone conversationalist there was. What did you say to someone you'd just seen at a graveyard?

"Everything's great. Well, not great, obviously." A pause came on the other end. "That was awkward. Anyway, I wanted to invite you to dinner."

Everly waited for the punch line. When Leigh didn't offer anything else, and the silence began to drag, Everly cleared her throat to buy some more time. Was this a Carrie situation? Did they want to invite her to dinner to throw pig's blood on her? Her first instinct was to say no, but the longer the hush wore on, the more she wanted to say yes. The fact that Leigh even thought to ask her was a big deal.

"Sure, I'll be there."

"Great!" Leigh shrieked in her ear. "Oh, sorry. Dinner is at seven. Do you remember the disgustingly huge house on the corner of Wood and Caramillo? That's us."

"Oh shit, you live in the Decomposition House?"

Decomposition was a low-budget horror movie shot in Splendid in the '90s. Most of the film was shot in the house Leigh now lived in, the place they called the Decomposition House, and it was disgustingly huge, but they could afford it … and nine more if they wanted to. Fletcher and Leigh had made a killing in the gaming industry. He was the CEO and owner of Cerberus Games. Leigh was the creative talent.

"Wow, that's so cool. I've always wanted to see inside that house. I bet Rose was in heaven when you bought it."

Leigh laughed. "Yeah, I've never seen her so excited to help someone move."

Everly smiled to herself. "Thanks for the invitation, Leigh. I'll be there at seven."

Everly was about to hang up the phone when Leigh blurted, "Just for full transparency, Rose will be here, and probably Charlie, too."

The weird flip inside Everly's stomach turned into full-blown nausea. "Okay. I'll see you later." She hung up the phone. She had thought for half a second that she would cancel, then she felt the hairclips, still gripped in her hand. She had a few things to say to Rose; besides, the opportunity to see the inside of the Decomposition House was too great.

The Tudor-style house, only five minutes away from her own, was everything Everly remembered. The massive home extended almost the entire block, the dark wood trim around the windows and under the eaves straight out of a German fairytale about little kids and the witches who eat them. Leigh and Fletcher had refreshed the exterior. Everly remembered the paint as being a dark tan. The surface was now a light cream, which looked beautiful with the dark wood of the trim. The windows, the many windows, looked brand new. The wrought iron gate, made by the same man who made all of downtown Splendid's fences, including the one around Everly's house in the late 1800s, was still beautiful, its fleur-de-lis finials pointing straight up to the sky.

The sun was still out and would be for another couple of hours. Despite this, Everly could see lights everywhere in the house. She left her rental car parked on the street. She hadn't dressed up. Everly's uniform was the same as it had always been— jeans, flannels, concert tees. Some things never changed.

Leigh met her at the door, pulling it open before Everly made it to the doorbell. Leigh looked brighter-eyed than she had at the funeral, her pale skin glowing with more life. She wore a breezy pair of palazzo pants with a loose tunic top, her head wrapped in a bright azure scarf.

"You look ready for the beach." Never knowing what to do, Everly reached for a sort of half-hug. Then, she handed

Leigh a bottle of wine she'd swiped from her mom's cabinet.

"I'm more ready for a vacation than you know." Leigh stood aside, motioning for Everly to step inside. "I'm fine, so that you know."

Everly looked down at Leigh as she closed the door. "I'm so glad to hear that, Leigh. I didn't know what the protocol was. Should I ask, or should I not? I've never been good at that stuff."

Leigh smiled at her. "I know. And the funeral wasn't exactly the place to get into it. I had breast cancer, but I'm all clear now. Just have to regain my strength and regrow my hair." She laughed, touching her scarf with her free hand.

"You look great. Really." Everly reached out a hand, clasping Leigh's elbow. Again, she was struck by the oddity of being ill in Splendid. "I'm so relieved that you're going to be okay. You were always the silent, strong one."

Leigh chuckled again. "Well, I'm hoping my days of being strong are over. Come on in. Everyone's in the back. The kids are with my parents for the week, but I'd love for you to meet them next time."

Relief bloomed in Everly's chest. She wasn't great with kids, and her stress level was already through the roof. Pretending like she was excited to talk to children was one less thing she now had to worry about, and since there wouldn't be a next time, she'd never have to.

But of course, Everly was the last one there. That meant when she entered whatever room they were in, they'd all be comfortably seated and watching her. Everly cursed herself for not being earlier.

Leigh led her past room after room. Everly's neck snapped from right to left, trying to take it all in.

"Don't worry," Leigh said over her shoulder, "I'll take you on a tour after dinner."

They turned a corner and entered the dining room. Everly didn't remember this room from the movie, but the wainscoting was a soft, muted green, a modern lantern-shaped chandelier over the giant cement-topped dining table. Leigh led the way, the bottle of wine still clutched in one hand. "Everly's here, everyone. Everly, this is Charlie." Leigh stopped behind the handsome young man from the funeral.

He leaned forward, his hand outstretched. "So nice to meet you, Everly."

"Nice to meet you." Everly shook his hand, trying not to make eye contact with anyone else. Out of the corner of her eye, she could see Rose seated across from Charlie, Fletcher at the far end of the table.

"Sit down, Everly. We're all ready to eat," Fletcher said from his veritable throne.

Everly tried not to roll her eyes. She had been late, after all, something Fletcher always gave her shit for in high school. He used to say, *"She can be on time for class, but never for us."*

Leigh sat at the opposite end of the table from her husband, indicating a vacant chair next to Charlie.

Everly sat directly in the line of Rose's evil eye.

Leigh cleared her throat to get Everly's attention, and when she had it, passed her a bowl of roasted potatoes. "Tell us about your job, Everly. Is it true you hunt ghosts?"

"Yes, Ever. I'm dying to know how you went from being terrified of everything that goes bump in the night to seeking out the unexplained." Rose cradled her chin on a palm, ignoring her plate of food.

"That's not fair, Rose. Everly wrote *Haunted Happenings* and ran all those cemetery meetings," Leigh offered.

"*Haunted Happenings* was an excuse for her to investigate what she thought happened at Red Manor, and the meetings were originally my idea. Ever hijacked what was supposed to be my true crime club."

Everly stared at Rose for one long minute. The little gold hair clips were in the back pocket of her jeans. She'd slipped them in there, along with a stupid note, thinking she would give these things to Rose, and maybe, somehow, they could return to 1994.

Everly could stare at Rose all night, and Rose would never crack, she'd never look away. At this moment, Everly had two choices. She could chuckle and say something dismissive or tell the truth. She decided on the latter. Hadn't she hidden enough in recent years?

Looking Rose dead in the eye, Everly said, "Everyone at this table knows why I became a paranormal investigator, and why I took on the *Haunted Happenings* column in school. You already said it, Rose. Something happened to me. Something happened to me, and no one ever believed me."

Rose cracked, then. Her eyelashes fluttered as she dropped her gaze from Everly's to stare at the table. She wasn't expecting Everly to be so forthright, so forceful. Everly wasn't expecting it herself. Her stomach bubbled, her ankles quaking under the table. Confrontation was not her strong suit. She dropped her gaze, too.

Fletcher raked his hands through his hair with a grunt. "It's not that we didn't believe you, Everly. It's the way you went about things, the way you went after people. You became unhinged."

"Fletcher." Leigh threw Fletcher a look that could kill across the dining room table.

"It's fine. Whatever." Everly set down the bowl of potatoes, which she realized she still held, then pushed back from the table, her chair legs biting into the floor.

"It's not fine, Everly." Leigh reached out a hand to grab Everly's arm. "Please don't leave like this. Stay. I can't speak for them, but I can speak for myself. I was wrong for the way I treated you back then. I should have done more to help you, done more to listen. You needed us, and we backed away. Nathan regretted it, too. We talked about this a lot in the last few months. You should know that he wanted to reach out. During our last conversation, he said something about believing you."

"What do you mean? Believing me?" Everly's chair was away from the table, but she remained seated.

Leigh shook her head. "I don't know. A lot of weird

stuff was happening, and I was sick from the chemo. Maybe Charlie has more insight." Leigh looked at Charlie, a hopeful expression on her face.

Charlie also shook his head. "I don't have any insight. I wish I did." His voice cracked, but he took a breath and continued. "He didn't talk about you, Everly, not to me, but I'm not surprised. In the last few weeks, he was obsessed with something he'd found in the museum archives. He wouldn't give me specifics. He kept saying he needed to do more research before he could talk about whatever kept him so busy. But that wasn't unusual for Nathan—he was always researching something."

"There was one weird thing, I remember." Fletcher took a deep drink of his wine. "It was about three weeks before he died, the night we gathered at The Peak to celebrate Rose and her Netflix deal. Leigh hadn't stayed long; she was tired and went home. Charlie took Rose home because she couldn't drive herself. Nathan and I stayed to have another. He told me he was working on something exciting but couldn't say what it was. I nagged him a bit and tried to get him to tell me. He leaned in with his whisky breath and whispered something about symbols and graves. I was as drunk as he was, so I couldn't track exactly what he said. We ended up laughing until we almost fell off our stools. Jonathan called us a car and cut us off."

"Jonathan?" Everly interrupted. "His dad still owns the bar?"

"Jonathan owns it now," Leigh answered, looking at her husband. "What do you think Nathan meant by symbols and graves?"

Fletcher shrugged. "No clue. We were drunk, like I said. He was probably messing with me."

Everly pulled her chair back to the table. She opened her mouth to speak, then snapped it shut.

The tree-trunk grave at Everwood with the infinity symbol.

Could that be what Nathan meant when he spoke of graves and symbols? The Everly of old would have presented this to the group. Everly from 1994 would have excitedly told her friends all about the graves she'd discovered at Everwood the day of the funeral and how she had traced the unusual symbol with her finger, the same character on a brick outside her house. But the Everly of now knew better. She knew better than to start spouting what would sound like another conspiracy to people who'd had enough of her more than twenty years ago.

And then there was Jonathan, the boy she still couldn't forget all these years later. Her mind was in turmoil. She had to admit to herself that she'd hoped he'd be there at the dinner, that he would have attended the funeral. She'd looked for him around every corner of Splendid since she'd arrived.

Everly grabbed the open bottle of wine on the table, pouring herself a tall glass. As she set the bottle down, she locked eyes with Rose.

Rose's brow was crinkled in a way Everly was familiar with. That crinkle meant Rose had something on her mind that was worrying her.

She looked away from Everly, replacing the crinkled, worried brow with a bright, fierce smile. "If I knew Nathan, and I did, he was messing with you. Nathan knew what the rest of us know, Fletch. You are easy as hell to mess with."

Leigh laughed, her shoulders dropping as if she'd been holding tension in the back of her neck, and Rose had made it melt away. "Totally," she said as she continued to laugh.

The table descended into silence. They continued to eat, but no one spoke other than to make awkward, random comments about sports and the weather.

After dinner, Everly helped clear the table. She was ready to bolt, prepared to leave that place far behind. The Decomposition House, her former friends, and Splendid.

"Thanks for the invitation, Leigh," Everly said as she placed her plate in the sink. "It was nice to see everyone." She tried to smile through the lie as she backed away from the group crowded around the kitchen island. "My mom is expecting me for a late-night movie." Another lie. Her mom had gone to bed before she'd left for dinner.

No one made a move to stop her. Fletcher held up a hand in farewell. Charlie smiled and nodded. Rose looked at the ground. Everly had never known Rose to look down so much.

Leigh half-smiled and moved toward Everly with her arms wide. Leigh hugged her, patting her back twice before stepping back. "Safe journeys back home, Everly. Thanks for coming."

Everly tried to smile one last time before turning on the heel of her Converse. She fished the hairclips and note from her back pocket, tossing them on the kitchen counter. Why she did this, she would need help to answer.

She bolted to the door in a half-walk, half-run, the back of her throat tightening. Tears were not something Everly shed often, but she might shed them before she got to her car. She'd been on the verge of tears all day. Being in the presence of these people who had once been her world and were now nothing more than strangers was almost more than she could bear.

She wrenched open the massive front door, tripping over the threshold onto the porch. Before falling on her knees, she caught herself on the porch banister.

"Ever, wait."

The door closed behind her. Everly didn't turn around, but she knew Rose was there. She took two deep gulps of air to try to keep the tears at bay.

Rose moved alongside her to the edge of the porch, her arms crossed in front of her chest. "I might believe you."

"What?" Everly turned toward Rose, leaning her back against the banister. "What do you mean?"

Rose's body didn't move, but she turned her face toward Everly. The waning light of the setting sun played in the ringlets of her hair, setting her skin on fire. There was no trace of a smile on Rose's face. "What you always said about something weird happening to you as a child, about seeing something the night we broke into Red Manor. I might believe you now, and Ever, I'm sorry."

Everly ignored the apology. "Why do you believe me now, all of a sudden, almost thirty years later?"

Rose glanced away, the side of one mouth quirking down. "I'm not sure, and that's my honest answer. Nathan's death, something is wrong there, apart from the obvious. No one has been allowed in his office. The museum refuses to give Charlie access to his personal belongings. They're saying it's so the office can be properly cleaned, but why? There weren't any fluids. Something is wrong, and I think you're the only one who can help me figure out what. Fletcher wouldn't dare, and Leigh doesn't have the strength."

Everly huffed a laugh, astounded by what she was hearing. Disbelief rolled through her. She narrowed her eyes as she studied everything about Rose, her posture, her facial expression.

"You're telling the truth."

Rose turned fully toward her then, dropping her hands to her hips. "Of course I'm telling the truth. I may be many things, but have you ever known me to lie?"

Everly shook her head. "You realize the irony of asking me for help after giving me the shaft?"

"I get it. Think about it this way, you're not doing this for me. Do it for Nathan." Rose had that look in her eye. A look Everly was more than familiar with.

"I know what you're thinking." She stared open-mouthed at Rose, another huff escaping her lips. "You want to break into his office, don't you?"

Rose smiled, and for a second, Everly was transported to senior year, to the night they broke into Red Manor, the night everything changed. "Don't tell me you're a chicken?"

AD BRAZEAU

CHAPTER SIX

1994

"It's staring at me." Everly shifted uneasily on the sidewalk, her body half-turned away from the house. She could feel something unnatural there, and hated even walking by the place in the daytime. There was something about it that screamed *Run.* "Doesn't it creep you out with its weird reflective windows? Like, what are they hiding, the undead?"

"You're afraid of everything, Ever. It's just an old house. I doubt there are actual ghosts inside, just a bunch of privileged old white men with nothing better to do with their time than to lounge around and plot the end of existence. It will be so cool if there are, though. The undead, I mean." Rose stood with her hands on her hips, her gaze trained on the imposing red brick, almost gothic structure, with its peaked windows, turret, and black iron spires. The turret with its witch's hat cupola was topped by an enormous metal dragon finial that seemed a warning in itself.

The club for men only was one of the first in the country.

It stood as a relic, a monument to another time, a time Everly was glad was far behind them, though not far enough. Red Manor stood out on a corner of downtown Splendid, adjacent to the park, alongside office buildings, shops, and restaurants. It didn't belong.

The house did have beauty to it. The men who gathered inside its walls, excluding anyone different, couldn't take that away.

Everly bristled at Rose's comment, rolling her eyes to the side even though Rose wasn't looking. "I'm not afraid of everything. I don't want to get caught. So why do you insist on always trying to get us into trouble?"

Rose tossed her enviable mane as she glanced at Everly over her shoulder. "When have I ever gotten us in trouble? And don't say last year, because one tiny trip to the principal's office doesn't count. You're terrified of ghosts here, which I don't get. It's not like ghosts exist, and even if they did, you don't find spiders ten times more terrifying? Those long, crooked legs crawling over your face while you sleep?" Rose shuddered. "Gross."

Everly laughed at her like she always did. Rose thought her feelings were innocent, childish ones. She didn't realize that the fear kept Everly up at night, and at seventeen, she still slept with a light on and her bedroom door open. That way, if she did have a nightmare, she could run to her mom faster. Ghosts weren't the problem. Whatever Everly feared was a little more complex—blood, dark rooms, the cold— these images inspired feelings of terror that stayed with her long after she woke from her regularly scheduled nightmares. Now, Everly's best friend pushed her to break into the oldest men's club in Splendid to poke around in the dark.

The building was famously haunted. A local author wrote a book on the subject, and a ghost-hunting team from Los Angeles even investigated the rumors. But unfortunately, there was so much activity that those men left before they could finish spending the night. A group of four grown men couldn't handle the place, but Rose thought they could.

Cold sweat gathered under Everly's arms and dripped down the small of her back. Rose loved pushing the envelope, and usually, she was right there with her, but this, this had Everly near fainting. The hauntings weren't so much the problem as Red Manor was itself. There was something inherently creepy about all the secrecy.

Rose must have seen her discomfort because she stepped in front of Everly and moved her face with her fingertips until Everly looked levelly into her eyes. "This is the crown jewel, Ever. Think of the bragging rights. To break into a club that is the epitome of white male dominance, think of it. We're just going to check it out. No harm, no foul."

Stomach acid began to work through the already tender lining of Everly's guts. She couldn't say no. If she did, Rose would go by herself and get caught. Because, as she always said, Everly was her lucky charm. Together, they could find their way out of any trouble. They'd been doing that since they learned how to spell their names.

Everly took a deep breath, swallowing the bile in the back of her throat. "Fine. But we're in and out. Just to say we did it."

Rose smiled and threw her arms around Everly. "Of course, babe. You know me. No unnecessary risks."

Everly did know her. That was part of the problem.

"We could always talk about Jonathan to distract you." Rose bumped Everly's shoulder as they crept closer to the side of the building. "I have it on good authority that you snuck him into the crow's nest the night before last."

Everly rolled her eyes. "Is Nathan telling on me again? Believe me, I have one or two secrets I could share about him."

"Nathan shouldn't have to tell on you. You should have told me yourself." Rose huffed a little. Everly tried not to laugh.

"Rose, do I have to give you a play-by-play of every moment of my day?"

"Absolutely, but give it to me later." Rose scaled the low brick wall that fenced in the back side of Red Manor, then Everly followed her over.

"Stay down, Ever. It's like you're trying to get us caught." Rose crouched, pulling Everly down next to her. The night was warm and not particularly dark. Although there was no light from the nearly invisible moon, Everly was afraid they would be seen by the glaring light of the streetlamps out front, but the downtown roads were deserted at three in the morning. There hadn't been a person or a car in sight.

They were dressed all in black, Everly's short hair and Rose's long hair swept up underneath thick black caps. There was no way they could look any more like obvious criminals.

Rose crouch-walked ahead of her. "Come on."

"You're sure about the cameras?" Everly tried to keep up with her the best she could. Rose's slim, athletic legs made everything look easy. Everly was glad there was no one behind her to judge the awkward way she teetered.

"I already told you. Jack took care of it."

What if he didn't? Jack was stupidly in love with Rose and had been since he moved to Splendid in the second grade. He didn't seem to get that she wasn't into dudes. He worked in the kitchen at the club and, luckily for them, was also a computer geek. He promised to cut the camera feed inside and outside the property after he closed at midnight. All they could do was hope he was true to his word and as much of a hacker as he liked to believe.

Everly's head began to sweat beneath the cap, so she pulled it off and stuffed it into the back pocket of her jeans. October first, and the weather was still warm on most days. She did everything she could to ignore the thoughts bubbling in her mind. What if this old place was haunted? Would they see ghosts? Would the ghosts see them?

Everything she had read about ghosts, and she had read a lot, said that they could see the living and manifest themselves in different ways. Spirits could reveal themselves as a cold spot, a ball of light, a hazy or shadow figure, or even appear as a full-bodied apparition. Depending on how strong the entity was, it could move objects, speak, and touch you, in some instances leaving marks behind as proof. This last thought almost drove Everly over the edge. Her breath went shallow, and she felt dizzy. *Breathe, Everly.* It was all she could do not to bolt. The only thing that kept her moving toward the back door was Rose. Everly would never leave her alone, not for anything.

Before she was ready, they were standing on the back stoop. Rose reached up and ran her hand along the top of the door frame. There was a scrape of metal against wood right before Rose pulled down a silver key that she held between two fingers. It glinted in the light, flooding the back stoop from the street. "Jack's going to get a little treat for this." She made a face. "Not that kind of treat, obviously."

Like Everly didn't already know that.

Usually, Everly would make a smart remark, but all she could focus on was not puking from the fear pumping through her veins. This was happening.

Rose slipped the key into the lock and looked back at her. "Here we go," she said.

They entered what appeared to be an enclosed porch. Rose clicked her tiny flashlight on, and Everly took her first full breath in ten minutes. The air was stale and smelled a little like red meat. Something else that made her want to gag.

Everly wrinkled up her nose. "Smells like they served roast beef for dinner."

Rose giggled. "They probably eat roast beef every night." She turned to face Everly. There was such an eerie glow around her dark eyes that Everly took an unintentional step back. Rose didn't seem to notice. "We have less than an hour, so let's get going. I want to explore as much as we can."

Rose turned and took off down the narrow hallway, sweeping the light around them. She seemed to have forgotten her promise that they would be in and out. Everly was about to reach out and grab her sleeve when a shiver ran down the back of her neck. She shuddered and wrapped her arms around her chest. "Why did it get so cold?" Had there been more light, she would surely have seen her breath billowing in and out.

Everly's best friend in the world ignored her. Rose kept walking, moving the flashlight to see the pictures hanging on the walls along either side of them. "Every one of these guys looks exactly the same. Like, seriously. Are you seeing this? White and old. White and old."

Everly did her best to focus on what Rose was saying and not the weird feeling in the air that seemed to settle around her shoulders. "The wallpaper is pretty." Of course it sounded dumb as soon as she said it, but focusing on the darkly embossed paper wrapping the walls gave her something to hold on to.

Rose faced Everly and flicked the light alongside her face. "The wallpaper." In the dimness of the long hallway, Everly could see Rose purse her lips. "Shake it off, Ever. You're fine. There's no one here but us."

That was part of her fear, being alone in a dark, scary place with nowhere to run. Everly's breath started to come faster, her chest tightening under Rose's disapproving gaze. The hallway was suddenly closing in. It was like being in a tunnel. Everly knew there was a way out. She just couldn't see it. Her fear was all in her head, and she tried to breathe through the panic, but the longer she stood there in the oppressive cold, the more the dark walls seemed about to eat her alive. Finally, she pushed past Rose and rushed into what must have been the main entryway of the old house.

"Ever. Take a deep breath. Seriously, girl, everything is fine. This place is pretty cool. I mean, if we were to move in, we'd have to majorly remodel, but some of this old stuff is okay. Like that, for example." Rose swept the light toward the ceiling to illuminate the ornate crystal chandelier. "And look over there." Rose lit up the top of the staircase, spotlighting a portrait of a tall man. "Isn't it comforting to know that your ancestor is always near wherever you go?" As she did so, a white mist caught Everly's eye.

"Did you see that?" Everly said, a little too loudly. She grabbed Rose's hand to point the light at the top of the staircase. Her heart hammered in her chest. She was so dizzy that she had to take a step back.

Rose reached up to take the flashlight in her other hand, so she could hold Everly's, sweaty as it was. "Okay, I can see I've made a huge mistake in bringing you here. I won't be the one who gives you a heart attack. We came, and we conquered. Let's go."

Before Everly could feel any relief that they were leaving, a door slammed. Her heart, previously racing, now skipped several beats. "Was that the back door?"

She could make out Rose's face in the dim light. Everly thought she detected a flash of something, perhaps fear, behind Rose's eyes. "No way. And if it was, I'm sure it was a draft. Come on."

Everly wanted to point out there was no draft or wind on this warm, still night.

With Everly's hand still clutched, Rose took off back down the hallway, pulling Everly behind her. Everly held her breath the entire way down the hall.

"What the …" Rose dropped Everly's hand to grab the handle of the now-closed door. She turned the brass knob and pulled. Nothing happened. Rose grunted and pulled again.

"What's happening?" Everly whispered, terror pulsing through her body like electricity.

Rose continued pulling on the door. "I …"

Before she could say anything more, the slamming of another door echoed behind them. Everly twirled around, her hands up in a defensive posture. There was nothing there. "Rose, what was that?"

"I bet it's the old guys messing with us." Rose was panting behind her. Her bravado was wearing off. Everly could hear it in the raised inflection of her voice.

"Let's try the front door. I don't care who sees us." Everly reached back for Rose's hand and bolted down the hallway. She hoped this would be their final time passing the hollow faces of the men on the walls. Although her heart continued to hammer away, and sweat soaked through her shirt, she couldn't freeze. She was all flight. They were getting out of there, even if that meant throwing a chair through the front window.

They ran together so fast that Everly misjudged the distance in the dark and slammed into the heavy, wooden door. Her forehead made sharp contact with the wood, causing her to see stars. She shook her head to try and clear it; she'd gladly take the concussion if it meant freedom on the other side. Rose had gone uncharacteristically silent. Everly pulled her hand free and began sliding back the first bolt. A wave of nausea washed over her so heavily that she had to stop and take a deep breath. She'd hit her head harder than she'd thought. On the exhale, dizziness wrapped around her, and she fell to the floor. Everything went black.

PART TWO
Revision

CHAPTER SEVEN

Rose sat cozily in her breakfast nook, a cup of steaming chamomile tea clasped in both hands. The sunlight streaked through the leaded glass windows, bathing everything around her in soft light. Pancake, her rescue cat, was curled in a ball next to her leg. She looked around at the kitchen she'd renovated after painstakingly picking out every detail. The gold-tone drawer pulls she'd waited months for, the monstrous slab of Carrera she'd had flown from Italy.

This house was essential to her because it was her own. She bought it with the advance from her second book. She paid it off with the advance from her third. The house on Cascade Avenue was only two blocks from where she'd grown up in another grand place, but it felt like a world away. Her parents were long dead, killed in an avalanche while skiing in the mountains. She and her older sister, Lily, had inherited the house they'd grown up in, but Lily had renounced worldliness, going off the grid with some weirdo cult in Utah.

What to do with their childhood home had been up to Rose. Her decision wasn't difficult—she couldn't sell the place fast enough. She'd rather die than live in the same space her mom had occupied for so many years. The kitchen where she smacked Rose on the back of her head with a slotted metal spoon for asking for a snack before dinner; the bathroom where her mom brushed her hair until her scalp bled; the backyard where she'd been slapped for kissing a girl. The house could rot for all Rose cared.

The money earned from the sale had been divided, with Rose putting Lily's half into an account should her sister ever emerge from the insanity of her current life. Not that Rose could blame her for disappearing, for becoming another person, not with the way they'd grown up.

Sitting in front of Rose while she sipped her tea were two little gold hairclips and a folded piece of paper. Rose had recognized the clips as soon as she saw them, slipping them and what she assumed to be a note into her pocket as fast as she could before running after Ever.

Last night had not gone the way she'd planned. The plan was to have it out with Ever, to word vomit all her feelings, come what may. Instead, she'd somehow enlisted Ever to help her break into Nathan's office. What was it about Ever that infected everyone around her? Rose had even gone so far as to admit that she believed her. That's what she said to Ever's face. But did she? Or was she temporarily appeasing Ever to gain an accomplice? It was harder to see conspiracies around every corner in the light of day. Maybe she believed that Ever believed it. Ever was a lot like Lily. Neither of them belonged in Splendid. Both lived in their made-up worlds, each escaping reality the only way they knew how.

Rose set down her tea, pulling the note toward her. She hadn't opened it yet. Last night had been exhausting, and she'd been too drunk from all the wine. All she'd wanted to do was crawl into bed, her sanctuary, the one place she could wrap herself in softness and forget.

She opened the piece of paper. It looked torn from a journal, the page lined, the inner edge jagged.

Found your clips on the bean bag in the crow's nest. The denim one you always claimed for yourself. Not a big thing to leave behind— little hair clips—but for some reason, the sight of them tugged at old feelings. I remember the day you bought them. What a weird thing to remember, but I do. We were at that little new-age store down the street from The Peak. You tried them on, and the lady behind the register said they looked so pretty on you that she gave you half off the price. There's no way you should be without these, so I scooped them up.

Rose tossed the note. She fondled the golden clips, butterflies etched around the edges, thinking back to that day more than thirty years ago. She'd worn the clips every day until she'd left them at Ever's. Rose had wanted to go back and claim them, but by then, she and Ever had stopped talking. The hair clips were a sacrifice she'd been willing to make.

Rose dropped the clips, leaning back in her cushioned nook, her head turning to look out the window at the street she'd walked down a thousand times.

The back of her throat burned, and her shoulders felt tight. Crying was dreadful. She'd cried so much over Nathan's death, always in private. She felt like she was made of raw flesh, inside and out, like her whole being had been scraped down to the tissue. Still, tears rolled down her cheeks as she envisioned her and Ever walking hand in hand down that very street. They practically skipped as they laughed, cracking jokes to and from school and their friends' homes. She missed that Ever, the Ever her friend had been before they'd broken into the damned Red Manor.

That one event had tipped Ever over the brink. She'd gone from having nightmares to worse, having nightmares and suspicions. She believed something, an entity, had attached itself to her that night. She started calling Rose at all hours, waking up Rose's parents, never helpful, to whisper crazy things like the town was eating her. After about a dozen of these phone calls, Rose couldn't take it anymore. She called Elsie Palmer to tell her Ever needed help, and then she bailed on the friendship. Rose bailed on her soul mate because she was young, just trying to survive herself.

Rose wiped her tears with the back of her hand. There were other, more pressing issues. The grief had to be put away, locked up tight with every other emotion she'd ever felt. She pulled her phone off the table, stabbing out a text.

Meet me at The Peak—1:00 pm.

There were only about twelve other equally fantastic places to meet for food and strategizing, but Rose wasn't the only one who deserved an apology from Ever. Jonathan, too, deserved some retribution. Jonathan and Ever had been each other's first everything. Nathan had been the last one of the four to tap out, but Jonathan had tried much longer to hold on to Ever. As a result, he'd been completely blindsided when she'd left Splendid.

Three little dots appeared while Ever typed her answer. Rose knew after the previous night, when Rose had asked her if she was chicken, that Ever wouldn't suggest they go somewhere else. No one raised in the '80s and '90s could bear the thought of being a chicken.

Fine.

Rose couldn't help but grin. After twenty-nine years, she still knew exactly how Ever would respond.

The lunch crowd was starting to filter out when Rose arrived. The bar, all dark wood and floor-to-ceiling glass windows, looked more like an English pub than a Colorado brewery. Vintage paper skeletons clung to the windows, and a few small gourds were scattered along the bar. This was all new since yesterday.

She waved at Jonathan as he talked with a table full of patrons. His stance was wide, casual as always, a little ginger gristle on his cheeks and chin. As far as men went, he was still an attractive guy, tall and slim, his figure athletic like a swimmer. He wore an untucked white T-shirt, good-fitting jeans, and a pair of white Vans.

He inclined his head toward her, raising a finger in the universal gesture of *I'll be right there.*

Rose slid onto a seat, choosing the same high-top table in the center of the bar she'd occupied yesterday. The whole thing was shady on her part, and she didn't care one bit. The only person she felt for in this scenario was Jonathan.

When Ever walked in two minutes later, looking pretty hot in skinny jeans and a cool Siouxsie and the Banshees concert tee, she stopped dead in her tracks for ten seconds.

Jonathan, too, seemed to freeze, his gaze on Ever and no one else.

Rose glanced back and forth like she was watching a tennis match, waiting for one of them to break. She saw Ever's shoulder twitch right before she smiled, too big and too bright, like the biggest dork on the planet. She waved one awkward hand. Jonathan waved back, his face still one of shock. His mouth was set in a straight line, not a smile nor a frown.

Ever tossed her long chestnut hair over her shoulders, then fixed Rose in her narrowed gaze.

Rose looked Ever straight in the eye, a vivid smile on her face like she hadn't a clue what she'd orchestrated.

"I hate you," Ever whispered as she slid onto the seat across from Rose.

Rose shrugged, a wry grin on her lips. "I don't know what you mean. The Peak has the best burgers in town."

Jonathan strode up behind Ever, his face one of confusion. Rose again felt terrible for him. He was no doubt flicking through everything he could say now, as anyone faced with an ex would be.

He came to a stop between them. "Everly, it's been a long time," Jonathan said in his deep, soft voice, his hands on his hips, then down at his sides.

Rose thought he might go in for a hug, but his back tensed, and he remained where he was.

Ever looked up at him. Rose could see Ever's chest rising and falling, her breath a little rapid.

She blasted Rose with a fiery look before turning her body in the chair. Ever still had a beautiful figure. Not as tall as Rose, but close. Ever was slim, but not overly so, her hips and behind shapely, her face still plump in the cheeks. Age hadn't sunk her yet. Her skin, the attribute Rose had always found the most beautiful thing about her, was still smooth, the line or two around her eyes barely noticeable. Ever's hair had been short in high school, but now it was long, curled in a beachy wave, almost as long as Rose's. All in all, Ever was still a beauty.

Ever smiled up at Jonathan, her shoulders as tense as his. "It has been a long time. I heard you own the bar now. That's fantastic."

Jonathan shrugged. His brow crinkled a bit, and Rose wondered if he was hoping for a more dramatic reunion with the girl who'd broken his heart. This was tepid at best.

"I suppose. It beats real work. Did you come back for Nathan's funeral?"

Ever nodded. "Yeah. Not staying long, in any case. I go back to New Orleans the day after tomorrow."

"Well, it was nice of you to come. I know you were all tight"—Jonathan paused—"in high school. I didn't go myself. I hate funerals. Donated to the museum in his name, though."

"I'm sure he would have appreciated that, Jonathan." Rose picked up her menu. She didn't want to talk about the funeral, and although she'd enjoyed Ever's discomfort, she was ready to move on to the real reason for this meeting.

Jonathan must have taken her hint because he asked, "What can I get you two?" His hazel eyes were still on Ever.

"I'll have a plain cheeseburger and an iced tea, please." Rose handed him her menu.

Ever scrambled to take a look at hers. "I'll have the black bean burger and water. Thanks." She handed her menu to Jonathan, staring at his hands rather than looking into his eyes.

"Sure," he said, turning from them with a sad, faraway

look in his eye.

Ever folded her hands on the table. "Feel better now?"

"Not really. I thought I would enjoy that more, but now I feel bad for Jonathan." Rose gazed into Ever's eyes. There were about a thousand questions Rose wanted to ask, and if there was ever a time, this was it. She had Ever right where she'd always wanted her—alone. There was no one to interrupt her or pull Ever's attention away. Except for Jonathan, maybe. But instead of asking all the things Rose felt she had a right to understand, her resolve melted.

Ever looked behind her. Jonathan had disappeared into the back.

Rose chewed on the inside of her lip. They should have gone somewhere else. "Why don't you go back there and talk to him?"

Ever turned back toward her, one eyebrow raised to the heavens. "Right. Like Jonathan would love to talk to the bitch of Christmas past." She rubbed her eyes before continuing. "Let's just talk about the whole break-in situation. Do you have a plan?"

Rose quirked a smile. She always had a plan. "The best way to do this will be during the day."

Ever's mouth dropped open for half a second. "During the day? Are you nuts?"

Rose narrowed her gaze, rolling her eyes about halfway. Only one person at this table was nuts, and it was not her. "There's too much to contend with at night. The whole place is alarmed by cameras and security guards. We'll be shot before we get halfway up the front steps. Long gone are the days of easy break-ins."

"The break-ins were never easy, Rose. But, you wouldn't take no for an answer."

There wasn't much of a police presence in Splendid, but touristy locales did protect themselves against out-of-towners.

"You had fun. Don't pretend like you didn't." Rose closed her mouth. Jonathan was on his way to their table with their drinks.

"Don't you have someone to wait on tables?" Rose asked him as he sat down the water and iced tea.

"Marty just left. Cramps or something. I didn't need the details."

Rose laughed, but it was Ever he glanced at before taking off again. Rose would have given anything in the world to know what happened between them, but that's not why they were there.

"Anyway," Rose said. "Melody, the front desk intern, doesn't know you, which makes this perfect. I'll distract Melody from her desk while you pick the lock to Nathan's office. Then I'll join you inside. Simple."

"Aren't there cameras and guards during the day?" Ever had one hand around the water glass, turning it slowly on the tabletop.

"There's one guard who works during the day. He usually mills around the front door. On my way inside, I thought I'd tell him I saw someone suspicious messing with the windows at the back of the museum. That will get him out of the way. The cameras are what they are. We can't disable them, but we'll be long gone by the time anyone figures it out. I don't think anyone in a booth is actively watching the feed."

"And then we'll get arrested for breaking and entering. Isn't that still a felony?"

Rose took a sip of her iced tea. "We won't get arrested. You're a direct descendant of the founder of Splendid, for god's sake, and I'm … Well, I'm me. All we're doing is gathering a few personal photos and knick-knacks. Property that technically belongs to Nathan's mom. Believe me, I'm ready to get down and dirty if I have to. Let's shoot for tomorrow afternoon. I'll pick you up at noon."

Ever looked up at the ceiling, then back down at Rose. "Fine, but then how do we get out? They'll see us walking out with his things."

Rose took a deep breath. Ever always had to make

everything so complicated. "I'll have a tote bag to take Nathan's belongings out of the museum. Stop overthinking this. It's simple."

"Simple, except I think I remember you telling me something like that before." Ever took a drink of water, glancing over her shoulder at Jonathan, who was cleaning up the table behind them.

"What happened between the two of you? You had just started dating when we stopped talking, like really dating. I remember teasing you about him at Red Manor, but that was just the beginning of the relationship. So, I heard. Nathan said that you two were pretty hot for each other. According to Fletcher, you ripped out his heart when you left." Rose had kept her curiosity to herself for as long as possible. It was time Ever spilled one or two of her secrets.

Ever looked down at the table, tracing the wood grain with a finger. "I don't remember. Who cares, anyway? It was a million years ago, a lifetime ago. I could ask you the same about that Anna girl. Weren't the two of you a couple? I saw you holding hands at graduation."

Rose watched Ever trace lines all over the table. "I'll tell you what happened with Anna if you tell me what happened with Jonathan. We may as well talk about something while we wait for our food."

Ever stopped her tracing, leveling Rose with one glance. "Fine. You first."

Rose rolled her eyes. "Of course, me first." She cleared her throat, adjusting her seat. Talking about Anna wasn't the most comfortable thing in the world, and Ever probably knew that. "We were a couple. She was my first real girlfriend. I couldn't take her home or even hang out much with her after school because my mom suspected something and didn't want me to see her. So most of our relationship happened at school between periods, at lunch, at school events." Rose smiled to herself. She hadn't thought about Anna in some time. The beautiful girl with the eyebrow piercing and the stars tattooed on her shoulder. "I thought

69

after graduation, since I had finally turned eighteen, that we'd get to spend more time together. But she went off to New York to model. She did pretty well for a while, but then she fell off the map. I'm not sure what she's doing now. My first experience with heartbreak. Which is why I could always relate to Jonathan."

It was Ever's turn, and Rose made that clear by resting her chin on her fist. Finally, she was ready to listen.

Ever's head bobbed up and down. "Yeah, well, I guess I did to Jonathan what Anna did to you. Except I didn't give him any warning, I just left. I didn't even leave him a letter or anything, and I never contacted him again." She looked down at the table. "Pretty shitty, I guess. But I had to get out of here, and he and I were so … intense, so in lust with each other, that I knew if I told him about my plans, he'd either try to stop me or want to go with me."

"Why not let him go with you? Especially if you felt the same for him."

Ever shook her head. "I don't know, Rose. I was so young, so immature. I was so dead set on getting out of Splendid that it was all I could focus on. I couldn't take the chance that he would thwart my escape somehow. But, believe me, Jonathan is one in a very long list of regrets."

Rose leaned back in her seat, stretching her back. "Jesus, Ever. You talk like you were trying to escape from a cult or something. No one would have stopped you from leaving, for god's sake. You got out of here, didn't you? There wasn't a SWAT team at the border demanding you turn around."

"Very funny. You don't know what I felt like at the time, Rose. I felt like something here was consuming me, and not one person I cared about believed me. Not even Jonathan."

Rose chewed on her lip as she and Ever stared into each other's souls for several seconds, neither talking but working out what to say next.

Ever spoke first. "Did you mean what you said last night? That you believe me?"

Rose took a deep breath. She was a little wobbly and

unsteady, and she wasn't sure why. All she'd had to drink was tea. "I'm not saying I fully believe. Let's get that clear. But something is fishy with the whole mayor thing. I didn't tell you that part, but why in the hell does the mayor have to clear Nathan's belongings? It's weird and reminds me of the weirdness from the night we were caught at Red Manor. I can't explain why, but it does. That's all."

Ever's face went blank with surprise. Rose couldn't read her at all. Was she registering shock, or was this some trauma response, and Ever had retreated into herself?

"Ever?" she asked.

Ever's hands clasped over the top of the table, kneading themselves together. "What do you mean, Rose? Is there something from that night that you kept from me? I always thought there was, that you were deliberately holding back." Her voice was quiet, except for a slight shrill inflection when she said *that night*.

Rose pulled her hair up, twisting it into a knot at the back of her head, then letting it fall over her shoulders. She shouldn't have said that. She shouldn't have said anything about that night. Only it seemed related in some bizarre way to Nathan's office being off-limits. So how did she articulate what she'd seen without Ever losing her shit in front of half of Splendid? There was decorum to be maintained, that placid, Splendid mask, to always be kept in place.

"Okay. I didn't exactly keep this from you." She paused, guilt forming a knot in her stomach. "Okay, I did because the mayor and your mom asked me to." She looked down, grabbing hold of her iced tea like it was an anchor. "I was a kid, Ever, the same as you were with Jonathan, so give me some grace. The whole thing freaked me out, and you know how my mom was. I couldn't risk them calling the police or telling my parents what we did."

"What happened, Rose?"

Rose put up a hand. "Let me get there because it wasn't any one thing. It was a series of strange things. I need to start from the beginning."

And that's what Rose did. She reached back into the far reaches of her memory, pulling out details from a single night twenty-nine years ago.

CHAPTER EIGHT

1994

For a second, Rose thought Ever might be dead. Cold sweat broke out on her lower back and her upper lip. Moisture coated the back of her hand as she wiped the sweat away, panic causing her heart rate to spike and her mind to go blank.

The red meat smell hung heavy in the air, only making her nervous nausea worse.

Ever lay in a heap, face down, by the front door of Red Manor. They were still locked in. Rose dropped to her knees, hooking her hands under Ever's limp body to roll her onto her back. A lump the size of a knuckle had formed on her forehead, right under her hairline.

"Shit, Ever. Wake up." Rose felt for a pulse. Ever was alive, and her pulse seemed normal. These were minor reassurances, as they were currently somewhere they shouldn't be. Ever was unconscious, the house was dark around them.

The floor creaked behind her, and Rose, already on heightened alert, yelped as she jumped to her feet.

She blinked rapidly, trying to make out anything in the darkness. What was she seeing? The foyer was so dark. There was a click, and the room flooded with light, so bright Rose had to shield her eyes.

Splendid's mayor, a man average in every way, stood in front of her. "What on earth is going on here?"

Rose swallowed the knot forming in the back of her throat. She pointed down at Ever. They were caught. There was nothing she could do to fix that now. The only thing that mattered was getting Ever help. To hell with the punishments that awaited her at home. "I'm sorry, sir. We were looking around, and we got scared, and my friend ran into the door, and she was hurt. We need to call an ambulance." Rose's words came out in a rush. All the bravado she'd felt during the initial phase of their adventure had left her as quickly as the lump on Ever's head had swelled.

"You were looking around?" Mayor Hart stood there with his hands clasped in front of him like he was getting ready to lead a sermon. For the first time, Rose realized her principal was probably this man's son.

While she was thinking this, she noticed what the mayor was wearing. He was covered from his shoulders to the floor in a black cloak. Rose blinked some more as she tried to make sense of what she saw. He looked like he was graduating. All he needed were the cap and tassel.

"Y-y-yes," she stammered, glancing down at Ever again, then back at the mayor. There was only one way to get out of this. Splendid was the nepotism capital of the world. She stepped back, revealing Ever's face on the ground behind her. "You know Everly, sir, Everly Palmer. She knocked herself unconscious when she ran into the door."

That did it. The mayor stepped forward as he gazed down at Ever, the deep line between his brows melting. "Don't move, young lady. I'll get Dr. Sprague."

Rose froze where she was, even though she had never been so confused. The mayor was going to get Dr. Sprague?

Wouldn't time be saved by calling an ambulance and having the doctor meet them at the hospital?

She didn't have much more time to think about this. Dr. Sprague, an elderly and stooped figure, emerged from nowhere like magic. He, too, wore the same black robes as the mayor. Rose stepped back, too bright to mention the odd way they were dressed. That was something to consider at a later time.

The doctor kneeled next to Ever. He felt for her pulse, opened her eyelids, and then felt her head. "She knocked herself out, all right. She's out cold and will be for a while."

"Is she all right? Does she need an X-ray, a CAT scan?" The mayor loomed over the scene, his gaze glued to what was happening on the floor.

The doctor shook his head. "She's fine. She might be slightly concussed, but if she is, it's minor. It's swelling outward, which is a good sign. She smacked a part of her head that isn't generally associated with brain bleeds. I'd say all she needs is to be tucked into bed. She'll have a headache tomorrow, but that's about all."

Dr. Sprague struggled to his feet. He must have been seventy years old, or at least that's how old he appeared to Rose, fresh as she was in life.

"Well, that's a relief. Elsie is on her way." The mayor looked at Rose. "She'll take you both home."

Rose nodded. This was slightly relieving. It didn't appear that the police were being called. She kneeled back down by Ever. "You're sure she doesn't need to go to the hospital?"

Dr. Sprague laughed, which took Rose aback. She stared up at him, one hand on Ever's shoulder.

"She'll be fine. Everly is a Palmer. That means her head is about as hard as they get."

The mayor laughed, too. Rose tried to smile, forcing a chuckle past her teeth.

Mayor Hart looked down at Rose as she crouched by the grand front door of an establishment where she wasn't welcome. She felt all this and more in the directness of his gaze. "I'm sure this goes without saying, Rose, but this is a stunt you'll never try to pull again, I trust?"

"No, sir." Rose shook her head, a shiver running up both her arms. The mayor knew her name. How did the mayor know her name? One thing was sure, she'd rather die than try to enter Red Manor again in her lifetime. "And it's probably best if you don't mention that the doctor was here this evening. I was here, working late, and that is all anyone needs to know."

Mayor Hart didn't say anything about their strange clothing, but Rose wasn't born yesterday. He would expect her to continue to ignore the cloaks when she spoke of this night. She caressed a hand over Ever's hair, worrying not only about her head but her friend's emotional state, too. There were days Ever was so tired from lack of sleep, her hands jittery, her eyes hollow, that Rose feared she might have some sort of breakdown. Nightmares were the bane of Everly's existence, her mother refusing at every turn to let her talk to a counselor.

Lights swept through the windows, bathing the foyer in even brighter light. A car door slammed, followed by footsteps running up the walk. Mayor Hart nudged Rose aside, bending down to pick up Ever. Then, as Rose stood to move aside again, she noticed another strange thing: two dots of something red blotted the white shirt collar peeking underneath the mayor's black robes.

Rose looked down, hoping her face wouldn't register what she'd seen. The mayor didn't seem to notice as he swept Ever in his arms. He carried her out to Elsie's car, laying her across the back seat. Rose buckled herself into the front, relieved to be removed from Red Manor and the strange men contained within.

While Elsie drove her home, rambling on about how disappointed she was in them and how lucky they were to have avoided getting into worse trouble, Rose stared out the windshield with one hand stretched behind her, clasped around Ever's wrist. Her pulse was strong under Rose's finger, and that's all she cared about.

Elsie was right; the night could have gone so much worse. They could have been arrested. Ever could have been more seriously injured. But all Rose could think about were those black robes and those two drops of blood.

"Rose," Elsie said. "Rose, did you hear me?"

Rose's mind was busy flicking through all the possible reasons for the blood on the mayor's collar. Shaving? Pimple popping? Vampirism? Shaving, it was probably shaving.

"Rose." Elsie reached her hand over, giving Rose's arm a slight push.

"Sorry?" Rose blinked the image of the blood from her mind. "What did you say?" She continued to stare out the windshield, her right hand still stretched behind her, attached to Ever's arm like a barnacle.

"I said you're home."

Rose looked out the side window. They were parked next to the sidewalk, two houses down from where she lived. She looked back at Elsie.

There was a sympathetic tilt to her head. "I'm guessing you snuck out, too. I won't tell your mom about this, Rose. There's no need to get her involved."

"Thank you so much, Elsie." Rose meant every word. She was grateful for Elsie's discretion. Getting in trouble with her mom was an almost daily occurrence for the most minor offenses. Had her mom gotten wind of this, who knew what kind of punishment Rose would face?

"You're welcome. Of course, you can do me one favor in return." Elsie tried to smile in a childlike, innocent way, but instead of looking sweet, the glow from the streetlamp set her eyes aglow like she was possessed from within.

Rose returned Elsie's fake smile. She should have known better than to assume Elsie cared for her welfare. You could never trust adults, a fact Rose had learned early on in her life. "Sure, Elsie. Whatever you need."

Elsie's attempt at a smile devolved into a glare. "I know

you noticed the robes, Rose. You're a smart girl. Goodness, but everyone in your little group is so smart. You may have even noticed the spots on the mayor's collar. Did you? I sure did. Men aren't as tidy as women, are they?"

Rose was adept at keeping her emotions under wraps. Growing up with a manipulative mother, someone who used every feeling Rose ever had against her, she'd grown accustomed to dropping a blank mask over her features whenever the situation called for numbness. She did this now, her face betraying none of the fear and trepidation she felt inside. Her pulse may have quickened, and sweat may have been collecting between her shoulder blades, but she betrayed none of this. Instead, she simply said, "Spots?"

Elsie narrowed her eyes. Ever's mom wasn't as skilled a poker player as Rose. Elsie was trying to see through Rose's defenses, see past the hollowness of her eyes, but Rose knew there was nothing for Elsie to see.

"Anyway, whatever you think you may have seen, you saw nothing unusual. The mayor was there working late, and that is all. The doctor was called, and all was determined to be well. So no harm done, and here we are."

A groan issued from the back seat as Ever began to stir. Rose looked back. The color was returning to her friend's cheeks.

"Don't worry about Everly. I'll get her tucked into bed. I want to ensure we understand each other before you go."

"Nothing unusual happened, and no harm was done. Exactly as I remember it." Rose put her hand on the door handle. "Goodnight, Elsie." She swung the door open, stepping out onto the sidewalk, the fresh night air welcome after being trapped with the stink of Elsie's pineapple-scented air freshener.

Breaking into Red Manor had been her idea. Rose thrived on the prospect of getting in trouble, and she'd never really been sure why. Getting into trouble with her mom would bring punishment no one should run toward. Ever tried to analyze this need in her once. Ever had said that since Rose never received any positive attention from her mother, she thrived on the negative. She'd take any attention she could get. Rose had been upset and had told her to shut up. They hadn't spoken for two miserable days until they'd both finally apologized. Maybe Ever was right, perhaps negative attention from her mom was all Rose could get, and she'd learned to take what she could. Even so, something about Elsie had never seemed quite right to Rose. Almost like she tried too hard to be too perfect. Rose hated anyone who tried too hard.

Elsie rolled away the second Rose shut the car door. She didn't need to wait to ensure Rose reached her home safely. No one was ever murdered or even assaulted in Splendid. Not ever. The last murders in the city happened over a hundred years ago. The terrible axe murders on Dale Street. Rose had nothing to fear, and she knew it. Still, the night seemed alive around her, raising gooseflesh along her arms. Crickets sang so loud the sound was almost startling. Cricket song was usual during the summer and fall months, but the sound was typically soft and calming even when one opened their window to the cool night breeze. Tonight, the sound was raucous, almost violent.

The canopy of tree limbs that crisscrossed the street was so dark and heavy that it was like walking through a tent. An owl hooted overhead so loudly she heard it over the roar of the cricket song. She had an inexplicable feeling of being smothered by the flora and fauna of Splendid.

A pit dropped like a stone in Rose's stomach as she hurried along the walk toward home. The sooner she snuck in through the window she'd left open in the living room, the better. Home had never been a welcome place for Rose. That's why she spent so much time at Ever's, so much time studying at the library, and so much time anywhere but there. But tonight, she couldn't wait to get back inside her mother's palace.

Rose would do as Elsie expected. She wouldn't mention the robes, and she surely wouldn't mention the blood.

Whatever those old freaks got up to after dark was none of her business, and whatever she'd seen on the stairs was just a figment of her frenzied imagination.

CHAPTER NINE

The uneaten veggie burger sat untouched on Everly's plate, the cheese congealing and rubbery around the edges. Rose had paused her story only once when Jonathan had brought their meals from the kitchen. Everly could see him watching her from the corner of her eye. She mumbled a thank you as he walked away, her blood pressure rising and receding based on his proximity. There was so much going on at the moment, and processing everything was hard. This was what she'd wanted. She'd wanted so badly to run into him, but now that they were in the same room, she was frozen. Her stomach hurt, her heart thudding in her chest.

She sat across from Rose, the person she'd thought was more than her best friend. She and Rose had referred to each other as soul friends throughout their childhood, convinced they'd been connected in previous lives. Everly's mom had always thought there was more to their relationship, that the two girls, once they hit high school, were romantic, but what they shared was more profound than sexual attraction. Rose had read about Anam Cara in one of the twenty-five thousand books she read in high school. Anam Cara was a Celtic concept that meant soul friend, someone who knew you on a level no one else ever would. Rose had been her Anam Cara, which is why Everly had never been able to forget her and why she'd never been able to forgive her for turning her back when reality began to slip.

Not only this, but the only boy Everly had ever had real feelings for was now the most handsome man she'd ever seen, serving her water and a veggie burger, acting like they were nothing more than acquaintances who'd once gone to school together. Jonathan was always the best-looking guy she'd ever known. In high school, his six-foot-five frame had been almost a little too lean. Now, he'd filled in the perfect amount. His arms looked muscular, well-developed biceps flexing below his short-sleeved T-shirt, with defined pectoral muscles pressing through the fine cotton. She even liked the dusting of white mixed in with the ginger of his facial hair. Not quite a beard, more of an afterthought. Jonathan was always kind, always polite, so she shouldn't have been surprised by his relaxed behavior. She didn't know what she had expected when they'd locked eyes for the first time in so long, but this detached civility wasn't it.

These two people, two of the three people who'd meant the world to her, now in her direct vicinity, would have been enough to deal with. They weren't. She also had to sit on her hands so she wouldn't chew her nails, a habit she kicked long ago, and listen while Rose told her something else had happened that night over two decades ago. The night she thought she'd lost her mind.

Neither of them touched their food while Rose talked. And boy, did Rose talk. Everly didn't interject once. The information she was receiving felt like a cancer diagnosis, or at least, that's how she imagined it. Her mind and heart were numb as she tried to absorb what Rose was saying, panic building somewhere in the back of her brain. Something in her wanted to react, but she didn't know the correct response. Everly wasn't good with emotions on the best of days—something she and Rose had in common. Rose's repression came from a childhood of abuse. Everly's from a childhood of unknown trauma, nightmares, night terrors, gaps in her memory, and a mother and friends who were never willing to help or even believe her. The tears she'd spilled the night before, only a couple, had come from a build-up of weirdness and pain. Now she thought she might scream instead. Mature, emotional regulation had always eluded her.

Rose stared hard into her eyes. "The main reason why I distanced myself from you was that I felt so guilty over keeping this from you."

When Rose finally finished, she heaved a huge sigh before reaching for her iced tea. Almost as if the weight of this secret was finally free to leave her. She took a deep drink, her eyes fluttering as she watched Everly. Everly knew Rose was waiting for a reaction, but what? What sort of reaction should she give? She always knew that something else had happened that night. Something she'd seen or some vibe the house had given off had triggered a remembrance deep within her psyche. She'd been haunted by visions and hallucinations ever since, a hazy spot in the corner of her eye that never cleared and couldn't possibly exist, according to optometrists and other doctors. So the revelation that there had been more to the story hadn't been much of a revelation. It was the fact that Rose had known all along that something bizarre had happened that night. She'd known and allowed Everly to feel crazy for thinking there was something more to the story.

Everly pushed the untouched burger to the edge of the table. The smell of cold black beans and the congealing oil on the fries turned her stomach. If she'd wanted to make a scene, she could push the plate onto the floor and storm out like a pissed-off cat, but what good would that sort of thing do?

She could throw her water in Rose's face. The thought sat in her mind as she gripped the glass, condensation dripping off the sides, but one thing she could never do was commit violence against Rose. Rose was just as fucked up as she was.

Rose had had enough of the silence. Rose couldn't stand silence, and Everly knew it. She cleared her throat to draw Everly's attention. "Are you going to say something?"

"What am I supposed to say, Rose? Thank you for telling me. Is that what you want to hear? Okay, then. Thank you for giving me the information I should have had almost thirty years ago. Thank you for telling me, the girl you called your Anam Cara, the truth after all this time." Everly pierced Rose with a cold stare. "What about what we saw on the staircase?"

Rose squirmed again in her seat. Everly had never seen her squirm so much, not once. "I told you back then that I didn't see anything on the staircase. But about the rest of it, I'm sorry," she practically whispered the words. "I was a child, too, and I was scared."

Everly thought Rose might cry. She hoped she would. To see the mighty Rose spill a little emotion might be some consolation, flimsy though it felt.

"I'm sure you are. It's easy to be sorry now. What I wonder is, were you sorry then?"

Rose flinched.

Everly slid off the stool, fishing cash from her pocket. She dropped a twenty on the table.

"Ever, wait. We have things to talk about."

Everly snorted a laugh. "We have nothing to talk about, Rose. Not now and not ever again. You're right, we were both kids, but we're adults now, and neither of us has to put up with anything less than we believe we're worth ever again." She moved toward the door, grateful to have a plane ticket out of the Splendid hell hole. She'd gladly sit inside the bathroom if it meant the plane would take her out of Colorado.

"What about Nathan's office?" Rose called behind her.

"I don't give a shit about Nathan's office." With that, she pulled open the massive double glass doors, a

Halloween skeleton waving to her as she went, not daring a look behind.

.

CHAPTER TEN

Back at home, the leaves were beginning to pile up in the front yard and along the brick walk, golden and fragile. They turned to dust under Everly's feet. There was a unique fall smell, earthy with a touch of wood smoke, in Splendid that she had to admit she missed. She inhaled deeply, remembering the falls of her youth, of pumpkin carving, costume shopping, and sipping whatever strange tea she and Rose had newly concocted.

She hovered over the brick with the strange symbol, staring down at it as if its meaning would become clear simply by giving it the evil eye. Then, crouching down, Everly traced the figure eight as she'd done at the cemetery. The tree with exposed roots, sitting inside the left loop, the wing in the other, stared back at her. Everly felt challenged by the stare, but there was no way she'd win a staring contest with a fixed image.

"Everly, what on earth are you doing?" Mom called from the front porch, startling Everly so severely she almost fell over, lost in her thoughts as she'd been.

She righted herself, still in a crouch. With one hand on the stamped brick, she looked up at her mom, sitting in her wheelchair with a book in her hand. Everly had been so out of it that she hadn't even seen her on the porch. "Mom, what is this?"

Her mom craned her head to get a better look. She glanced at Everly with concern. "A brick?" The inflection at the end of her answer meant she thought her daughter had once again lost her marbles.

"No, Mom." Everly shook her head. She was exasperated from head to toe after the lunch with Rose and the awkward encounter with Jonathan. The last thing she needed was her mom looking at her like she belonged in a straitjacket. "What is this symbol stamped onto the brick?"

Mom dropped her book in her lap, pressing herself slightly more upright in her chair. "I don't know, Everly. I can't see it. What does the symbol look like? It's probably a maker's mark."

"I don't think so." Everly slid her phone from her back pocket, snapping a photograph. "I'll show you; hold on."

She jogged up the walk, crushing leaves underfoot, then bounded up the front steps, dodging pumpkins, her phone held out in front of her.

"There's an infinity symbol with a rooty tree in one loop and a wing in the other." She said all this as she handed the phone to her mom.

Her mom expanded the image, bringing the phone closer to her face. She was wearing her glasses, but still squinted at the photo. "I've no idea what this is. Do you know I've never noticed it before? How strange." She continued to stare at the picture. Finally, after a couple more minutes, she returned the phone with a shrug. "You know this house has been here for over a hundred and twenty years. I imagine the symbol is some old sort of maker's mark, as I said."

Everly took the phone, glancing at the image one more time before clicking it off and sticking it back in her pocket. "I guess, but I saw it on a grave, too. At Everwood, the day of Nathan's funeral."

"Was the grave an old one?"

Everly nodded. "Yeah, the late 1800s."

"There you go, then. Whoever made our bricks probably made the gravestone, as well."

"Probably." Everly leaned against the porch railing, gazing toward Nathan's old house. In her mind, she saw them at his sister's tenth birthday party playing croquet on the lawn, chocolate icing smeared on both their faces.

Her mom glanced that way. "Nathan loved that house. He wanted to restore it for him and Charlie to live in. Did you know that?"

Everly shook her head.

"No, I imagine you didn't." Mom probably didn't mean for this accurate statement to cut Everly to the quick, but it did. "He spent much time there in recent weeks, measuring and making plans."

An ache bloomed in Everly's chest. Nathan had been making plans for his future, which he never had the chance to have.

"Are you going to be home for dinner? I'm making a casserole."

Casserole was a generic term her mom used for many different dishes. These dishes consisted of meat, an assortment of frozen vegetables, and whatever sort of canned cream soup she had in the cupboard.

"Sounds great, Mom. Do you need some help?" Everly gripped the railing behind her as she leaned against it. The rough texture of the old wood felt good as it pinched her, reminding her that she could still feel something other than the pain of being in Splendid.

"I do not. I freeze my casseroles now. Audrey comes over, and we make a day of putting several together. Then I pop them in the freezer and pull them out when I'm hungry. Easy."

Everly wanted to laugh at the idea of Audrey, with her crazy wigs and smeared red lipstick, helping Mom with anything. "Okay, then. I'll be upstairs in the crow's nest. If you need me, text me, and I'll come down."

Mom reached out a hand. "Before you go, dear, I was wondering if you've seen Jonathan? Perhaps I should invite him over for dinner."

Everly gripped the railing tighter, a splinter of wood scratching her palm. "I don't think that's a good idea, Mom, but it was a nice thought."

"The two of you made such a good couple, and I know from Audrey that he's still single." Mom offered a sympathetic tilt of the head. "Don't discount him just yet. You've both matured so much."

What did Everly say to this? She bit the inside of her lip, willing a response to materialize in her brain. Instead, all she could say was, "Not tonight, Mom."

"All right, then. You're the boss." Mom smiled, picking up her book in the universal signal of *thank you next*.

Everly gladly took the cue.

The soft, worn fibers of the couch were a comfort after the crappy afternoon she'd had. Bright sunlight streamed in, and the room was so warm that her eyes began to droop. A little catnap before dinner might not only be welcome, but sleep would also make the day go by faster, bringing her several hours closer to the time she had to be at the airport.

She kicked off her shoes, intending to lay her head on the faded yellow pillow at her elbow, but her journal, lying half open on the crate, caught her eye.

Picking up the pink diary, she flipped, this time to the front, to the beginning. The very first entry was dated February 1992. Everly read the first two lines before tossing the book back on the crate. She knew the entry well and remembered vividly sitting on this couch to write the words on a cold afternoon.

Everly leaned forward, dropping her head in her hands, pressing the heels into the sockets of her eyes. She didn't want to think about the journal entry. She didn't want to think about anything but knew sleep wouldn't come for her, not in the middle of the day.

Something her mom had said stuck in the back of her mind, other than her bringing up Jonathan out of the blue. Mom had said Nathan had been coming to his old house with a tape measure to begin plans for renovations. On his own? Without a contractor? That didn't seem like Nathan. Her old friend had been many things, but a builder wasn't one of them. Of course, he could have taken up the hobby in recent years. What the hell did Everly know? But, as wealthy as his family was, richer than her own, that didn't seem very likely.

Everly stood up, drifting toward the window that faced Nathan's. She ran a hand over the warm glass, her breath fogging it up as she leaned closer. There was that piece of paper still taped on his window. What the hell did it say? She squinted, pressing her forehead against the glass. There was no way she could see the words, not at this distance. Maybe it was one of those papers, like a permit, that builders stick in the windows of houses they're renovating. But then again, Mom hadn't said anything about contractors. That's something her mom would not have missed. That woman was always keenly aware of everything that happened in the neighborhood. A wheelchair wouldn't have stopped her from pulling out her opera glasses to get a closer look at who Nathan had hired to fix up his house.

Everly tapped the glass with a fingernail. There was only one way to find out what was stuck to the window. She had to go over there and see for herself.

Her mom had once had a key to the Strattons' back door in case of emergencies. They'd had one to Everly's house for the same reason. The key, attached to a Batman keychain, was kept on a hook by the back door. Nathan's dad loved superheroes. So if her mom were still on the porch, this would be the easiest break-in of all time. No Rose needed.

Everly got up, ignoring the diary as she walked by, open to the details of her recurring nightmare. Walking down memory lane was probably fun for most people. For her, it was just another layer of hell.

Everly's Journal
February 21, 1992

The nightmare came back. After six months, the nightmare came back. It was the same as always. I'm in a dark room with no walls. There's some kind of flicker—candles, maybe? I'm strapped to a cold metal table or chair, my eyes are always too bleary to see, with my arm, always my right arm, hanging over the edge. There's a sharp pain as someone, I can never see who, slices into the soft inside nook of my elbow. Blood drips down my arm, splattering onto the floor. I can hear each drop as it falls and hits the ground. I always wake with a start, my pajamas soaked with sweat. This time, like all the times, I ran into Mom's room. I threw myself on her, sobbing and sweating. She doesn't like that. She patted my head and told me the same thing she says every single time: It was a dream. You're fine. *Mom says the nightmares are from when a nurse took my blood for a routine test. I was tiny. The nurse was new, in training or something, and she didn't know what she was doing. She kept stabbing my arm, missing my veins, and in the end, my whole arm was black and blue, leaving me with the scar I now have. Mom says I was traumatized by that nurse and that I need to let it go. She says it was a long time ago, and I'm fine now. I don't feel fine. I argued with Mom. I asked her how one event could give me nightmares for ten years. An event, Mom says, wasn't a big deal. I asked Mom if I could see the counselor at school, and she shook her head like she was mad.* Palmers don't go to therapy, Everly, *she said.* People will talk, and we can't have that. You have to forget it. *I told her I've tried, over and over, to ignore it, but I can't. I'm meeting Rose, Nathan, Fletcher, and Leigh at the mall today. I'm going to ask them what they think. I don't feel fine.*

CHAPTER ELEVEN

1994

The bell rang ten minutes before she was ready for it. Everly couldn't find her psychology book, her disaster of a locker, and her foggy brain conspiring against her at every turn. The image staring back at her through the half-thrashed locker mirror looked every bit as haggard as she felt. Her head throbbed, a raised lump the size of a quarter near her widow's peak. Whatever had happened last night, she'd found herself tucked into bed this morning. She took out a brush and smoothed down her short, tangled hair. She adjusted the smashed collar of her flannel and tucked in her REM concert tee.

"Ms. Palmer, did we not hear the bell, or are we ignoring the rules this morning?"

Everly jumped, her heart threatening to stop. Mr. Hart, Splendid High's young and not unattractive principal, hovered about ten feet away, one eyebrow raised.

"I can't find my book, sir, but I'll see if I can borrow one." She banged the locker door shut and scurried past him, her face pointed at the notebook in her hands as if she found it the most fascinating thing in the world.

Mrs. Moore side-eyed her as she entered the class at the beginning of the lecture. Everly slunk into the front row desk, doing everything in her power to look as small as possible. She was never late to class, not once, not ever. That was Rose's MO, not hers. Rose, who sat next to her during their first-period psych class, wasn't there yet. Not unusual for her.

She sauntered in about five minutes later, her hair a shocking purple.

"When did you have time to do that? And are you going to tell me what happened last night? My mom wouldn't say a word to me this morning," Everly whispered as Rose took her seat.

"Couldn't sleep. I was too keyed up after being caught, you know?"

"We got caught?"

"Yeah, you hit your head and passed out. Thank the goddess Mayor Hart was there so late. He called the doctor and your mom." The news that they had been caught breaking into Red Manor by the mayor was not welcome. "The doctor said you were fine, no concussion, and your mom took us home. She was nice enough not to tell my parents what happened, and Mayor Hart said he wouldn't call the cops. We got lucky. You don't remember any of this?"

Mrs. Moore cleared her throat.

Everly shook her head. She didn't remember a thing after running into the door. Rose kept whispering that what Everly saw on the staircase was nothing, an overactive imagination, but hadn't it been fun? She liked to be scared. Haunted houses and horror movies were two of her favorite things. Sometimes Everly wondered why they were friends—there could be no one more her opposite than Rose.

"Everly?"

Oh, shit. Mrs. Moore stared pointedly at her. She must

have asked a question. Everly swallowed. "Yes, ma'am."

"Can you answer the question, or should I ask someone else?"

Snickers in the back row.

"Can you repeat the question, please?"

Mrs. Moore closed her eyes for a second, probably to roll them behind her lids. "Yes, Everly. From Friday's reading, the question was, name one of Jung's four Archetypes and explain it in two to three sentences."

After what they had been through the night before, Friday seemed like a hundred years ago. Everly squirmed a bit in her seat. Psychology was her favorite class. Rose even called her Mrs. Moore's pet student, but right now, she felt off, like her balance had shifted, and her head still hurt like hell.

Then it came to her. "The Shadow. The Shadow is all about repression, what we don't want the world to see. Like, our prejudices and our, um ..." She was hoping Mrs. Moore would rescue her, but her teacher just stared, her hands clasped in front of her. "Our sexual desires."

More snickers in the back.

"Excellent, Everly. Anyone else?" Mrs. Moore shifted her focus to the rest of the class as several hands shot in the air.

Everly risked a look back, and Jonathan—the cutest boy in the world—was staring right at her, a little smirk emphasizing the dimples on his beautiful face. She jerked her head back around before he could see her cheeks flush.

While Angela was talking about the Persona, another of Jung's Archetypes, Everly took a moment to close her eyes. She was one of those people who needed a lot of sleep. Again, the opposite of Rose, who could stay up all night and never feel it.

She thought about the Shadow and last night. Maybe an entity is nothing more than leftover feelings and desires from life, the thoughts and emotions they never got to express. That's why ghosts couldn't always communicate.

They were nothing more than base instinct. As Everly was having these thoughts, she shivered. She was freezing in her flannel shirt in a building older than the city with no working air conditioning.

She opened her eyes. A disturbance in the air, right next to her face, startled her so badly that she jumped out of her seat, sending her notebook and papers flying.

"Everly, what happened?" Mrs. Moore was startled by movement, as was Rose, who put out a hand to grab Everly's elbow before it contacted her nose.

"Nothing." Everly dropped to her knees, gathering her work. "It's just that I don't feel well. Do you mind if I go to the office?"

"Of course not. Go and take the pass."

Everly half-ran, half-walked, the soles of her sneakers squeaking across the 1970s green and yellow linoleum. Running in the halls wasn't allowed, and she didn't want to risk another face-to-face with Mr. Hart.

The nurse's office was the quietest room in the whole building. They didn't have an actual nurse, so Mrs. Dobbs, the secretary, let her lie down on the cot, all alone in the blissful silence.

"Do you want me to call your mom, dear?"

For a split second, Everly considered it. Mom would excuse her, no problem. The issue was that she was at work and not talking to her. So, not only would Everly have to swallow the fear of calling her mom, but it also meant that once she got home, she would be alone until four o'clock. Toughing out the day was preferable to being alone at home for that long.

"No, Mrs. Dobbs. It's just a headache. I'll be okay in a little bit."

Mrs. Dobbs, a saint, gave her an aspirin, then let her catnap through second and third periods. She went to fourth, Colorado History, and was blessed with a video on the creation of the Pikes Peak Highway, which meant more napping.

By the time the bell rang, it was lunch, and Everly was rested enough to appear half alive. She met Rose across the street from the school in Acacia Park, her crumpled brown bag lunch clutched in one hand.

"Dear god, you look like an extra from *Night of the Living Dead.*" Rose sat on a bench, a notebook in her lap, a piece of sour licorice in one hand.

"Lunch of champions, I see," Everly said as she collapsed next to Rose. "I feel as exhausted as I look. How are you so awake?"

Rose shrugged, munching on her licorice. "I'll sleep when I'm dead."

Everly met Rose in preschool, really more of a glorified daycare. Rose was the most talkative kid in class. Their teacher moved Rose every week or so, hoping she would find someone Rose wouldn't talk to so much. Everly was the last move. When Rose learned her name, she informed Everly that she would only call her Ever since they would be friends forever. Everly hadn't been able to shake her since. Not that she ever wanted to.

"So, let me guess," Rose talked between chews, "you couldn't sleep because of the haunted house." She said haunted like Fred might say it when teasing Shaggy and Scooby.

Everly pulled down her sunglasses so Rose would know she was serious. "You saw it, too, didn't you?"

Rose swallowed, her gaze falling to the ground. "What?"

"The ghost, or whatever it was. A form, a hazy form that looked like a dog, maybe."

Rose huffed a laugh. "Maybe you do have a concussion."

"Whatever. I don't want to talk about it. It was weird. Let's chalk it up to that, and I did sleep because of the concussion, as you said." She pointed to her head. Talking about last night was the last thing Everly wanted to do. She didn't want to talk about how she had to sneak out of her house all alone in the pitch black, how she had to creep through the yard, an owl hooting in a tree, more afraid of being murdered than she was of waking her mom, even though no one in Splendid had been murdered in a hundred years. She didn't want to talk about how she hadn't felt right since entering Red Manor, like something had attached itself to her brain, a demented lesion that she could continually see from the corner of her eye.

"Definitely weird and done." Rose swallowed her last piece of candy and pulled out another from the backpack at her feet. "Let's talk about why it's so goddamn hot in the middle of October. We're all doomed."

"Yeah, another thing our generation gets to deal with. Nathan left a note about Environmental Club. We're meeting tomorrow after school."

"How does Nathan have time to run this club with football and his general nerdery? It's like, we get it, Nathan, you're the shit. Calm down."

Everly blurted out a laugh. "Be nice to Nathan."

Nathan Stratton had been their friend forever, and he was, most definitely, the shit. He had so much going on as quarterback and captain of the football team, mathlete, organizer of clubs, and intern at the local history museum that just thinking about it made her tired.

"You know I love me some, Nathan. Speaking of, did you invite him to attend *our* little club meeting? When should we start? I'm thinking the sooner, the better. Friday?" Rose picked up her notebook to show Everly the first page as she ate her sandwich.

The first thing Everly saw was *Murder Club* in Rose's looping scrawl at the top of the page. This was Rose's dream. She had been planning the formation of this club all summer while Everly did everything in her power to avoid it. There weren't many more excuses she could make. Not only were they to be the founding members of this group, but Rose also wanted to use the little room at the top of Everly's house that they called the crow's nest for the club's meetings. Rose's house, where her parents fought incessantly, and her mom was constantly mean to her, was out of the question. With her older sister at the University of Colorado, Rose spent as little time there as possible.

"Fine. I'll tell Nathan. Who else should we invite? Three people seem a little light for a club."

"Fletcher and Leigh, and I'm inviting Anna, and you"—she bumped Everly's shoulder with hers—"should invite Jonathan."

Anna was a model-like blonde Rose was currently obsessing over. Jonathan was out of the question. "I don't know if I'm ready for everyone to know."

Rose laughed in her husky way. "Babes, everyone already knows. I'm adding him to the list, and I'll talk to Anna in sixth. I've told you she sits right in front of me, right?"

Everly rolled her eyes. "Only about a thousand times. Anna and the stars tattooed on her shoulder, Anna and her plaid mini-skirts, Anna and her lemon-scented hair."

"I said sun-kissed hair, but whatever. That's at least seven and a good number of bodies to start with. Get it? Bodies." Rose laughed as she stuffed her notebook in her backpack. "I can't believe I'm about to be so damn responsible, but we can't have you late to two classes in one day. Let's go."

AD BRAZEAU

CHAPTER TWELVE

Mom was still on the porch, but Everly tiptoed through the house like she was sixteen and sneaking out. In her haste to get downstairs, Everly hadn't put her shoes back on. She knew she would regret this, but there were worse things than walking barefoot through the grass.

Everly rounded the corner from the kitchen to the back door, vanilla from a lit candle reminding her of Rose. The key rack still hung as it always had, right next to the door, a project she'd made in eighth-grade woodshop. She fingered the keys. The collection had grown over the years, but toward the back, on the third peg, hung the familiar Batman keychain. Everly almost squealed. The only impediment now would be if the locks were changed.

She held the keys together in a bunch so they wouldn't jingle and pulled them off the peg. The Batman keychain went into her front pocket while she put the other keys back in their place.

She glanced up, a portrait above the key rack catching her eye. Her great-grandparents stared out at her, vacant expressions behind their eyes. Her great-grandfather stood behind his wife, a rose stuck in his lapel, while she perched cross-ankled in a chair that still sat in the front room. This portrait had once hung in her mother's bedroom. It was strange to see it relegated to a back room.

Everly refocused on her task. She opened the door, poking her head out to ensure the coast was clear. Of course, it was. Finding someone stalking around her backyard would have been highly unusual and a great cause for alarm—people didn't do that here.

The Strattons had been their closest neighbors, the only house they had a clear view of unless you were in the crow's nest.

The back porch steps stopped where a winding path of brick started, much like the one at the front of the house. This path wound around a small pond and then continued to the back shed, which hadn't been painted to match the new house colors. The pond water gurgled through a fountain, Koi fish, the size of Everly's head, swishing beneath the surface. She made a beeline away from the pond, off the beaten brick pathway. There was a brief thought to check these bricks for the symbol out front, but this would have to happen later. She only had a moment to get over to Nathan's house, see what was in the window, and get back before Mom decided to cook her frozen casserole. A forty-six-year-old woman, still afraid of her mother, was pathetic.

The grass was cool, a bit sharp underfoot, as it had been recently mowed. Nevertheless, the scent of cut grass was pleasant, and Everly kicked at the ground to stir up more of the smell that reminded her of a childhood spent running barefoot through sprinklers and drinking from hoses.

Nothing separated her house from Nathan's except a sizeable flat expanse of lawn and a few hedges to mark the property lines. The Stratton home was twice the size of her own, rivaling only the Decomposition House in terms of size. Unlike hers, which was a Queen Anne, and the Decomposition House, which was a Tudor, the Stratton home was Italianate in design. The creamy stone exterior with a flat façade looked like a villa you might find along Lake Como or high in the hills above Florence. Everly, Rose, and Leigh liked to tease Nathan by calling him Romeo because not only did he live in an Italian palace, but he was also handsome, rich, and accomplished. Nathan hated the nickname and quickly began to call the girls the Weird Sisters after the three witches in Macbeth. Leigh wasn't happy about the moniker, but Rose and Everly thought it was perfect. "*No one's weirder than we are,*" Rose would say.

Everly crossed the property with a glance over her shoulder. No one was around. While she wasn't looking, she tripped over an uneven paver but managed to stumble forward to keep her balance. She was on the back patio now, struck by how overgrown everything was, how the stone pavers had begun to crumble around the edges. Weeds, up to her knees in some places, grew between cracks and crevices. The grand fountain at the center, three times the size of hers, with its statue of the faun, was green with slime, a fetid smell wafting off the putrid surface. Mr. and Mrs. Stratton would have hated to see their property in such disrepair. Everly couldn't help but wonder why Nathan had let it degrade to this state. Maybe he hadn't meant to. Perhaps he'd been too busy living elsewhere to worry about the upkeep. There was certainly a lot to keep up with. As she stood, staring at the faun, remembering all the times she and Nathan had waded in the fountain, their jeans rolled up to their knees, an etching near the faun's foot caught her eye.

Her empty stomach turned over on itself as she pushed aside the tall weeds. The stench from the stagnant water worsened the closer she walked, but she had to make sure what she saw was real.

Young eyes wouldn't have had to get so close. Standing by the fountain's edge, Everly tried to breathe shallowly, the symbol coming into sharper focus. Even standing in the warm sun, a chill washed over her. What did it mean? This figure eight she now seemed to see everywhere she went.

Everly bounced up the back steps to the verandah, sticking the key in the French door's lock with a prayer that it hadn't been changed. It hadn't. The key turned without the slightest protest, the door opening without so much as a squeak.

The air inside was musty but not awful. What more could you expect of a house that hadn't been lived in for ages? She walked into the kitchen, which was much the same as Everly remembered. Maple countertops and white appliances, every surface almost surgically clean as if the counters had been recently wiped down.

Everly passed through the dining room—the same oak table and chairs where she and Nathan did homework, sitting in the center—the chinoiserie wallpaper still looking good, then passed through the sitting room, also unchanged. Nathan's mom had been fond of pink and white and probably had never encountered a wallpaper she didn't like. This room sported an antique sofa and chairs, all upholstered in tufted pink silk. The same chinoiserie wallpaper from the dining room continued in here. The house was like a museum of their childhoods. She and Nathan played in and hung out in every single room. Everly had to reach out a hand to grip the doorway for a few deep breaths before she continued.

The parlor gave way to the formal sitting room, also unchanged. However, there was a more modern set of furniture in this room, white couches that would have been the height of sophistication in the early '90s, and more wallpaper, this one a white and silver stripe.

At the front of the house, standing in the grand foyer under the massive chandelier, Everly paused. She knew no one was there but wanted to take a moment to stand quietly and listen, the first thing she always did when assessing a house for a paranormal entity. After several minutes of silence, she ascended the curved double staircase to the second floor. This was where she would find Nathan's room with the window that faced the crow's nest. She felt nothing unusual, just the oddness of being in the house after so long.

She stood in the doorway, amazed by what she saw. Like the rest of the house, nothing had changed. With the same navy duvet he'd had in high school, Nathan's double bed sat to the right, pushed up against the wall. The matching dark oak furniture remained, and the dresser where he kept his football trophies was still covered in their school team stickers. Splendid High's mascot, the Miner, was still splashed all over the top and sides, one hand on his hip, the other holding a pickaxe over his shoulder, his comically large hat askew on his head. Everly couldn't help but smile as she ran a finger over the stickers, then trailed a hand over the top of the trophies that spanned from elementary school onward.

She glanced up at the mirror hanging over the dresser, crestfallen by what she saw. Except for one little round section, the entirety of the mirror was covered, as it had always been, by pictures she'd forgotten about. Pictures of them, of their childhood. Romeo, the Weird Sisters, Fletcher, Jonathan, and Anna. They were all there and all accounted for. Everly was the most represented. She was in nearly every photograph, sometimes smiling, sometimes not, depending on how she'd slept the night before. Everly caught her face in the exposed piece of mirror. She looked like a ghost. She didn't recognize herself. It was hard to reconcile the woman she was now to the girl she'd been then. Despite the fear permeating her nights, she'd once been full of hopes and dreams. She'd been happy, in love with her friends and the distraction they provided. Yes, the nightmares had always been there, but she'd been able to compartmentalize and put them away because she had them. She had these people who made that trauma seem so small. If only she and Rose had never broken into Red Manor. It's hard to say what would have happened, but Everly was reasonably confident her life would have continued in the same, primarily happy way.

Everly sank onto the edge of Nathan's old bed, her gaze

tight on the pictures.

Whatever Rose had seen, she had no right to have kept it from her for so long, to let Everly think she'd lost her mind that night. The robes. How could she not have told her about the robes? Rose had said that the mayor and the doctor had materialized from behind the stairwell. A basement? A hidden room? They were both wearing strange cloaks, and the mayor had something that looked like blood on his collar.

That was the detail Everly had been least interested in. Men were always cutting themselves while shaving. But the robes were bizarre. Also strange was that the mayor hadn't been too keen on getting the police involved or sending Everly to a hospital. Instead, they'd called her mother, who took the word of those men that her daughter was fine, loaded up her unconscious body, and drove away.

Everly thought back to that long-ago time. The day after, when Everly had woken with the worst headache of her life, her mom hadn't said a word about anything. Everly had walked on eggshells around her mom that day, and then like magic, her mom had returned to normal.

Nothing about that night made sense, and now, looking back on it, the night made even less sense.

Everly's gaze wandered from the photographs over to the window. The curtains were wide open, a single thread of spider silk wafting from the valance in the breeze coming from the vent below.

A piece of paper was taped into the corner with regular old scotch tape—nothing special about it. Everly went to the window, careful to keep herself hidden behind the curtain that matched the navy duvet. Whatever the sign said on the other side, from this side, she could see it was plain white printer paper.

She peered around the edge of the curtain to the grass below and then over toward her house. She didn't see anyone, but that didn't mean much. Her mom could easily be watching from the corner of the porch or any of the numerous windows facing this direction.

Kneeling on the floor, Everly reached out a hand, keeping it low, and peeled the paper from the window. She pulled it toward her, then slunk back to the bed where she could examine it out of sight.

When she turned the paper over, the shock of what she saw caused her to drop it on the duvet as if the words could poison her.

Weirdo, if something happens, find the notebook. —Romeo

More shocking than the words was the symbol drawn into the corner of the paper. It was so tiny that most people would probably overlook it or assume it was nothing more than a doodle. But at this point, Everly would recognize the looping figure eight with the tree and wing anywhere.

"Nathan, what the fuck?" she whispered to the room. Everly almost wished Nathan would answer, but there was no one there. Not a single entity that she could feel. She was cold suddenly, down to her bones.

Everly was still a bit of a skeptic, even after all her years as a paranormal investigator and as someone who regularly wrote articles about the undead for various online blogs. She'd never come across any full-blown evidence of hauntings, but she had had a couple of strange encounters, including the one at Red Manor, and the presence she knew resided in her mother's home. Strange enough that she was sure there was something to the whole ghost thing and to whatever had attached itself to her that night. Despite this, most of what she wrote was overblown exaggerations. No one could blame her for trying to survive in this world. Money was money.

Find the notebook.

Everly looked around the room. Nathan had given her permission, from the beyond, to ransack his room. So, she did. She turned out every drawer, pulled every box from the closet, and looked under the bed and the mattress. It took her ten minutes to turn the room upside down, and the only notebook she'd found was full of essays from senior

English. None of which seemed relevant. She had a vague idea of what she was looking for—a book that wasn't a book but a hollow box. Back in junior high, Nathan had gotten hold of a marijuana joint. This was during Nathan's brief stint as a rebel, which lasted through two puffs of weed. He had invited Everly over to smoke this joint with him in the backyard while their parents were at some charity gala event. He'd hidden the joint inside a box that looked like a hardcover copy of *Dracula*. If Nathan had something to hide, the *Dracula* box would be a good place, and one that Everly was familiar with.

There was only one other place Everly could think of where Nathan might keep something important: his office. His home, which he shared with Charlie, didn't feel right. If you want to hide something, you keep it away from your spouse. Spouses were a mystery to her, but she knew one thing, if you had a suspicious spouse, no amount of snooping was off-limits.

Everly pulled her phone from her back pocket, then scrolled until she found Rose's name.

Okay, I'm in. Don't come to my house, though. I'll meet you in the museum parking lot at 11:45 tomorrow. So let's forget about what happened at the bar for now.

Everly folded up the piece of paper, sweeping one last look over the message. Whatever had happened to Nathan, and she was now convinced it wasn't natural, he'd expected her to return. Why? He could have left this message for any of the others, but he chose Everly. Again, why? None of it made sense, and she wasn't sure if sharing this with Rose was the best idea. Not yet, anyway. There was a reason Nathan left this for her. Maybe the reason was as simple as their close childhood relationship.

Two minutes later, Rose responded.

Fine. 11:45. DO NOT BE LATE.

Everly rolled her eyes. She wanted to retort but left it. There was no point.

She stuck the paper in her back pocket with her phone.

She tidied the room, putting everything back in its original state. It didn't feel right to leave the bedroom a mess. Before she left, she pulled a photograph off the wall. One of her and Nathan reading on the yellow couch in the crow's nest, his feet in her lap.

She wasn't sure if she would find this mysterious notebook, but assuming she had time before her flight, she'd turn over every rock in Splendid before she gave up.

CHAPTER THIRTEEN

The rental car was starting to get on her nerves. The blinker wasn't working, sending Everly into a thought spiral. Had it ever worked? Was she going to be charged for this? How much did a blinker cost? More than she had in her bank account?

She pulled into the parking lot, practically in the shadow of the impressive clock tower jutting from the top of Splendid's Museum of the Founders. The building was much the same as she remembered it. Every school-age child in Splendid has visited the museum at least three times. Once in elementary school, once in junior high, and once in high school.

The museum sat square in the middle of its city block, surrounded on all four sides by open green spaces, mature oak trees, winding walking paths, and sculptures by local artists, making the area feel like the grand park of a much larger city. The building itself was imposing, in a classical style of architecture that Everly wouldn't have been able to identify had her life depended on it. She knew the place was huge, built of some stone, granite probably, the interior lined floor to ceiling in cold, red marble. The afternoon was warm, as always, the sun bright, prompting Everly to keep her sunglasses on.

She exited the car, then plunked several quarters into the parking meter. Two spaces down, Rose and Leigh sat inside a Mercedes SUV with Leigh in the driver's seat, peering out the windshield at Everly like she was watching a street performance. Rose waved her over.

Everly shoved her hands in the pockets of her jeans, annoyed that Leigh was there. This didn't need to be any more complicated than it already was. Leigh, law-abiding and sweet, would probably panic halfway through.

Rose rolled down the passenger side window as Everly approached. "I thought in case we needed another distraction or help to get out, it might be useful to have a third. Leigh is going to stay in the car unless I text her."

Leigh leaned over the center console, a white scarf tied around her head. "Please don't tell Fletcher. He'll have an aneurysm."

"Of course not." Everly couldn't imagine a scenario where she would ever speak to Fletcher again.

Leigh smiled. Her cheeks had some color, the skin around her eyes a little plumper and brighter.

Everly stepped back as Rose stepped out, looking put together as always in a cream pencil skirt and a sky-blue silk top. Everly felt a little shabby in her ripped jeans and a black T-shirt.

"Here's the plan." Rose unbuttoned the top buttons of her blouse. "I'll go in first and tell the guard that I saw someone messing with a basement window at the back of the museum. Then, when he's gone, you slip in while I talk to Melody. I'll pull her away from her post so you can pick the lock. Do you have what you need for that?"

"Yes, Rose. I'm not an idiot." Everly only needed one tool for the job, which was tucked tight inside her sock, jutting against her ankle.

Rose smiled, that devious glint Everly knew so well in her dark, amber eyes. "Just like old times."

Rose took off, striding up the long, cobblestone walkway in her four-inch heels like a pro. Everly didn't know how Rose would manage those heels on the slick marble floors, then realized she didn't care. Not her problem.

She meandered under the shade of a hundred-year-old oak tree, watching the entrance to the museum. Several couples milled about, one white-haired and bespectacled lady reading a book on a bench. Sparrows chirped overhead, a few magpies poking the grass for crumbs. About two minutes after Rose went inside, a jiggling, middle-aged man in a uniform jogged out the double doors, down the steps, and around the side of the building. Everly darted in behind him.

She paused inside the doors. Not far off, Rose was performing, bawling her eyes out while Melody hugged her. A second later, Rose pulled Melody off to the side, asking the young woman to get her a glass of water. Melody, who reminded Everly of an ancient librarian, her hair in the tightest bun Everly had ever seen, even though the girl couldn't be more than twenty-two, rushed around a corner.

Everly didn't need to be told twice. Before Rose could give her a nod, she was off, speeding down the hallway, following the directions Rose had previously given her.

Nathan's office was near the end of the hall, right off the main lobby. The window was glazed for privacy, not allowing Everly so much as an idea of what lay beyond the stained wood door. She bent down, pulling the screwdriver from her sock, then dropped to her knees. No matter what Rose said, they didn't have the time to pick a lock. They were working against the clock here. Rose wouldn't be happy, but there was no way around it. Everly shoved the working end of the screwdriver into the lock, then gave the butt end one hard slam with the palm of her hand. The door gave way just as Everly knew it would.

She was inside with the door closed behind her in less than ten seconds. Rose would join her as soon as she'd sipped her water and let Melody know she would use the restroom.

Everly stood aside so Rose would have quick access to the room.

Professional offices were not places that Everly frequented, but this one was about as stereotypical as it got. Heavy wooden furniture, probably oak, dominated the room. The desk was massive, swallowing up more than half the space, with a monitor sitting toward the back and a keyboard resting on the brown blotter. Bookcases lined the wall behind the desk, each shelf jammed with books. Two stiff-looking dark leather chairs sat against the wall to the left. Old maps of Splendid graced the walls.

There was nothing of the Nathan who Everly once knew in the room. Not a single football trophy sat on the many shelves, and most shocking, there appeared to be nothing from which to play music, not a radio or even a wireless speaker of any kind. The only personal item Everly could see from her quick perusal was a photo of Nathan and Charlie and a single plant, some sort of succulent.

The door opened and closed so fast that Everly didn't have time to jump.

"You haven't even started gathering his things?" Rose moved to the desk.

"There isn't much to gather unless we're taking all these books out of here." Everly went to the first bookcase behind the desk, running her fingers along the spines. "If you want to do that, we'll need more than a tote bag."

"Charlie said he wanted the picture, the plant, the copies of Nathan's newest book, and whatever we found in his drawers that looked personal. You grab the books. There should be around eight copies on the bookcase somewhere."

Everly didn't acknowledge this, she just kept looking at the spines. She was in that office for a very different reason, a reason she hadn't shared with Rose. There was a notebook somewhere with her name on it, but she knew it wouldn't be obvious. The notebook wouldn't be in a drawer or somewhere out in plain sight. Not if Nathan had gone to all the trouble to tell her about it via a cryptic note stuck to his old bedroom window.

"We don't have much time, Ever. Do you have the copies of his book?"

Everly heard Rose behind her but didn't answer. The copies of Nathan's local history book were not on her radar. All morning, Everly had been thinking about the *Dracula* book box. She was now positive this was where the notebook would be hidden.

Everly continued grazing the spines of each book on the shelves. Finally, she struck pay dirt when she reached the second shelf from the bottom. Her fingertips grazed wood, not leather, the fake spine reading *Dracula* by Bram Stoker. Her heartbeat quickened as it does when you know you've won a game. She pulled the box from the shelf, opened the lid, and almost stopped breathing when she saw a notebook the size of a paperback novel nestled inside. She yanked out the notebook, putting the decoy book back on the shelf.

"What is that?" Rose asked, standing so close behind her that Everly could see the tips of her expensive pumps.

Before Everly could answer, the door to the office slammed open. She and Rose both jumped.

Rose squealed, a hand held over her heart. "Was barreling through the door necessary?" she cried.

Everly stood, but not before tucking the notebook down the front of her jeans. She pulled her T-shirt out to hide the lump.

"Rose Hibbard?" Mayor Hart stood in the doorway. Behind him, out in the hall, stood the guard to one side and Melody, her face screwed up like she was in pain, to the other.

Rose straightened her shoulders in the way only Rose could, and her chin tipped up toward the sky. "Hello, Richard."

Everly knew Rose well enough to know she wasn't using *Mayor* to address Mr. Hart on purpose. Instead, she was putting him on the same level as everyone in the room.

The mayor bristled, a slight scowl marring his still attractive face. He, like Rose, didn't look like he'd aged much. His blue suit was pristine, fitting him in a way that probably meant it was bespoke. His gaze moved from Rose to Everly. "Everly Palmer?"

Everly nodded. "Hello, sir." Sir is what Everly had called him when he strode through the halls of Splendid High like the king of the hill.

"Well, I can tell you girls one thing. This is not how I expected my afternoon to go."

"We're not girls anymore," Rose said as she clutched the tote bag closer to her body.

"I can see that, Ms. Hibbard." The mayor held out his hand. "You can't take anything out of here. Not until the room has been sanitized."

Rose scoffed. She wasn't about to give up the bag. "Enough with the bullshit. All Charlie wants are a few of Nathan's personal effects. Don't try to act like he had Ebola or something. Ever and I are leaving with the contents of this bag, which include nothing more than a framed photo, a few personalized pens, and these copies of Nathan's book." Rose turned her back on the crowd, not giving an inch. She grabbed the few copies of Nathan's book off the shelf, cramming them into the bag, then spun back around. "And also, this plant." She picked up the succulent, shoving it toward Everly, who took it gratefully as another shield to hide the bulge in her pants.

The mayor moved forward, his mouth open to speak.

Rose cut him off. "And if you so much as try to stop us, I'll use my national platform to go on TV, social media, you name it, to tell the world what a douche you are for denying personal effects to our friends' gay lover. Would you like me to do that, Richard?"

Everly turned her head to look at Rose, who stood with a triumphant gleam in her eyes. Everly wanted to throw her arms around Rose at that moment and praise her for being such a badass. This was the Rose she missed, the Rose who didn't take shit from anyone except her horrible mom and who was always Everly's guiding star. But unfortunately, they were in familiar territory at the moment, and Everly knew to stand back and let Rose do her thing, a pink and green cactus gripped in her hands.

The mayor took a step back. He licked his bottom lip, a hard sigh escaping his nostrils. "Fine," he conceded. "But take heed, Ms. Hibbard. I do not want to see either of you again within a hundred yards of the museum."

"Take heed, my ass." Rose stormed down the marble steps of the museum. She spoke so loudly that the schoolchildren getting ready to enter the museum stared at her, a few laughing behind their hands. "Hart can shove his heed up his ass."

"Okay," Everly said, joining the kids as they snickered at Rose's rant. "I'm not sure how that would work, but I'm with you on the sentiment."

Rose halted, Everly almost slamming into her back, and turned to Everly with a hand on her hip, the tote bag slung over one shoulder. "I mean, what was that, anyway? Some warning? What exactly are we being warned away from?"

Everly wasn't sure what to say, but before she could think of something, Leigh jogged up behind Rose. She was flushed from the exercise and out of breath as she said, "What happened? I saw the guard go back in, and then the mayor came rushing from City Hall." Leigh pointed to City Hall, a square, oddly squat building that looked like it had been built sometime in the '70s. City Hall was across the street, about forty yards from the museum. "I didn't know what to do, and since I hadn't heard from Rose, I stayed put."

Rose screwed up her mouth as she stared across the street. "Nothing you could have done, Leigh. We got caught, but it wasn't a huge deal. Other than the strange, cryptic warning we received from mayor douchebag."

"You got caught?" Leigh, who had never been in trouble a day in her life, stared at Rose with her eyes wide open, her mouth gaping.

"It's fine. As I said, it wasn't a huge deal. Just weird." Rose looked at Everly, standing rigid with her arms around the terracotta pot of the succulent like she would fight to the death to defend it. Her gaze was on the ground.

"Ever? Are you going to chime in? That was weird, right?"

Everly glanced up at her, her face feeling like stone. She knew there was no expression, that her face was blank, but she had nothing to give. "I don't know what you want me to say, Rose. Do you want me to agree with you, because I do, and we can go back down the road where I tell you there's something wrong with this town. Or do you want me to smile and nod and suggest we go have a beer like nothing's wrong?"

Rose pulled the tote bag to her front, hugging it to her body like Everly was hugging the plant. Rose's face changed. The annoyance of the run-in with the mayor blinked away, replaced by something softer. "Can't we do both?"

"Excuse me?" Everly wrinkled her brow, unsure what Rose meant.

"Can't we go have a beer *and* talk about what may or may not be wrong with Splendid?"

Leigh, having caught her breath, perked up. "I could go for a cider right about now."

Everly looked at the group of school kids, getting antsy while their two teachers took a head count. Part of her wanted nothing more than to sit down with these two childhood friends, people she wanted to trust, and show them the note from Nathan and the notebook. There were the symbols at the graveyard and her house, too. There was much to share. Then there was the realization that she'd been through this all before, with these exact people. They'd laughed at her all those years ago, pushed her away. Her heart began to harden inside her chest. She couldn't let them in again. But, if there were a chance they'd believe her now, a chance that they would help her figure some things out, maybe she should take it. Everly was at war with herself, but she was thirsty. She could decide at the bar if she wanted to bring them in.

"Yeah, fine. I'll meet you there."

They all knew where they were going without even naming the place. The Peak seemed to be the only bar as far as Rose and the others were concerned. Jonathan was an old friend who would be the recipient of their business. Everly hoped that today would feel more comfortable after the awkwardness of their first encounter the day before.

It didn't.

Everly waited until she knew Rose and Leigh were already inside. She'd handed off the plant, which now sat on Leigh's backseat, and worried over what to do with the notebook. Should she leave it in the rental car or take it in with her? The thought of leaving Nathan's book, pages he'd hidden for one reason or another, inside a cheap rental car with doors that seemed to lock only intermittently made her cringe. The safest place for the notebook was with her, but she didn't have her purse. So, once again, the leather notebook went down the front of her jeans. At least it was small enough that her T-shirt covered the weird-looking lump it made.

Everly kept the book where it was, uncomfortably pressed into the tender part of her abdomen, and went inside to face more torture. She hated to be dramatic, but hell was precisely what being in Splendid felt like.

Rose and Leigh sat at the same high-top table where they had eaten the day before. That must be their spot, perfect for surveying the landscape and the street outside.

The bar smelled like the same mix of wood polish and cooking meat. There was certainly a lot of wood to polish. The floors, tables, and bar top were all a deep mahogany, and they all shone as if well cared for. About half the tables and three or four bar stools were occupied. There was more of a crowd than yesterday, which made Everly feel good. The more people there to take Jonathan's focus off her, the better.

Everly walked over to Rose and Leigh. She stood by the table but didn't sit down. Instead, she felt the notebook press against her flesh and thought about how time was running out on her stay in Splendid. The return flight to New Orleans she'd booked the day of Nathan's funeral, was tomorrow. She didn't have the hours to sit and fake a pleasant conversation with two people who would never believe that something was going on.

"Ever." Rose snapped her fingers in front of Everly's face. "What's the matter? Jonathan isn't here today if that's what's freaking you out."

Everly looked calmly at Rose. Leigh hid behind her menu, only her eyes visible as she watched Rose and Everly with a curious gaze.

"I'm a forty-six-year-old woman, Rose. I'm not freaked out about running into an ex-boyfriend."

Rose looked at her, the annoyed expression she'd served the mayor clear on her face once again. "Okay, then. What's your problem?"

"My problem, Rose, is multi-layered. Let's start from the beginning, shall we? I come home to attend the funeral of an old friend. I then found out my mother has MS and never bothered to share this rather important information with me. I get invited to a dinner where my former best friend interrogates me, makes me feel like a freak, and then invites me to break into a museum with her. Talk about whiplash. Let's not even talk about how I'm feeling about seeing Jonathan because that seems secondary to all the other weird shit happening. Because next, I found this piece of paper stuck in Nathan's childhood bedroom window. Intended for me."

Everly pulled the folded piece of paper, the note left inexplicably for her, out of her back pocket and smoothed it out on the tabletop. Rose and Leigh leaned over it but didn't pick it up. "So then, what do I find after we forcibly enter Nathan's office? This." Everly pulled up her shirt and then dug out the notebook. She showed them the cover but didn't hand it off. "This was hidden in his secret hidey spot. A spot I remembered from when we were kids. He knew I would find the paper, and he knew I would find the notebook. How he knew I'd return from New Orleans is another mystery I can't understand. But this symbol on the cover matches the symbol on the paper, which is stamped on a brick outside my house, and the symbol I saw on a very unusual gravestone at Everwood. Which is where I'm going right now." Everly pushed the notebook back down the front of her pants and began to refold the paper.

"Wait. What?" Rose held out her hands.

"Nathan left the note for me to find. It was taped to his bedroom window, the one that faces the crow's nest. I used our key to go over and grab it. You know the rest." Everly was tired of explaining herself, so tired she'd much rather have taken a nap than go over the particulars one more time.

"Ever, is this bullshit? Did you read what's in the notebook?"

Everly leveled Rose with one glare. She wanted Rose and Leigh to hear her loud and clear while also keeping her voice down. She wasn't an idiot. If she hadn't been on the town's radar before, after the stunt at the museum, she was now. "The fact of the matter is this, Rose. I refuse to let anyone gaslight me again. This is not bullshit. I know you know that, but for some reason, you can't wrap your brain around the fact that bad things have happened. We know they have. Everyone in this bar knows they have, but they refuse to open their eyes because they enjoy the Splendid lifestyle. A life where everyone has an opportunity, and money, no one ever gets hurt, and everything, even the weather, is perfect. But the three of us all know this place isn't perfect. People die mysteriously, but somehow always naturally, and people disappear. I need to figure some shit out, and I'm starting at

Everwood."

"I'm coming with you." Rose grabbed her handbag as she slid off the seat. "Leigh?"

Everly shook her head, tucking the message left by Nathan back into her pocket. "I don't know if that's a good idea."

"Ever, it's the only idea." Rose held on to the edge of the round tabletop. "I don't know what any of this means, and I don't know if I buy all the conspiracy stuff, but I've already conceded that something strange is happening. You can't be out there by yourself getting into trouble. If you're going to get in trouble, so am I."

Everly didn't know what to say. So instead, she folded her arms across her chest. Rose looked at Leigh, her eyebrows raised.

Leigh shook her head, glancing around to ensure no one was listening. "I can't. Part of me wants to. I mean, I want to know what's going on with the note and the secret notebook, but I don't have the energy yet. You two go. Maybe come by the house tonight and fill me in?"

"You got it," Rose said. "Have a drink for me."

"Rose," Leigh called. "You're going to need flats. Grab my flip-flops out of the car."

They left Leigh at the bar and made their way outside. On the sidewalk, Everly turned to Rose. "Leigh was your ride, right? I have the rental over there. We can take that."

"Great." Rose took Everly's arm as she moved away. "I'll probably be apologizing for what happened senior year for the rest of my life, Ever. I'm truly sorry if you felt gaslighted. I don't know what's going on now or why Nathan has left you these crumbs, but I promise I will help you figure out why. I miss you. I miss us. I hope it isn't too late."

This was the Rose that Everly remembered. The soft, sweet Rose with only the occasional edge. Everly wanted to believe everything Rose said. She wanted to wrap her arms around her friend and breathe in the warm, familiar scent of her. But Everly had been burned before, and like a dog beaten, she was wary.

Everly tried to smile but knew the warmth didn't quite reach her eyes. "One thing at a time."

AD BRAZEAU

PART THREE
Research

.

CHAPTER FOURTEEN

Everly's Journal
October 30, 1994

    Even though I hate this stuff, I've taken on a column for the paper. I'm calling it Haunted Happenings. *Rose is annoyed, but I think that's just because she wanted to form a true crime club, and I'm hijacking her meetings to talk about stories for the column. Splendid is a puzzle, and I'm going to solve it.*

1994

The inside of her locker was a disaster. Books and papers, some of them probably way past due, were piled at the bottom like the base of an avalanche. A sour smell emanated from somewhere down there, underneath the jutting of papers and the corners of books, but Rose wasn't brave enough to go fishing through the mess.

She tossed her psychology book on top of the teetering pile, pulling her new Cover Girl lip gloss from the top shelf, the only shelf she kept halfway neat because it housed her collection of cosmetics she wasn't allowed to own or wear at home.

Her locker was across the hall from the boys' locker room, and every time someone opened and closed the door, she got an unwelcome waft of teen spirit.

Rose slathered her lips in pink glitter, staring into the crappy locker mirror that made her face look wavy. Her stomach had felt sick all night. She was telling Ever the truth when she said she'd been too keyed up to sleep. Dying her hair purple in the middle of the night was the only thing she could do to take her mind off what had happened at Red Manor. Her mom had been gone when she came down for her usual bowl of cereal, her dad ignoring her as he always did while reading the paper. The second her mom saw her hair, she'd be grounded for the rest of the month, but the sweet distraction the hair had provided would be worth it. The added benefit to grounding would be the opportunity to distance herself from Ever, at least until she forgot about what had happened.

Last night had been an epic failure, and it was all Rose's fault. She was the one who pressured Ever into going with her. She was the one who planned the whole thing. And what had happened? Ever had gotten so scared she'd knocked herself unconscious while Rose had seen something she wished she could erase from her mind.

Add to that, Ever having had some sort of episode in psych class and currently being in the nurse's office. All Rose wanted to do was crawl inside her disgusting locker and never come out.

A pinch on her arm brought her out of her thoughts.

"Hey." Leigh stood beside her, her shaggy brown hair twisted into a claw clip. Leigh's other accessory, Fletcher, stood so close behind her that his front was touching her back. "What happened in psych? Everyone is talking about it. They're saying Everly freaked out."

Rose pushed the lip gloss applicator back into the bottle, then placed it on the top shelf. She shook her head. "Ever didn't freak out. She's not feeling well, a headache or something. Fell and hit her head, I think."

"Oh, crap," Leigh said. She was the only one of Rose's friends who didn't use actual swear words. "I hope she's okay."

"She's totally okay. Where are you two heading?"

"English. Aren't you coming?" Leigh dropped an eyebrow as she studied Rose. "Are you okay?"

"Great." Rose plastered a fake smile across her face. "I'll see you two in there. I need to run to the restroom first."

Fletcher pulled Leigh away, and they were swallowed by the hordes of high schoolers flooding the halls like schools of fish, feet stampeding over the linoleum.

Usually, Rose would have told the entire school about her and Ever's middle-of-the-night adventures, but the strangeness of last night was haunting her.

Ever's mom hadn't said not to tell anyone about being at Red Manor. All she'd said was don't tell Ever, or anyone else, about the robes, and Mayor Hart had said not to mention the doctor was there. It seemed like a warning. A strange warning. The whole night had been strange, from start to finish. The back door had slammed and locked. That hadn't been an accident, and Rose was sure of that now. The emergence of the mayor and then the doctor, from where Rose couldn't tell. The robes, the blood, or whatever the hell was on the mayor's shirt collar. All of it spelled trouble. Rose knew all about adults and trouble.

And there was something else. Something else in Red Manor that night. Something she'd never tell Ever, not if her life depended on it. What Rose had seen was not something she could even explain. The image lived in her head, where it would stay until the day she died. Ever was scared enough, plagued with nightmares. She didn't need any more. Rose now knew that Ever's fear of Red Manor had more of a foundation than Rose could have ever guessed. Aside from the weirdness that the men of Splendid were up to in the middle of the night, Rose could now say that ghosts were real.

The sunlight streaming in from the windows of the crow's nest was so warm that Rose wanted to stretch out like a cat and nap. But she was too shocked by what Ever had told her. So all she could do was sit on her favorite denim bean bag and stare.

"Your head injury must be worse than I thought. Maybe we should schedule you for a CAT scan."

Ever had been scribbling notes in the back of her pink diary. Finally, she stopped to look up at Rose with a roll of her eyes. "My head feels a hundred percent better. I'm telling you, Rose. I saw something at Red Manor last night, and I don't care if you believe me."

Rose licked her lips, thinking of what to say. "You think you saw a ghost dog?"

"Please don't condescend to me, Rose. I know what I saw. At the moment, I was terrified out of my mind, but the more I thought about it today, the dog wasn't scary. He was just a dog. His expression was almost sad."

"A sad ghost dog. And you're sure it was a ghost and not a real dog. How?"

"He was gray and not fully embodied." Ever continued scribbling in her book.

"Embodied? Ever, listen to yourself. You've been terrified of ghosts and everything that goes bump in the night since we were little. And now, after one possible encounter, you want to turn my true crime club into some ghost hunters club? I think we should call the doctor." Rose got to her feet, concern for Ever's mental state causing conflicting emotions. She, too, had seen something she couldn't explain that night. The haze hadn't taken any particular form for her. It didn't look dog-like or person-like. For the last twenty-four hours, she'd been trying to convince herself that what she saw was nothing more than a spot in her vision, although she knew it wasn't. But if Rose was good at anything, it was denying the truth when it was right in front of her face.

"I'm still terrified, Rose. You don't shake off fears like mine in one night. I can't explain what I felt to you. All I can say is that the more I think about it, the more I realize that the entity wasn't threatening. It looked sad. You know how a dog looks when it's in trouble, its tail drooping? Then it drops its ears, and its eyes get all big and round? That's what this guy looked like." She stuck the end of the pen in her mouth but kept talking. "I already spoke to Mr. Hassell, and he loved the idea of a column that examines some of the haunted histories of Splendid. There's a lot. I'll call it *Haunted Happenings,* and it would be so fun if you guys helped me with it."

Rose appraised Ever, hands on her hips. She hovered over Ever, who sat on the couch. "You only want us to help, so you don't have to explore this stuff alone."

Ever smiled, placing the pen in the journal and closing it. "Obviously. I'm scared of this stuff, as I've already demonstrated. But with you and the others around me, I'll be able to explore my fears, as you said, in relative safety. I feel like I have to do this, Rose. I can't explain why, but being in Red Manor last night made me feel something familiar, like I'd been there before." She gave Rose the saddest puppy dog eyes ever, more tragic even than her alleged ghost. "Please, Rose. Think of all the times I've gotten, or nearly gotten, in trouble with you. Now I'm asking for something. And it'll be fun. We can meet here and in the cemetery."

"What?" Rose's mouth went wide. Now she was sure that Ever had permanently damaged her brain. "Ever, I'm concerned here."

Ever waved her away. "Don't be. I feel very firmly that facing my fears is something I need to do, and I already know what our first case will be."

"Case?" Rose asked. She wanted to groan, but also didn't want to keep talking about what had happened the night before. "What is the first case?"

Ever smiled, her head tilting slightly to the right. "Red

Manor, of course. We already know it's haunted, which will give me a legitimate excuse to go back and interview some of the club's members. I mean, it's for the school paper, and my mom is, like, an important community member. You've said so before. That kind of dumb shit is important around here."

Rose had to think fast. Returning to Red Manor, interviewing members, and possibly crossing paths with the mayor again, was the worst idea imaginable. She settled back into the denim-covered bean bag, beans snapping under her as she swished her backside into the cushion. What would sour Ever on the idea of investigating Red Manor? Rose could only think of one thing. Ever hated being like everyone else, hated being a daughter of Splendid, someone who was always expected to look and act in a certain way, which is why she always wore dirty sneakers and ripped jeans. The only way to make Ever switch course was to point out that she was treading in waters that had already been swum.

"I like the whole hauntings column for the paper idea. I think that's great," she began. "But the thing with Red Manor is that it's been done to death. I mean, there was already an entire documentary filmed there. Everyone has seen it." Rose played with a loose thread sticking out of a seam on the bean bag as if her thoughts were just streams of consciousness with nothing behind them.

"Well, what does that matter?" Ever dropped her notebook on her lap.

Rose knew she had her attention, so she continued, "I guess it doesn't. Someone will probably still read the article. But if you want to get people interested, I would start with more obscure stories. Not something that's been told a hundred times." She pulled the thread loose.

"A hundred times," Ever said, more to herself as a spoken-out-loud thought. "Maybe you're right. Just to get started, to gain interest in the column, but I'm sure going to investigate Red Manor before the end of the year."

Rose looked up at her with a smile. "Smart."

Moving past what had happened the night before was all Rose wanted out of life for now. The more the day went on, and the further away from last night they got, she felt surer that what happened at Red Manor had been a series of strange coincidences. Adults did things that didn't always make sense; this was a fact she'd learned relatively young. The sinister feeling she'd had while standing in that foyer was dissipating in the light of day in the company of her best friend, who now seemed fine. Still, even if the weirdness was dispersing, she was good with staying far away from that place. Ever's mental health could be fragile sometimes, and Red Manor seemed like a place that could zap away all your positivity.

"You know," Rose said, her hand behind her neck as she stretched out her legs, "a great place to start would be the axe murders that happened down the street. That was over a hundred years ago, and Splendid's last murders. People would love to hear more about that. We could even hold a séance on the empty lot."

The Dale Street axe murders were instantly infamous when they occurred in the early 1900s. Everyone knew the general story, but there were sure to be some forgotten details they could dig up that would keep Ever occupied for a while.

Ever's eyes went wide at Rose's suggestion. "A séance?" She blinked. "Only if everyone comes."

"It's a séance. Of course, they'll come." Rose had to giggle. Ever only had so much bravado.

AD BRAZEAU

CHAPTER FIFTEEN

The cemetery was not where Rose wanted to spend her afternoon. Not only did the cemetery bring her grief over Nathan to the forefront, but she wasn't dressed for the occasion in a Dior pencil skirt and a silk blouse. At least, thanks to Leigh, she could exchange the high heels for a pair of flip-flops. They were a size too big, but walking the graveyard would be a bit more comfortable.

The graveyard was quiet as they drove through, gravestones dotted over rolling hills. Two cars sat by the main gate office, and so far, they'd only passed one grounds worker, riding along on a mower, who'd waved at them. All was somber, the graves like soldiers lined up for an eternity, each one facing the snowcapped peaks to the west.

Ever drove down the main drag, parking right in front of the grave where Rose, Leigh, and Fletcher had confronted her the day before yesterday. Late afternoon was lovely, as that day had been, warm and sunny, crisp, golden leaves a blanket over the still green grass.

Rose took a breath, adjusting her feet in the flip-flops. "We should have brought flowers for Nathan. God, I miss him." She stared out the car window, the top of the Stratton family mausoleum in the distance. "Being in his office was weird. I guess everything is going to feel weird from now on."

"I'm sure it will." Ever pulled the keys from the ignition. "At least you three got to spend so many years with him. Imagine how I feel."

Rose felt the familiar stab of guilt in her chest. "You could have come home, Ever. Whenever you wanted."

"Right." Ever pulled the notebook from under her thigh where she'd stuffed it while they drove.

Rose had wanted to flip through the pages, but Ever wouldn't have it. "*He left this for me*," she'd said.

"Why do you think he left you these clues? Why wouldn't he leave them for me, Leigh, Fletcher, or Charlie?" Rose eyed the notebook with envy. They had been Nathan's true friends. The friends who'd been his partners for trivia Tuesday, who'd gone to see matinees with him on Sundays, marking every single holiday and important event.

"I don't know, Rose. Maybe he thought I would understand."

Rose wasn't sure what that meant. Understand what?

Ever held the notebook in one hand as she caressed the strange symbol. "You don't know what this means? You've never seen it before?"

"No." Rose shook her head. "I've already told you. It's familiar, like I said, but I can't identify it."

"The symbol is familiar because it's all over Splendid. I didn't realize it at first, but not only is it in the cemetery and at my house and Nathan's, but it's also outside the museum. I saw it etched into the marble at the front door. My hunch is we'll also find it at Red Manor. That's my next stop." She opened the car door. "Before we dive into the notebook, come look at this grave. Really look at it."

Rose reluctantly exited the car. She felt fickle, someone who agreed to something at the moment, then changed her mind. The conspiracy angle was hard to wrap her mind around for any length of time, especially when there were so many other things to think about, like deadlines and dead friends.

They stood in front of the grave, Rose in flip-flops, Ever in her practical Converse. The grave was unusual; there was no denying that. Made out of what Rose guessed was plaster, the sculpted tree trunk was taller than both of them, branches jutting off the sides. The symbol, clear as day underneath the epitaph, was large and obvious.

"Well, no one is trying to hide the thing. You could probably see the symbol from across the path, and this grave is massive. There's no subtlety about it. This guy, William Scott, was a prominent Splendid-ite from back in the day. Like the days of the founding."

"I thought so." Ever pointed past the tree trunk headstone. "There's another one there. Come on."

Ever took off, much surer of her footing than Rose, who flapped along behind her, doing her best to keep up. The shoes Leigh had lent her slipped off with every step she took in the slick grass, but she refused to appear incapable. They approached another grave, a tree trunk made out of the same rough plaster. This one had the requisite branches, leaves, and even a plaster squirrel.

"I'm kind of loving these," Rose said as she ran her hand over the textured bark. "I think I want one."

"You're probably a prominent enough citizen to get one," Ever said, crouching down to read the epitaph.

This one was in rougher shape, the words hard to make out.

"The symbol is here, but what is this name?" Ever pulled out her phone to snap a picture.

"Pretty sure it says Richard Hassell, ancestor of our journalism teacher. He was an ironworker. Made all the wrought iron fences in our neighborhood, yours included."

Ever stood, her phone in her hand. "Holy shit, there's another one."

Ever tried to go, but Rose grabbed her arm. "Hold on. I see it, too. There's also another one over there." Rose pointed north. "But what is the point of this exercise, Ever? These are all prominent early residents of Splendid. We get it. Whatever this symbol is, it's probably on all these graves. What I want to know the most about right now is the notebook you refuse to open."

Ever screwed up her mouth, sliding her phone back into her pocket. "I guess you're right." She pulled the notebook from the other back pocket, thumbing through the pages but not opening it all the way.

"What are you afraid of?" Rose asked.

Ever shot her a hard glare, which softened when she met Rose's eyes. "I'm not sure."

"I know you, Ever." Rose peeled off the flip-flops, standing barefoot in the grass. "You may not like to think I do, but I do. You're thinking it's connected somehow. You think whatever is in that book is connected to that night at Red Manor."

"Which is connected to my nightmares and my general uneasiness about being in Splendid." Ever shrugged. "Maybe."

"There's only one way to find out."

Ever continued to finger the notebook, caressing the spine, flipping the whole thing over in her hands.

"Come on." Rose was taking charge of the situation. She was tired, needed to get home to feed her cat, and was ready to move on. She didn't think there was going to be any great revelation within the pages of the notebook. Nathan was a nerd, like they all were, but his brand of nerdism was special. There was probably nothing more inside the book than an apology to Ever. That's why he left her the trail of breadcrumbs. They'd been tight growing up, so tight that sometimes Rose had been jealous. He felt bad for senior year, just like they all did. "Let's go sit by Nathan and open this thing up."

She didn't wait for Ever. With Leigh's flip-flops dangling from one hand, she walked barefoot, past gravestones, past trees, watching for rocks and branches that could become splinters. There was something about having Ever home that made Rose feel like a kid again. When was the last time she walked barefoot in the grass, any grass, even her own? She forgot how good it felt, how the spikey blades bent under her feet, the soft earth cushioning each footfall. For a second, she almost felt carefree. Then, reality hit once more.

She stood in front of the Stratton mausoleum. A giant building built in the Greek style, all stone and columns, with the name of Stratton, carved into the pediment. Nathan was in there. Well, not Nathan. Not the smiling, athletic, brilliant Nathan. He wasn't in there, but his ashes were. That's what he was now, ashes. A week ago, he was flesh and bone, joking about how badly she needed to get laid while he put the kettle on in her kitchen, looking so alive with his fake tan and a new haircut. Now he was nothing but ashes.

Rose didn't cry. She wasn't much for crying, and she'd already done enough of that. She'd learned early on in life that crying didn't get you anywhere and that it never made her feel better, only worse, so, for the most part, she'd sworn off crying. That didn't mean she didn't feel, though. She felt it inside when her mom hit her, and her dad did nothing. She felt it when Ever up and left without a word. Rose felt it when every woman she ever fell in love with ended up leaving. She felt it when Charlie called to tell her the awful news. Leigh sometimes called her the Grinch. Leigh thought she was being funny, but the truth was Leigh wasn't wrong. Rose had a heart. Of course, she had a heart, but with every horrible event in her life, she let it wither smaller and smaller.

"Let's sit. Not sleeping is catching up with me." Ever jumped up the two short steps to the porch. If that's what it was called. Rose wasn't sure. Did mausoleums have porches? Rose had almost forgotten Ever was behind her.

Ever leaned her back against one of the columns, pulling her legs into a cross-legged position. Rose dusted a spot with her hand, dismayed by how much dirt there was. She sat anyway, a flash of lounging on the floor with Ever in grade school crossing her mind. Across from Ever, leaning her back against another column, the stone cold and hard against her, she blinked the thought away.

"What have we got?" she asked.

Ever dropped her scowling pretense and looked at Rose like she had decades ago. Like she needed support. Rose hadn't given it to her then, but maybe she could now.

Rose scooted on her rear end, in her designer skirt, across the dirty marble flooring until she was sitting alongside Ever. This was the closest she'd been to Ever since she'd come home. Rose laughed.

"What?" Ever glanced at her, the scowl back.

"Do you still use Herbal Essences?"

"Yes, it's the best, and no one will ever convince me otherwise." Ever pulled a lock of hair up to her nostril and sniffed.

Rose laughed again. "Well, it's still working for you. You smell like coconut, and your hair is as shiny as ever."

"Thanks." Ever tossed the lock of hair over her shoulder and took a deep breath. "Okay." She opened the front cover.

Property of Draco

This statement, written across the top of the inside front cover, had been crossed out and replaced by *Property of Nathan Stratton – thoughts*

"Thoughts," Rose said. "Nathan, you little oddball. But who was Draco?"

"No idea. But this has to be the notebook Nathan said he found in the museum archives."

"Keep going." She nudged Ever with a shoulder.

Ever turned the page.

"What the hell is that?" Rose drew closer, squinting her eyes at a drawing spread across two pages.

"A map. Maybe? They look like tunnels." She flipped another page. It was blank. She flipped another.

Drawn across these two pages was an aerial map of

Splendid. She and Ever studied the drawing.

"These are the original buildings of Splendid. Red Manor, the museum, which at that time was the courthouse, the first library, City Hall, the Miners Hotel, and the Sisters of Mercy Church." Ever held up the book to see the drawings better.

When she did that, Rose got a flash of something underneath. "Wait. Do you see that?"

"What?" Ever tilted the book toward the sunlight.

"The drawings on the first two pages. Holy shit. Give me the book."

Rose took the book from Ever, and a sense of excitement washed over her. Rose loved nothing more than puzzles, escape rooms, and murder mysteries. Figuring out a solution was such a thrill. She set the book on the ground, then carefully tore out the first two pages.

"What the hell?" Ever tried to grab the notebook away.

"Hold on." Rose pushed her hand, handed her the first two pages, then tore out the map of Splendid.

"Damn it, Rose. What are you doing?"

She took the first two pages from Ever. "When you said these were tunnels, I think you were right. Look." Rose put the drawings of the tunnels underneath the drawing of Splendid and held the whole thing up to the light.

"Woah," was all Ever said as they both stared. "All of the original Splendid buildings are connected. Did you know this?"

"Nope, but look at the edge. There's your house. Yours is the only house on the map." Rose moved her thumb over to the edge of the page.

"Oh my god."

AD BRAZEAU

CHAPTER SIXTEEN

Staring at the paper was all Everly could do as a sense of dread rolled through her body, nausea making her belly contract. Gooseflesh raised on her arms even though the temperature was seventy degrees.

Rose continued to hold the pages to the sun, the veins of the tunnel system seeping through to the map of buildings on the top. Everly held up a hand, her index finger tracing a line from her house to Red Manor. The chill on her arms intensified. She then took her finger and moved to the museum, tracking its tunnel back to Red Manor. "I'm assuming you've never seen a tunnel entrance in your cellar."

"Never. I haven't been in that basement in a long time, but I don't recall a doorway. I'm sure if there is one, it's hidden by something large or maybe sealed."

"Maybe not," Rose said, causing another shiver to spike down Everly's back.

The thought of having lived in a house with a secret tunnel was unnerving, but the entrance might have been sealed long ago. There was a possibility that her mom didn't know about the tunnel either.

"Everything goes back to Red Manor." Rose's hand

began to shake a bit as she held the maps together. "I never realized that the Manor is smack in the middle of everything."

"It's the center of the city," Everly said. "How did we never know that?"

Rose dropped her arms, setting the maps on the stone they sat on. "Because we were always taught in school that the statue of Eli Palmer, your ancestor, sits on the original city center."

Rose was correct. This was an acknowledged fact that anyone who'd gone to elementary school in Splendid could tell you. The statue of Eli Palmer, astride his horse, smack in the middle of the intersection next to Splendid High School, was the original center of Splendid, Colorado. Since then, the town had spread in all directions. Who knew where the geographical center of the city was now, but back in 1871, the location of the statue was it. Only it wasn't. According to the map drawn in Nathan's secret notebook, Red Manor was the true center, only one block away from the statue.

This had significance, but what?

"I don't get the deception." Everly voiced her thoughts out loud. "Why teach that the geographical center is where the statue stands? I mean, what's the big deal in teaching that the center is Red Manor?"

"Maybe people don't know. This seems a silly thing to be purposely deceptive about." Rose adjusted her legs. "I mean, everyone in town knows that the Manor was originally a men's club. There's nothing..." Rose trailed off.

"There's nothing what? Secretive about it?" Everly huffed a laugh. "Well, we both know that isn't true, don't we?"

"Maybe we do, and maybe we don't. Let's not get ahead of ourselves here. We don't know what was going on that night, Ever. They could have been having some old man orgy. There doesn't have to be something sinister going on. You always go right for the worst possible explanation."

Everly was tired of explaining how she felt. It was true she couldn't always explain her feelings. Identifying emotions was difficult when memories of her childhood were murky or plain non-existent. But she'd always known one thing, there was something wrong with Splendid.

"Let's keep looking." Everly flipped to the next page in the notebook.

Draco
Leo
Orion
Eridanus
Aquila
Scorpius
Auriga

"Birth signs?" Rose asked in her ear, her left arm leaning against Everly's right.

"Constellations," Ever answered. "Maybe code names?"

"Or maybe whoever owned this notebook was just into astronomy."

Concentrating was hard, especially when Everly was assaulted by memories at every turn. Right now, all she could think about was the last time they were this close. She may still smell like coconut shampoo, but Rose still smelled like vanilla. The scent was more sophisticated than the vanilla perfume she used to buy at the drugstore; there were other notes to this scent, but vanilla was still there. The last time she'd been close enough to smell Rose's vanilla-scented skin, they'd been huddled under a blanket watching *Pet Cemetery*, Leigh and Fletcher making out so loudly, Rose and Everly yelled at the couple to get a room.

"This is boring, turn the page." Rose nudged Everly with her shoulder.

Everly did as she was told.

Written on the next page was one phrase, bolded with deep trough marks of black pen ink.

Roots and Wings Forever

"Roots and wings? What the hell does that mean?" Rose

asked.

"The symbol," Everly breathed. She pulled her phone from her back pocket with so much force that she almost ripped her jeans. Flipping through her photos, she landed on the one she'd taken of the symbol on the gravestone and expanded the image.

"Roots and wings. Don't you see it, Rose?" She held the phone up higher.

"I see it. I just don't get it. What does it mean?"

"I think Roots and Wings is a secret society started by these men." She dropped her phone and flipped back a page. "Who used code names for their secret dealings. And that is their symbol."

Rose chuckled. She leaned back against the wall of the mausoleum. "Secret dealings. Okay, so the old men of Splendid had some secret club. They probably fashioned themselves on the Masons or something like that. Again, not super shocking."

"Not shocking in itself, no. Unless they were up to something worse than orgies and secret handshakes."

Everly flipped to the next new page.

There was a beautiful pencil drawing of each of the three elements of the symbol, all detailed separately. The tree was first, the trunk shaded so well you could see the bark peels. The wing was more detailed than on the graves, shaded to show off each feather. Below both the tree and the wing sat the figure eight, more looping and delicate than the final product.

"Pretty. Whomever Draco was, he was an artist."

A thought flittered across Everly's mind as Rose made this statement, but the thought was lost as soon as Rose spoke again.

"What else?"

The next page was titled *Rituals & Spells*.

"Rituals and spells, but where are they?"

Everly ran her thumb down the center of the notebook. "There's only one; the rest are torn out."

"Not by Nathan. He would never ruin something so old," Rose said.

Everly shrugged. "He already crossed out Draco to put his own name in the book. Maybe he would." She flipped.

"What's on the page that's left?"

Everly froze, her thumb rubbing over the words, as if by doing so, she could erase them from history.

Rose, picking up on her apprehension, asked, "Ever, what does it say?"

"It's a spell for conjuring a hellhound."

Rose blurted a laugh. "Nathan." She shook her head. "He's fucking with us. Nathan did this on purpose somehow. He probably thought I would find this and planted it as a game, not expecting to die. He was really into escape rooms in the last few months. Let me guess, you have to make a blood sacrifice on the new moon or some shit?"

Rose wasn't far off.

Seeing the look on Everly's face, she laughed again. "He's used the hellhound story and the Dale Street axe murders as the basis for a game he was playing. That's all."

"I don't think so, Rose." All Everly could think about was the first article for the *Haunted Happenings* column, the one all about the axe murders and the hellhound sightings. Right now, she needed to press on with examining the notebook. She could let the rest of it sink in later.

The next page contained another list. Written in ink, not pencil, and was more current.

Richard Hart – Leo?
Stone Hassell – Aquila?
Mark Hunt – Orion?

"Surprise, surprise. The mayor's on there, along with our journalism teacher and Jonathan's dad. That one's a little weird."

"Yeah, but look at the numbers." The lines on the page were numbered by Nathan, one through seven. "Only the first three numbers are filled in. Who are the other members? It looks like Nathan was trying to pair the current members with the old code names. Orion is the hunter. Leo is the lion. What is Aquila?"

Everly flipped back to the original list once more while Rose searched on Everly's phone. "There are seven here, too."

"Aquila is the eagle. I wonder what the significance of these names is. Maybe Nathan was in the middle of figuring it out." Rose tossed the phone back into Everly's lap before shooting to her feet. "No, no. I don't like this. What are we saying here?" She descended the two steps, pacing back and forth on the grass, chewing on a nail.

"I didn't say anything." Everly watched her as she paced. "But I believe you may have implied that Nathan was in the process of completing this list when he died."

Rose stopped, pointing a finger at Everly. "I did not imply that."

"Okay, I'm implying it."

Rose raked her hands through her hair.

Everly ignored her as she continued to read through the notebook. "There's a set of rules on this page. These are in Nathan's handwriting," she said.

She held up the book, so Rose could see the page with the bolded, inked-in words: **RULES.** Followed by bulleted numbers, one through seven. Only the first four were filled in.

"Again, things are missing. Only four rules out of seven are written down."

"Seven, again. This is creeping me out." Rose continued to pace, her hands shuffling up and down her arms as if she were cold. "What are the four?"

"One," Everly read. "All dealings must be kept confidential. Two, meetings shall be held on the new moon. Three, a member is permitted two absences per year. Four, members must uphold high standards of dress."

Rose stopped pacing, staring at Everly with all the attitude of her teenage years. "I'm still not hearing anything too freaky, except for the missing Rituals pages. What else is there?"

"A couple more pages. This one is a drawing of some kind of instrument." Everly held up the book so Rose could see the picture of a tool with three legs connected by a hinge. Each leg of the tool had a blade resembling guitar picks, each a different size. "Looks like an antique surgeon's tool."

"No, wait, I've seen one of those before. There's one at the museum in a case with other old medical instruments." Rose held out her hand for Everly's phone, again typing in a search. "It's called a fleam. Fleams were handheld instruments used for bloodletting. Gross." She handed the phone back. "What's next?"

"The next page says *Mission statement*." Everly squinted at the page.

"Which is?"

"To connect the town of Splendid with its citizens to mutually ensure a beneficial existence for all." Everly shifted on the cold, hard floor. "The next page looks to be nothing but random thoughts. Scribbled at the top, the page is titled *Natural Deaths*. Then this, 'So many unexplained deaths in Splendid, all seemingly natural, but sudden and strange. Too close to the secret? Refusals to play ball?' and a line that reads, 'Where does the magic come from? Splendid?'"

"What the fuck does that mean, Ever?" Rose's hands had now migrated to her hips. An edge had entered Rose's voice. Everly knew she was losing her. Just like in the old days. Rose was happy when it was Rose wanting to wreak havoc, trying to get Everly into trouble at every turn. When the tides shifted, and Everly wanted to delve into secret places, Rose betrayed her. Of course, Rose had never cared about uncovering or discovering. Back then, she was an adrenaline junkie, acting out the trauma she was experiencing at home. Everly was the seeker. She'd been the one searching for answers to what made Splendid so strange and unique.

Everly closed the book, setting it on top of the phone in

her lap. "I don't know, Rose."

Rose let out a long sigh, one hand dropping off her hip to rub at an eye socket. "Okay, look. I don't know what else to do now, do you? So, Nathan left you a strange notebook. There isn't anything frightening in there, just bizarre. I, for one, would like to get back to my life. I have a deadline next week, and I have zero pages to send to my editor. I did what I set out to do: get Charlie the personal effects he was after." Rose threw up her hands. "I just don't know what else to do."

Everly smiled up at Rose. "It's fine, Rose. I'll take it from here." She grabbed the notebook and phone from her lap, pressing herself to her feet.

"Don't do that, Ever."

"Do what?" Everly picked up Leigh's flip-flops, tossing them to Rose.

"Do this. Shut down on me." Rose held the flip-flops in one hand, close to her chest.

"Rose, it's fine. This is what I do. I investigate the unusual." Everly moved past Rose, her sights set on the car, fishing the keys from her front pocket. The afternoon was sliding into early evening, and a breeze moved the leaves on the grass and the hairs on her arm.

"You investigate the paranormal," Rose said behind her like that was different from what Everly had said. "Which I still don't get."

Everly halted, then spun to face Rose. "What is that supposed to mean?"

Rose made a face, rolling her eyes. "You know exactly what that means, Ever. You could have gone to Stanford with me. That was always the plan. You were going to be a surgeon. Out of a group of people, Ms. Moore called Splendid High's genius cluster, you were the most brilliant. And what did you do? You moved to New Orleans and became a paranormal investigator. Did you even go to college?"

Everly had never wanted to smack anyone more. She

sputtered for a moment before gathering her thoughts. "What does college matter? And for your information, I'm slowly getting my degree at LSU. But who cares? I enjoy what I do. I've learned a lot about myself through my job. I'm sorry I didn't follow your trajectory or Fletcher's or Leigh's. I never accepted money from my mom. I don't have enough to buy the Decomposition House or designer shoes that I can't wear through the grass, but I got away from Splendid, Rose, and that's all that matters to me. I wanted to do life on my own, away from the cradle of Splendid."

She wasn't entirely truthful. Her job was less of a career and more of a title she'd given herself. She lived well below the poverty line, which was why she'd taken the tour guide job and could take only one class every semester. Despite this, in one more year, she'd have a psychology BA, hopefully translating into a better-paying job.

Rose scoffed. "You and your obsession with Splendid."

Everly turned away from her, done with the conversation. Rose would never be on the same page as her. Even when Everly thought Rose might be her Rose, once again, she proved Everly wrong at every turn.

"Don't turn away from me, Ever."

"Stop calling me Ever. You don't get to call me that anymore because we're no longer friends." Rose's face fell, but Everly went on. "You can stay in denial all you want, but you and I just discovered that Nathan's death may not have been so natural after all. Open your eyes, Rose. Why is there no crime, such little illness? It's almost Halloween. Why the hell is it so warm? Why are the trees still in leaf even though there are leaves all over the ground? Something is wrong here."

"It's called climate change, Ever. A scientific fact that the whole world is studying. Get a clue." Rose threw her arms up as if to indicate that the beauty of Splendid was due to global warming.

"It isn't climate change, and you know it, Rose. If it were, the summer heat would be unbearable, but I know for a fact, because I monitor the weather here, that the temperature is always the same. Sure, the temp fluctuates some, but it never dips below seventy or rises above seventy-nine. Ever. When was the last time it snowed here, Rose? You get rain, sure, but snow? We're in the mountains, Rose. Every city around us gets truckloads of snow every winter, but not Splendid. *You* get a clue."

Rose didn't speak for several seconds. She blinked at Everly a few times, her arms crossed in front of her, her hands gripping the sides of her ribcage. She chewed her lip, her gaze flicking from Everly to the ground, back up to Everly. "I'm going to call Leigh to come and pick me up. I need to get Nathan's things to Charlie before it gets too late." She moved past Everly to the back door of the rental car. She opened the door, fishing out her purse and shoes.

"That's it? You don't have any response to what I've said?" Everly stood behind her, a few paces off the path, still in the graveyard grass.

"I need a minute, Ever. Several minutes." Rose typed in a text, presumably to Leigh, and pressed *Send*. "And like I previously said, I have work to do. Real work that pays me real money."

Rose turned in her bare feet, her purse slung over one shoulder, her heels dangling from her fingertips, the flip-flops shoved under an arm.

Everly scoffed, loud enough so Rose could hear her, then she said, "You always had to have the last word, the last parting shot. Typical Rose."

She expected Rose to turn around and volley a retort right back in Everly's direction, but she kept walking toward the cemetery's entrance.

"Fine," Everly said to herself. She got back into her piece of shit rental car, started the engine, and threw it into reverse. If Rose wanted to be a stubborn ass, who was Everly to stop her?

CHAPTER SEVENTEEN

Everly drove north, back toward home. She didn't have anywhere else to go except maybe to the museum or the library to do some research, but the thought of digging through decades worth of microfiche and dusty old books made her want to curl up and die. Maybe Rose was right; what did all this matter anyway? Everly was leaving tomorrow on the last row seat of an airplane that would take her back to New Orleans and her small, inconsequential life. Nathan was gone, and she wasn't a detective. Even if she could, by some miracle, come up with some evidence that his death hadn't been natural, who would take her seriously, and what would she be able to do about it? Not even her former friends could hang. And if the mayor was truly a member of this secret society, there was no telling who else might be involved. The entire police force could be involved, as far as she knew. There was no way she, acting by herself, could make anything happen.

Defeatist much, Everly? Yes, yes, I am.

The thought of asking her mom about this crossed her mind. Her mom had been called that night. She had seen the mayor and Dr. Sprague in their freaky robes, the same as Rose. But when Everly thought of her mom, moving around the house in her wheelchair, she came to her senses. Her mom was trying to survive. Everly wouldn't dare bring this to her doorstep. She'd caused her mom enough grief over the years.

As she drove home to face her failings as a daughter, she realized that was the last place she wanted to go. So, instead of turning right on Cascade Avenue, she turned left toward downtown. She was thirsty, and the kind of drink she wanted would be abundant at The Peak, even if she wasn't much of a drinker. She'd always been a lightweight. On the few occasions when she had crossed that line into drunkenness, she'd not made the best decisions, once even sleeping with the owner of the tour guide company she'd written for. But she couldn't think of anything else to do that would take away the pain of being home amid yet another mystery. Hiding and running away were the things she did best, after all, and hiding in a shot glass was pretty appealing.

Kismet must have been on her side, because there was a vacant parking spot right in front of The Peak, and the meter still showed an hour and a half remaining. The powers that be supported this decision, so it couldn't be all bad. She'd take it.

Late afternoon in downtown Splendid was bustling. Pedestrians strained the sidewalks, ladies gripping boutique bags in their slender hands; teenagers, earbuds in and heads down; and couples strolling hand in hand. The weather was perfect as always. The heat from the sun was warm but not overly so, while the breeze coming off the mountains looming in the distance was cool and delicious. Whatever was going on in Splendid, Everly wanted to ignore it. She focused on the double glass doors of The Peak, pulling them open to reveal a packed bar inside.

The sight of the crowded tables deflated her spirits, if such a thing were possible. They were already lower than a subterranean cavern and had been for some time. She stood on the threshold, one arm dangling, the other pulling on the skin of her elbow, as she pondered what to do. Retreat seemed the only option.

"Table for one?"

Jonathan popped up in her peripheral vision. Everly jumped.

"Sorry." He held out a hand but didn't touch her. He looked so good in a University of Colorado T-shirt about a half size too small across the chest, the same stubble from yesterday dusting his cheeks.

"No." She tried to make a sound resembling a laugh. "My fault. I'd love a table, but it doesn't look like there is one."

"There's space at the bar. Are you alone?" He looked at her like he always had, with such intense focus that she felt like the only person in the room.

"Yeah," she murmured.

"I got you. Come on." He turned, leading the way to the end of the bar and the only open seat in the joint.

Everly grabbed his hand. She wasn't sure what had come over her, but she had some things to say, and if she didn't get them out right then, she wasn't sure she ever would.

Jonathan glanced back at her, his eyebrows raised. "Everything okay?"

"I know you're at work, and this is weird, and I'm so sorry, but I have to talk to you. In private." She bit the inside of her lip so hard she tasted metal. "Is this okay? Can you give me, like, five minutes?" She held on to him like she was drowning.

He squeezed her back. "Sure. We can talk in my office."

Jonathan continued to hold her hand as he guided her past the busy tables, past the bar where Marty, the waitress, glared at Everly as she passed, and through the doorway that led to the kitchen. Were he and Marty a couple? Or was Marty just in lust with her boss? Everly couldn't blame her if that was the case; Jonathan was easily the sexiest man in the room. They continued past two workers. Everly couldn't tell who the chef was, neither wore a chef's jacket or glanced their way, but they worked diligently, the smell of grilling hamburger patties and fry grease strong in the air. Everly and Jonathan came to another door. This one opened onto a small room, a desk shoved against one wall, a chair pushed up under it, and a tall, old-school metal filing cabinet shoved against the other. There wasn't a window, so they had total privacy once Jonathan closed the door behind them.

Everly turned around, leaning her back against the wall by the filing cabinet. "I'm sorry," she said.

Jonathan shrugged, leaning his backside against the edge of his desk. "For wanting to talk? It's fine, Everly."

He was so close to her that she could smell his aftershave, something woodsy and clean, and she could feel his body heat. Or maybe she was imagining that she could, remembering what it was like when his body was pressed against hers. She had to take a deep breath to dispel some of the butterflies in her stomach. She'd almost forgotten this feeling. The feeling of wanting to be so completely absorbed by one person, the feeling of wanting only to feel his arms around her, warming her, cocooning her.

She shook her head, glancing down at the floor so she wouldn't have to feel the intensity of his eyes. "I'm not sorry for wanting to talk. I'm sorry about how I behaved back then. I owe you four or five apologies, at least. But since so much time has passed, maybe you'll let me get away with one blanket apology. One ring to rule them all." Her face warmed. "That was dumb," she murmured. She was too ashamed to go into specifics. During those few months they were together, they'd broken up a couple of times, Everly always the one to end things. She'd treated him badly, and she knew it.

"It was a long time ago, Everly. More than two decades. It's okay, really. Feels like another lifetime at this point."

She still couldn't look at him. Staring at the floor, she said, "I know. And I'm not crazy. I don't imagine that you still think about me. I just wanted you to know how truly sorry I am. I was going through a lot, emotionally and maybe psychologically, and what I felt for you was too intense for me then. I wasn't equipped to handle all that feeling on top of what I was going through."

From the corner of her eye, Everly saw Jonathan grip the edge of his desk, biceps flexing as he held on. "I understand. I wish you had been able to talk to me about it. I cared for you so much. All I wanted to do was be there for you, and you kept pushing me away."

Everly's throat closed up, her eyes beginning to burn. For what felt like the tenth time since being home, she was on the verge of tears again. The only thing she could think to do at that moment was bolt. Running was what she was good at. Rose had taken the moment away from her at the cemetery, turning Everly's best defense against her and taking off before she could.

"I should go. Sorry I bothered you." She bolted for the door, reaching out to grab the handle.

Jonathan took her hand before she could touch the doorknob. He held it gently, not forcibly, and he didn't move to block her. This is what Everly wanted, to be in physical contact with him again, so she held on. When he held her hand from the bar's door to the office, she felt seventeen again. She felt that spark of attraction that she'd never been able to replicate at any point in her life with anyone. The simple act of holding her hand, a hand that hadn't been held in any way—romantic or familial—in so long, broke the tide of tears she'd been keeping at bay for the last two days.

As the first tears dropped, her head still down, unable to look Jonathan in the eye, he pulled her toward him, snaking his other arm around her waist. He held her, her head against a still hard chest, while she unloaded all the pain of those last days. She cried out the moment her mom had called to tell her about Nathan; she cried out the pain and discomfort of his funeral; she cried out the awkwardness of being with her former friends; she cried out the agony of feeling, only briefly, the sunshine of Rose's smile; she cried out the pain of her mom being sick, and she cried out the pain of Jonathan's absence from her life. The absence of them all from her life. She'd done this to herself, this isolation, this loneliness. It had all been her fault. She had no one else to blame.

"Everly," Jonathan spoke over the top of her head, his breath warm on her scalp. "Why don't you come home?"

Jonathan said this as if he knew why her heart was breaking and what she was thinking.

She shook her head against his chest, her tears staining his T-shirt. "I can't. There isn't anything here for me. Not anymore."

"There could be."

He touched a finger to her chin, tipping her face up toward his. Even with her face soaked with tears, a little snot bubbling from a nostril, he kissed her. The kiss was gentle at first, a test to see what she would do. Everly knew this kind of kiss. This was reminiscent of the first time he kissed her in the rain, walking home from a movie. Her face had been wet then, too, and so had his. He'd touched his lips to hers with the lightest pressure, and she had reached up on her tiptoes, throwing her arms around his neck to devour him. That kiss had gone from chaste to flaming in a hot second. This one did, too.

Before Everly knew what was happening, Jonathan's mouth was on her neck, and she was tugging off his shirt. Her hunger for flesh-to-flesh contact made her throw all sense out the window. Footsteps echoed outside.

A single knock on the door had Jonathan reaching for his shirt as quickly as it had come off. "Just a sec." He grinned at her like he had when her mom had caught them making out in the crow's nest twenty-five years earlier.

Everly tried to grin back, breathless, hair tousled, but knowing that ached-for orgasm wasn't happening now made her want to cry again.

She straightened her T-shirt, then combed her hair with

her fingers.

Jonathan opened the door to reveal Fletcher standing on the other side. He looked tired, like he'd slept less than Everly, puffy bags under his eyes the size of lifeboats.

He cast a wary glance in her direction. "Hey, sorry. Am I interrupting something?"

"No, I was just leaving." Everly plastered a fake smile across her face. She was getting good at that.

"Don't go. Fletcher's here for our weekly beer. I can make him wait so we can finish our discussion." Jonathan's sly grin and how he leaned a careless arm against the door frame nearly made Everly weak in the knees.

It shouldn't have mattered what Fletcher thought. They were all middle-aged adults. If she and Jonathan wanted to have some afternoon delight in his office, they should have it. But the thought of Fletcher knowing, the thought of Fletcher watching her as she walked out of the bar after having sex with Jonathan, made her cringe. It shouldn't have, but it did.

"We can finish that discussion another time. I'm late for a thing, anyway." There was no thing, and everyone knew it. Everly smiled again, or tried to, patted Jonathan on the arm in a truly awkward way, and walked past Fletcher, who had stepped back for her to pass. She was almost to the door that separated the kitchen from the bar when she turned around. She was leaving tomorrow. If she let this opportunity pass her by, she'd regret it for another twenty-five years. She looked straight at Jonathan. "Come to the crow's nest tonight. It'll be like old times."

He nodded, a wolfish grin spread cheek to cheek.

Everly walked through the restaurant as quickly as she could. She was out on the street when she felt a hand on her arm. Assuming it was Jonathan, she whirled around for a goodbye kiss. The harrowed face that greeted her was Fletcher's. In the bright sun of midday, the bags under his eyes looked twice as puffy as they had been inside. The creases that lined either side of his mouth appeared deeper than they had before. His glare as he stared at her was anything but friendly. "Everly, I need to ask you a favor."

Everly tried not to seem taken aback. What sort of favor would Fletcher need of her? "Sure, what do you need?"

He gazed down at the ground, revealing a bald spot surrounded by salt-and-pepper hair. When he stared back into her eyes, a pleading cast to his brow, Everly worried that he, too, might be sick like Leigh had been. "I need you to stop with the crazy."

The worry she had felt for Fletcher and his health was over the second he spoke.

Crossing her arms helped Everly quell the desire to punch him. "I'm not crazy, Fletcher, and I'm not having this conversation with you." She turned toward her parking space.

"Oh, yes, you are." Fletcher took her a little forcibly by her elbow, spinning her back around to face him. "Everly, please understand something. Leigh is still healing. She is still weak. Yes, her scans were clear, but there is a chance of relapse. I can't have her stressed out in any way. Calm is the word of the decade in our house. You do not instill calm, Everly. You bring chaos. You are what we, in the industry, call a disruptor, only in your case, being a disruptor is as negative as it gets."

Everly didn't know what the hell Fletcher was talking about, but she knew when she was being disparaged. She took a deep breath, ready to release her diatribe against him, but he beat her to the punch.

"Rose is fragile, too," he began. "She feels a huge amount of guilt for pulling away from you in high school, and I'm scared that she'll do anything now in some sad attempt to make it up to you. Rose has been through a lot, Everly. I doubt you're aware. Also,"—Fletcher pointed to the doors of The Peak—"leave him the hell alone. I had to talk him off the ledge when you left, almost literally. Don't fuck with him again."

A punch to the gut would have been less painful. Everly

hugged herself, sweating in the warm sun while also feeling chilled. She felt sick, like she was coming down with the flu.

Part of her wanted to say *fine* and retreat. But Everly was getting tired of turning her tail and running. So, instead of disappearing into herself, she squared her shoulders and met Fletcher stare for stare. "Fuck you, Fletch." She turned on her heel, making a beeline for her rental car.

It wasn't much, but she felt like she'd stood up for herself in a small way. Her friends could not have made it clearer that she wasn't wanted here. Tomorrow couldn't come soon enough.

AD BRAZEAU

CHAPTER EIGHTEEN

Mom was sitting in the living room, working on a new mystery novel, when Everly walked in.

The wainscotting was the color of butter in the waning light of early evening, shadows seeping from the edges of the large landscape painting over the fireplace. Nothing in the room had changed except for the rug. The burgundy Turkish carpet from her childhood had been replaced by a plain cream rug that seemed to suck all the color out of the room.

Everly sat on the sofa, also cream. "What are you reading?"

Mom looked over the top of her book, reading glasses perched on the end of her pert nose. "The latest O'Shea." She flipped the book around to show Everly the cover.

"Cool," she said like she knew who that was. Everly was uncomfortable, had been uncomfortable since the moment she walked in the door the day before. She loved her mom, she did. They just never seemed to have much to talk about. "I don't know if I told you, Mom, but I'm leaving tomorrow. I have to get back to work." She didn't. Paranormal investigation work was not steady, although her landlord had informed her that he was raising the rent. The second she returned to New Orleans, she'd have to start pounding pavement to find a job, even if it was only minimum wage.

"Oh." Mom put her book down, holding it loosely on her lap. "That was fast. I had hoped you would stay longer."

"Me, too," Everly lied.

"Well, let's make sure to have dinner together. I'll order from your favorite, Manicotti's."

"Manicotti's, wow. Sounds great." Everly fidgeted. She needed to move her body and be active. Sitting and thinking about the strangeness of the last twenty-four hours was not something she was interested in doing. "Is there anything I can do for you, Mom? You know, while I'm here."

"Oh, no. I don't want to burden you with silly household chores." Mom smiled, pushing her spectacles back up the bridge of her nose.

"It's not a burden, Mom. Tell me what you need." Everly knew from Mom's tone that there was something Everly could do, only she didn't want to ask. The idea that there was a tunnel under her house connecting it to Red Manor had been playing in her mind all the way home. That and how toned Jonathan's body still was. It might seem strange to go into the basement without a reason, so Everly was hoping her mom would give her a chore that involved going down there while also helping her get something done.

"Well." Mom looked at her phone and set it back down alongside her chair. "The gardener was supposed to come yesterday, but he had a family emergency. The leaves in the back are driving me crazy. The pond is so full of them, I'm afraid for the fish."

"I can clear the leaves for you, Mom. That isn't a problem, and you know I like being outside." Everly smiled at her mom, trying to give off as much of a reassuring vibe as she could. "The rakes and pond skimmers still in the shed?"

Mom nodded. "Thank you, dear."

"Great, and I'll just run downstairs to grab some

gardening gloves."

Mom smiled as she returned to her O'Shea.

Conveniently, the basement was opposite the back door. Everly threw back the deadbolt, opened the door, and then descended the old, rickety wooden stairs. The usual musty, slightly damp basement smell made her think of cobwebs and centipedes.

She stood at the bottom, craning her neck to take in the large, cavernous space. The furnace, looking like a spider itself, with various ducts jutting up through the flooring, sat in the dead center. There were no doorways she could see from where she stood, so she walked the perimeter to be sure. An old, defunct washer and dryer were against one wall, no doubt collecting mold in their crevices. Another wall sporting shelving held boxes marked with words like *Books, Christmas,* and *Baby Clothes.*

There were a couple of paintings leaning against a box, landscapes by Eli Palmer. Everly bent down for a closer look. The fleeting thought she'd had in the cemetery rushed back. The drawings in the notebook were made by an artist, as Rose said. "You're Draco," she whispered to the empty basement. This made sense, of course. As the town's founder, Eli would have been right in the thick of Roots and Wings.

Everly peeked behind the boxes but saw nothing but a cement wall. The third wall was bare cement, but something made her pause. Some of the cement was a different color, darker and patchier.

She ran her hand over the space, large enough to conceal a doorway. Nausea bubbled in her stomach. This was the tunnel entrance. The tunnel that led to Red Manor. It had been sealed, probably some time ago, but realizing that this had been here all her life was sickening. Her hand recoiled, as did the rest of her body, and she shot back up the stairs, suddenly too afraid to be down there alone.

She rebolted the door, leaning against it to take a few deep breaths. There was nothing to be done about the entrance. Someone had taken care of it long ago, but she wouldn't be able to sleep in that house ever again.

Everly filled up a glass of water before heading out back. Hydration had been the last thing on her mind, a mind full of so many strange threads, so she was sure her kidneys would appreciate a little moisture before they began to shut down.

The sun was still bright in the backyard, sliding its way toward the mountains that Everly now faced. She'd have a good hour before the sun disappeared behind the peak as she did her best to shake off what she'd found in the cellar.

The shed, not original to the house, built sometime in the '60s, was looking weathered, in bad need of some scraping and a new coat of paint. Everly wrenched open the warped door, wary of what may lurk within. There had been an occasional wasp nest in the front right corner. The nest was removed repeatedly, but the wasps were determined; they always returned. Everly cocked her head to the side, trying to get a look at the corner without stepping inside. She didn't hear any buzzing. She craned her neck a little farther. No wasps in sight.

The second problem to keep abreast of was black widows. Everly had learned from a young age to watch her fingers and bare toes when she reached or walked into dark places. She leaned inside the shed, keeping her feet firmly on the grass, and grabbed for the rake. She gave it a little shake before pulling it out. Something small and black scurried toward the back of the shed, causing a shiver to spike along her arms. She tossed the rake on the grass and returned for the pond skimmer.

Once she had the tools she'd need, she slammed the door closed to give the spiders their privacy.

The pond wasn't as overrun with leaves as her mom had made out. The koi were fine, swimming and coming to the surface to beg for food like little dogs.

Everly steadied herself on the edge, glad to have a physical task to take her mind off past events. She refused to give any thought to the fact that Nathan had left her a note taped to his window and that he had hidden his notebook about Roots and Wings in a place she would know to look. She refused to think about Rose, Jonathan, or any of them, and she especially wasn't thinking about the tunnel.

All Everly wanted to do was enjoy the last rays of the day's sun, skimming leaves away from her mother's precious koi.

She started to get lost in the repetition of skimming leaves—thrust, pull, dump; thrust, pull, dump. When she heard a twig snap toward the property's edge, the sound barely registered. It wasn't until she heard what sounded like a scrape against flagstone that she glanced to the side.

There wasn't anything there.

She went back to skimming, but a chill raised the hairs on the back of her neck, theatrically, like she was in a scary movie. There was only one other time when she could remember the hairs on the back of her neck rising.

Everly dropped the pond skimmer—half in, half out of the water—with a splash and a clank. She faced the direction the sounds had come from, her feet planted in the grass, ready to run the second she had to. There was a little flush of foolishness, but if she'd learned anything, it was to trust her instincts.

There was the unmistakable sound of leaves crunching under feet. Everly's head swiveled left and right—there was no one about, no one she could see. Only, there was no doubt something was there, not far from where she stood. Not only could she hear the crush of leaves, but she heard what sounded like a huff, an animal exhaling through its nostrils.

The time to stand and fight had passed. Whatever was in the yard with her wasn't natural, and she was no hero. With her heart fluttering in her chest, she pivoted, ready to dash to the back door, to safety. But before she made it more than two steps, she was tackled from the side and pushed down hard, her hip and elbow biting into the gravel surrounding the pond.

Everly felt like she'd been hit by a train, only trains didn't tear into your flesh. Molten fear ran through her veins like lava as her heart pumped so much blood that she thought she would surely die of a heart attack. Pain sliced through her on both sides of her body, the side that had bitten the hard rock and the side that was being mauled by something the size of a lion.

Thinking was hard when all she could do at the moment was fight for her life. Every snap of the beast's jaws brought new pain, new terror. The thought of dying on the gravel, pond scum on the bottom of her shoes, brought tears. She was in a panic, working off pure adrenaline. She had to do something. She almost rolled over on her back, then realized that would be a mistake. She wasn't strong enough to take on whatever was tearing at her. She had to regain her feet and make it to the door.

She bucked forward, kicking at whatever had her in its grip. She couldn't see it and had no idea what it was. That it was a dog of some sort made the only kind of sense, although animals like cougars and bears were not uncommon in the area. They did live in the mountains, after all.

There was a satisfying yelp as Everly squarely kicked the beast, causing it to momentarily back off. She was on her knees, stumbling forward. All she had to do was make it fifteen feet or so to the back door.

She didn't make it. Before she gained even five feet, the animal was on her again. This time from behind. Everly lurched forward, her palms hitting the brick walk, flesh scraping off like her skin was made of nothing more than taffy. She now had no choice but to roll over and try to kick at the thing. Kicking had been successful once before. She was currently fighting for her life.

Claws cut into her back. She screamed for the first time. Why hadn't she thought to scream before? Someone would come. She screamed again, this time as she rolled. The beast rolled with her. Everly had closed her eyes for a moment, as the pain of rolling from her front to her back had been too great. When she opened them, she expected to see a snarling wild animal on top of her, saliva and blood dripping, but there was … nothing. Nothing was there, nothing that she could see. But she could feel it. Everly thought maybe her mind was playing tricks on her, that maybe through the terror of what was happening, her eyes were sparing her a sight that might send her into shock.

She screamed again, as loud and long as she could, while she worked both her knees up to her chest. With one good kick of her legs, she bucked backward, propelling whatever was attacking her as far as possible. There was another yelp, this one less satisfying, as Everly began to feel dizzy, her mind going fuzzy. She was sinking. Her worst fear was about to come true: dying in Splendid. Something shot by her in a rush of air, then more yelping. The sounds of two animals fighting, snarling, and growling confused her as she stared at nothing.

There was a loud bang behind her, maybe a door slamming open. Then there were footsteps, shouting, and tugging as hands hooked under her armpits. Everly felt herself going under. She fought for consciousness.

"Ever," Rose shouted at her, holding her upper body, while Leigh checked her hands and elbows. "Is it a stroke or a seizure?"

"Everly." Leigh dropped her arms, her small fingers digging into Everly's eyes to open her eyelids. "Maybe we should call 911." Fingers opened her eyes. "Everly, can you hear me? Can you say the alphabet for me? Can you get up and walk?"

Everly concentrated on what was happening around her. All was silent in the yard. She batted away Leigh's hand. Now that the beast or beasts were gone and Rose held her in her protective arms, Everly felt like she could finally take a deep breath and focus on getting her heart rate down. "It attacked me," she croaked through a dry throat.

Everly looked up to see Rose looking around. "Someone attacked you? Leigh, call the police."

Everly shook her head, frustrated that they couldn't see with their eyes that her wounds were from an animal attack. She was sure the tears and the claw marks were obvious. "Not a person. It was an animal." She was coming back to herself, pushing Rose away, and she pulled up her shirt. "I was bitten, mauled. Can't you see the wounds? And there was another animal that helped me."

Rose pushed Everly forward, pulling her shirt up farther. "Ever, there aren't any wounds here. The only wounds are on your elbows and hands, which look like road rash, probably from falling. I think we need to take you to the hospital and let them evaluate you."

Everly touched the pink, untouched flesh of her stomach, her side. "What the hell?" The pain had vanished, like smoke dissipating in the fresh air.

Rose rolled her shirt back down and then rubbed what was supposed to be a reassuring hand over her back. "It's okay, Ever. We've all been through a lot. Let's take you to the doc and let them check you out."

Everly pushed to her feet, teetering away from Rose and Leigh, where they still sat on the cement walk that led to her back steps. She looked at Rose, incredulousness on her face. "I'm not crazy, Rose."

"I didn't say you were, Ever, but you weren't attacked by an animal. That's a fact."

Everly crossed her arms in front of her like she was cold, even though she was sweating. "What did you two see when you came outside?"

Leigh stood up, casually dropping a hand into a pocket of her voluminous pants. "Your mom said you were out back. We heard you screaming from the kitchen and ran out the door. You were thrashing and kicking on the ground. It was really scary. I think maybe you had some kind of seizure." Leigh glanced at Rose, then back at Everly. "We should take you to the hospital, Everly. Just to make sure it wasn't a stroke or something."

Everly closed her eyes and shook her head. "I didn't have a seizure or a stroke. I was fully in possession of my faculties the whole time, and I feel fine now."

Rose stood for a moment, then took a seat on the back step. "Tell us what happened."

Everly wasn't sure she wanted to do that. Only moments ago, Rose had wanted to take her in for an evaluation.

The sun was starting to slide behind the mountains at Everly's back. Her shadow almost touched the tip of Rose's foot. The closeness she'd felt to Rose outside of Nathan's mausoleum, how much she'd missed not only that proximity to the woman who had once been her Anam Cara but the camaraderie, caused the pain in her throat and heart to increase. Everly hated to admit how much she dearly wished she could snap her fingers and make Rose her best friend again. There was nothing she had ever wanted more, except maybe to make out with Jonathan some more.

"Ever." Rose stared at her, compassion behind her eyes. Her lips quirked up into a soft smile. "I don't think you're crazy. Tell us what happened."

"I don't think you're crazy, either, Everly." Leigh still stood off to the side, the sun's waning light illuminating half of her face. "If I'm telling the truth, I never did think that."

Everly could not have been more shocked, and she had just been attacked by some phantom wild animal. "You didn't?" Not even Rose had gone so far as to say she'd fully believed her. She certainly never expected such an admission from Leigh, who rarely seemed to decide anything without Fletcher's nod of approval.

Leigh shook her head. Everly noticed for the first time that Leigh wasn't wearing a head scarf. She was wearing a wig, a pretty brunette one cut into a cute bob. It had an extreme effect on Leigh's features. She looked far less sallow than she had, with an almost glow to her complexion. "No. Splendid is weird. Strange things happen here, or don't happen here. It certainly isn't normal to live in a city this size with zero crime, is it? The local meteorologists explain our unusual weather by saying we live in a mountain valley that retains heat and keeps out snow. I don't think anyone believes that stuff. We accept it because it's nice here."

Everly didn't know whether to hug Leigh or slap her. "Why didn't you say anything then? Back when I needed people on my side."

Leigh shrugged, her beachy, loose tunic swaying as she moved. "We were babies, Everly. I wasn't comfortable speaking out. I'm never comfortable speaking out. That's why Fletcher and I work so well together. He's the extrovert, and I'm the introvert. He does the things that I'm not comfortable with."

Everly wanted to be mad. She wanted to rail at Leigh and call her a coward, ask her what kind of friend abandons someone who's going through hell, but instead, she nodded. Everly could understand Leigh's trepidation. Everly wasn't an introvert, but she wasn't an extrovert, either. For most of her childhood, she'd had Rose to grab her hand and lead the way, much like Fletcher had done for Leigh.

"Ever." Rose's voice caught, and Everly thought she might be on the verge of tears, but Rose cleared her throat and continued, "Please tell us what happened out here."

Everly looked straight into her eyes. "I was attacked, Rose. I was at the pond, skimming leaves, and I heard something stalking toward me in the grass. Only I couldn't see anything. I got the chills, and I tried to run for the door. Whatever it was, it felt like a huge dog tackled me from the side, mauling me with its mouth and claws. We fought. I tried to kick it off, but it kept returning for more. I thought it was killing me, Rose. I felt my flesh tear, its teeth penetrate me, and the blood drip down my side and back. Only I couldn't see the animal. Then there was another one, another dog, I think. It rushed past me, and they fought. When I felt your hands on me, they were gone."

Rose held Everly's gaze for a few seconds, then looked

down at the ground. She mashed her lips together, her fingers digging into her kneecaps. Rose had changed into more practical clothing after their jaunt in the cemetery. She now wore gray slacks with the same silky button-down she'd had on earlier. Gone, too, were the heels, replaced with black ballet flats.

Rose took a breath, glancing toward Leigh and then toward Everly, a softened expression behind her eyes. "You know what this sounds like, right?"

Everly shook her head.

Rose huffed. "How could you not? This was your big article for the paper, Ever. The topic of our first *Haunted Happenings* meeting in the graveyard. We just talked about it this morning. Think. What did you always maintain that you thought you saw at Red Manor?"

Everly's gut pinched with a cramp so fierce she thought she might hurl right there. She rubbed a light hand over her belly, disbelief coursing through her. She didn't want to believe what was right in front of her. As much as she knew she'd seen an apparition on that staircase all those years ago, seeing something and being attacked by the same something were two very different things. "It can't be."

"You're the one who's been pushing this narrative for over twenty-five years, Ever. You tell us what it was."

Leigh's hand flew to her mouth. She held it there as she stared at Everly.

"I was attacked by the Hellhound of Splendid."

AD BRAZEAU

CHAPTER NINETEEN

Rose was coming around, but it was hard. There was still that part of her that found it all too much, too far-fetched. She lived in the real world, adulting for herself and her older sister, meeting deadlines, giving interviews, and always meeting expectations. Besides that one night, she'd never seen anything unusual in Splendid. Ever talked like the town was alive, like the town acted purposefully. This was the stuff of novels, of movies, and Rose should know; all she did was create fictional realities.

Leigh walked ahead up the back servant's stairs to the crow's nest. It was clear when they passed Elsie, wheeling herself into the kitchen for some water, that she hadn't heard the awful screams coming from Ever in the backyard. Rose wasn't surprised. Elsie was older now, and she had been in the front parlor when Rose and Leigh had strolled through the kitchen on their way to find Ever.

"Woah," Leigh said, opening the door to the crow's nest and stepping inside.

Rose motioned for Ever to go first before entering herself and shutting the door.

Leigh walked around the small room, her mouth open in a gaping smile. "I can't believe this. I haven't been in this room in so long, and it's still exactly the same." She squealed when she saw the record player, sinking to her knees to thumb through the dust-covered albums.

"Yeah," Rose said as she sank into the bean bag. "Some things never change. If only our faces could be as unchanging as this room."

"Oh, stop." Leigh slipped a Siouxsie and the Banshees record from its sleeve. "Your face is as smooth as it ever was." Leigh placed the record on the turntable, lowering the needle. The record spun, the catchy song "Peek-a-Boo" spilling from the speakers. Leigh turned the volume down so they could talk, then settled herself on the floor, her back against the couch. "Remind me about the hellhound story. I think I vaguely remember talking about it in the graveyard, but that was eons ago."

Ever was still shaken up. This was evident to Rose in how Ever hugged her knees to her chest as she sat in the fetal position. She was shaking, too, her arms quivering as if she were cold, only the room was quite warm. The crow's nest was always warm.

Rose looked out the window. The sun had set, twilight casting a pale glow on the grass outside, making it look more yellow than green. Nathan's house sat in the distance, a sad and lonely reminder of a friend she would miss until the end of time. She pulled her gaze away. "The hellhound was a supposed apparition seen several times stalking the streets of downtown Splendid in the weeks before the final murders here took place."

"The axe murders," Leigh clarified.

Rose nodded, pointing a finger toward the south window behind Ever. "Yep. The axe murders took place about four or five blocks from here. A family of four was butchered with their axe, which was procured from their yard and left at the scene. A husband, a wife, and their two kids. There was a lot of speculation that the wife had a lover and that he was the perpetrator, but nothing ever came of that theory. The last theory, and the one that people came to accept as fact, was that a serial killer had come through town on the railroad, killed the family, and rolled right back out of town. The little house was torn down. There's nothing but an empty lot now. I'm not even sure who owns the lot. Someone has to, but nothing has ever been built there, not in a hundred and fifty years."

Leigh's brow wrinkled down the middle as she glanced at Ever before looking back at Rose. "But did the hellhound ever attack anyone?"

Rose nodded. "There were scattered reports of people being attacked by an animal they couldn't see, remember? The supposed attacks occurred around the time of the axe murders, but people shrugged them off as hysteria. The murders freaked out the whole town."

Ever remained in her strange, almost catatonic state, her arms tight around her knees. Rose knew she'd been through something. That was plain to anyone with eyes, but how could a specter take corporeal form and attack? As was usual with Rose, the longer she was removed from a strange incident, the more unlikely it began to seem.

She hated to make Ever talk, but they had to understand what was happening here. "Ever, do you remember the story you wrote for the paper? Can you think of a reason why it would hurt you, or try to?" The fact of the matter was that even if it had attacked Ever, she wasn't injured in any way. Not physically.

Ever squeezed her eyes shut, removed a hand from her knee-holding, and rubbed them. Rose heard her taking several deep breaths. Ever opened her eyes, dropping her feet to the floor. "The hellhound story was never corroborated by the authorities. It was all chalked up as a hoax." Her voice was shaky, hoarse from screaming. "But, if you get your head out of your ass for five minutes, Rose, you'll realize that I was just given a warning."

Rose leaned forward. A bean bag was not a good place to be when you wanted to act with indignation. "Excuse me? My head is not up my ass, Ever. I'm here, aren't I? Or are you trying your damndest to alienate me again?"

"Wait." Leigh sat up on her knees, a hand out toward Rose and a hand out toward Ever. Leigh, the peacemaker, was going to try and make peace. "Let's hear what Everly has to say, Rose. Although maybe she can say things more nicely."

Rose would have laughed if she weren't so pissed.

Ever took another shaky breath, her brow set in a way that Rose was familiar with—Ever was on the defensive. No doubt she felt she had to be. Rose leaned back, her arms across her chest. "Talk, Ever. I'm listening. We both are."

"Leigh doesn't know that I've seen the hellhound before, and I suspect that you, too, Rose, also saw the hound that night at Red Manor." Ever stared at Rose as if trying to see through to her innermost thoughts.

Leigh gasped, one of the hands she'd been holding out flying to her mouth in Leigh fashion. "The night you broke into Red Manor and got caught?" The words were muffled, said behind her hand, but Rose heard her.

"I," Rose started, then looked away, out the window. "I don't know what I saw. I'll grant that I saw something, and it may have been dog-like, but that night was so bonkers. I was so scared, my adrenaline was through the roof. And it wasn't the house that had me scared, it was the adults."

"Because you guys got in trouble?" Leigh asked.

Rose shook her head, still staring out the window. "No. Although, don't get me wrong, I was scared as hell of my mom and what she would do if she found out. What scared me the most was the weirdness of it all, like we had interrupted something dark, something scary."

"What do you mean?"

"What I mean, Leigh, is there are two things I never told anyone until I told Ever yesterday." Rose looked straight at Leigh. "The first was that when the mayor came out from wherever he had been, he was wearing a black robe, and he had two drops of what looked like blood on his collar." Rose paused so Leigh could digest this first bit of information. "The second thing was that the doctor was already there. No one called him. He also appeared from behind the staircase and wore a black robe."

Leigh's face registered shock. Her eyes, small though they were, had become saucers, her mouth hanging open.

"And that's not all." Ever explained the last two days to Leigh and the things she had found, starting with the symbols and ending with the notebook Leigh had already seen.

Rose heard Leigh gasp again, but something else had caught her attention. Rose wrenched herself out of the bean bag, a hand propped against the window ledge. She had to hold her breath to keep from fogging up the glass. "What the hell?"

"What?" Ever asked behind her. Two seconds later, Ever was at her shoulder.

"Do you see that?" Rose pointed toward Nathan's house. "It looks like a light, a moving light."

Ever moved her face closer to the glass. "A flashlight. Someone's inside."

"It's probably Charlie or maybe Nathan's mom or sister." Leigh had materialized alongside Ever.

"Why would someone who's allowed to be in the house use a flashlight?" Ever asked the question that Rose was already thinking.

They watched as the light disappeared from the first floor. Moments later, it reappeared on the second.

"Someone's in Nathan's bedroom," Ever said. "We should go over there."

"Are you crazy?" Leigh blurted the question, then immediately said, "Sorry, I didn't mean to say that. Maybe we should call the police."

"By the time they get here, whoever it is will be long gone," said Rose. She ran to the light switch, flipped off the lights, then made her way back to the window in the dark.

"I can't see much, but I can tell whoever is over there is male. The figure looks big even from this distance." Ever crouched down to see around the fogged-up window.

"I think he's alone."

"Rose, I don't like the tone of your voice." Leigh backed away from the window. "If you two are planning on breaking and entering, I can't join you."

"Probably best, Leigh. Ever, let's go." Rose tugged on Ever's sleeve.

Ever peeled away from the window to follow her to the door.

"Wait," Leigh called. "At least take a weapon. A knife from the kitchen or something."

"Great minds, Leigh." Rose opened the door.

Night had fully settled in by the time they had stalked their way to the back door of Nathan's house. Ever held a knife in one hand, a key in the other. Rose, also holding a knife from Ever's kitchen, stood back, quelling the butterflies in her stomach with deep breaths while Ever stuck the key in the lock. She tried to focus on how lovely the evening was, the soft, gentle breeze as it rustled the fall leaves scattered over the flagstone, the soothing sound of crickets singing their nightly song.

Ever turned the key. Without removing the key from the lock, she turned the knob with deliberate slowness, pushing open the door at the same snail's pace. Rose knew she was trying to be stealthy and quiet, but the longer they stood out in the open, the antsier Rose became. She jostled from one foot to the other.

Ever entered first. The kitchen was dark. There was enough light from the night sky shining through the windows to illuminate the room enough to keep them from digging a hip into a sharp corner. They tiptoed their way down the hall from the kitchen to the foyer, stopping every few feet or so to listen. The first time Ever stopped, Rose slammed into her back, almost dropping her stainless-steel knife onto the wood floor. After that, they'd entered a rhythm: stop, listen, go; stop, listen, go.

At the foot of the grand staircase, Ever took hold of the banister, shooting a look back at Rose. Rose knew what she was asking without Everly having to say a word. *Are you ready?*

Rose felt her heartbeat in her throat, her stomach so tight she felt as if she'd done a hundred crunches. Had she done this very thing, breaking into homes, buildings, graveyards, her entire childhood like it had been nothing? All she could do at that moment was nod. They'd gone too far to turn back.

Ever placed her right foot on the first step, testing it with part of her weight to make sure it wouldn't creak before taking her left foot off the floor. She repeated this process until they were halfway up the stairs. There hadn't been any sounds above them. Maybe they had been imagining things, or whoever had been inside had snuck out, and they were alone, sneaking through the house like a couple of idiots.

It wasn't until they were on the second stair from the top, Rose gripping the banister like she might drown if she let go, that she heard noise from down the hall. Ever crouched, Rose following suit. They both craned their necks to look over the railing toward Nathan's old room, which sat at the very end of the hall behind them.

Rose couldn't see Ever's face very well in the dark, but she could hear and feel the forcefulness of her breath. Ever was as nervous as she was. Rose nudged Ever forward. There was no point in stalling on the staircase. Unless they were going to retreat, which Rose knew wasn't going to happen, it would be better if they got to high ground, somewhere they had a better footing. The last thing she wanted was to be pushed down a hard set of steps.

They made the second floor. The light was better, but not by much. At least up there, the bright light from the streetlamp glowed through the window at the end of the hall, illuminating Ever, making her a silhouette in front of Rose. Ever held the knife firmly at her side. Rose did the same. They crept forward. There was a crash from up ahead, which sounded like furniture being knocked over.

Ever rushed forward. In her haste, she ran her hip into a small table. A vase, long empty of the colorful bouquets it used to hold, toppled over. Ever dropped her knife to try and catch the vase, but missed in the dark. There was a sharp, shattering sound as the vase hit the hardwood floor and exploded into a million pieces.

"Wonderful," Rose hissed as she grabbed the back of Ever's T-shirt. Her only thought was to dive into a bedroom and lock themselves inside. There was nowhere else to run unless they went back down the stairs. If they did that, they'd be seen for sure.

Just as Rose was about to turn and bolt, a fistful of Ever's shirt in her hand, a figure emerged from Nathan's old room. Someone squeaked. Rose wasn't sure if the sound came from her or Ever, but everything in Rose froze like she'd been plunged into ice water.

Ever put up her hands, the knife sitting useless on the floor. "Who the hell are you?"

Rose couldn't move, couldn't speak. All she could do was stare. Light spilled in from the window behind the figure, highlighting him in an otherworldly glow. From what Rose could tell, the man, she was sure it was a man, was dressed in black from head to toe, a ski mask covering his face and head.

The figure stood in front of them for a long moment. He looked from side to side, probably gauging the best way to escape.

Ever took a step forward, Rose's arm stretching with her. *Why couldn't she let go of the shirt?* "I said, who the hell are you?" Ever yelled the question this time. She was braver, much braver than she'd been when they were kids.

The man in the mask faced them dead on. Something went to mush in Rose's stomach, her breath coming so fast she thought she might faint.

Then, he rushed forward so fast that Rose didn't know what had happened until it was too late to do anything. The man shoved them to the side with so much force that Rose didn't know what hit her. What had struck her, she'd realized later, was the man's shoulder, pushing into Ever, throwing her sideways into the hallway table, then knocking into Rose, throwing her into the open doorway of a bathroom. She smacked the tile floor hard, driving her head against the toilet's base. The knife she'd been holding skittered across the floor like a rock skipping across a pond.

For a minute, she thought she might black out. Her vision went dark, sharp around the edges. She tasted metal, then realized she'd bitten her tongue when she fell. The cold floor felt good under her head, so she lay there, pain slicing through her brain like a saw slicing through wood.

"Rose." Ever was on top of her in the small bathroom, straddling her stomach, warm hands on her face, her head. "Shit. Are you okay, Rose?" Ever pulled Rose's head toward her.

"I think I'm fine, other than the spinal injury you're trying to give me."

"Oh." Ever moved off her. "Sorry. I panicked for a second."

Light flooded the room as Ever flipped the switch. Fresh pain sliced through Rose's head. She shielded her eyes, holding out her free hand for help. "I assume our friend is gone?"

Ever pulled Rose to her feet. "Yeah, heard the front door open and close."

Rose sat on the toilet, probing the top of her head. There was a bump, sore when she pressed it, but it didn't feel too bad.

"Maybe we should take you to the ER and get that checked out."

Rose shook her head. "I'm okay. I've taken worse knocks than this and survived. Remember when I fell off the jungle gym, headfirst onto the concrete?"

Ever leaned against the door frame. "I'll never forget that. The amount of blood was something out of a slasher film. Ms. Pace fainted when she saw you."

"Right? That was the '80s for you. A jungle gym built over cement." Rose closed her eyes to stand. She knew she'd feel faint if she didn't. She felt dizzy anyway, gripping the edge of the sink as she wobbled.

"Rose." Ever sounded parental.

"I'm fine, Ever." She opened her eyes. "Let's see what the damage is."

"To you?"

"To Nathan's room."

CHAPTER TWENTY

The sight of Rose teetering down the hallway didn't sit well with Everly, but there wasn't anything she could do. Rose was a grown woman. If she didn't want to go to the hospital, Everly couldn't do much.

She walked behind Rose, watching her wobble as she rubbed the top of her head. Everly felt bad about snapping at her in the crow's nest. Her relationship with Rose was such a complicated mess when all she craved was the relative simplicity of their youth.

Entering Nathan's room last, she sucked in a breath. The nicely kept room she'd been in the day before, the one she cleaned up after searching, was now a wreck. Dresser drawers were tumbled into a pile, and the contents spilled all over the floor. The mattress had been pushed from the bed frame, blankets were in disarray.

"Why tear the posters off the wall?" Rose stood in the center, surveying the damage.

"Maybe to see if there was a safe or something behind them." Everly took out her phone. "I'm going to tell Leigh to come over." She sent the text and then joined Rose in putting the room to rights.

"Do you think they were looking for the notebook?"

Rose stuck the drawers back into the dresser.

"I think that's pretty obvious. Either they had already searched his office and came up with nothing, or they hadn't had a chance to search before you and I were there."

Rose shoved clothes back in the dresser. "I can't believe he kept all these old clothes. There's a treasure trove of '90s apparel here." She closed the last drawer, standing to lean back, her arms folded. "They must know we have it, or at least suspect it. I mean, Hart caught us in the office red-handed."

Everly kicked the mattress back onto the bed frame. "Yeah, but all he saw us with was a picture frame and a plant."

"And the copies of Nathan's book."

"Right." Everly picked up the ruined posters, folded them, and laid them on the bed. It made her sick to see the once-prized pictures in tatters. There were John Elway and Dan Marino in their prime, along with two Teen Beat posters. One of Corey Feldman and one of Corey Haim. Another thing she and Nathan had in common was their love of the two Coreys.

Leigh rushed into the room so fast that Everly jumped.

"Sorry," Leigh said, breathless and smelling of the fall night air. She looked around her, eyes wide. "What happened?"

"Someone was here, trashing Nathan's room." Everly pushed the folded, torn posters aside, sinking onto the bed. "He rushed us, knocked me into a table, and Rose into the bathroom. She hit her head."

Leigh's hand went to her mouth. "Rose, are you okay?"

Rose nodded. "Fine."

"Did you two call the police?"

Everly shook her head, then glanced back at Rose. "This doesn't feel like a situation for the police."

"What are you talking about?" Leigh stared at Everly, incredulity in every line of her forehead. She changed tactics, moving her stare to Rose. "What is there to do but call the police? You were both attacked. Nathan's house was broken into and ransacked."

"I know it seems odd, Leigh, but I have to agree with Ever on this one. Whatever is happening, the police can't help us. There's a real possibility they won't help us."

Leigh stared open-mouthed for a minute before snapping her jaws shut and continuing, "What do you mean they won't help us? What do you think the two of you can do then, working independently with no official backing?"

"I don't know," Rose said. "I really don't."

Leigh huffed, throwing up her hands. "Well, I'm out of this. I love you both, I do, but I can't be breaking into private places, sneaking around in the middle of the night, and just generally breaking the law. I'm going home. Please promise me that you will both think seriously about the next steps and that you'll consider going to the police."

"We promise." Everly was getting good at telling lies.

After Leigh left them, still sitting in Nathan's childhood room, Rose suggested they lock up and return to the crow's nest. Everly didn't like being there any more than Rose did. Too many memories.

After leaving Nathan's and trudging back across the connected lawns, eyes and ears open lest they be attacked again, they resettled on the top floor of Everly's house—Rose in the bean bag, Everly on the yellow couch.

"Thoughts on who gave me a concussion?"

Everly laughed as she sipped a glass of water, sputtering as she tried to swallow. "My money is on Mayor Hart."

"Come on," Rose scoffed. "If the mayor is involved in all this, which I concede is likely, he wouldn't be the one to do the dirty work."

"You're right. He'll have a lackey or lackeys."

"Exactly, which is why the who doesn't matter as much as the why."

Everly set her glass on the table. "We know the why. The notebook."

"What's so damning about the notebook, though? The names? The tunnels? The torn-out ritual pages? I still don't see what the big deal is. So, a bunch of old dudes whack off in the basement of Red Manor while trying to summon ghosts? There's nothing earth-shattering about that. In this day and age, the rest of the world won't be shocked either. Nathan's notes were just speculation."

"Then, there's more to this, Rose. Why would these people, this society, go to such lengths for a notebook? Because there's more to it. I think they killed Nathan. We need to wrap our heads around that. Maybe they think there's more in the notebook than there is."

Rose leaned forward in the bean bag, surprise widening the features of her face. "Jonathan."

Everly was so taken aback by Jonathan's sudden appearance in the crow's nest that she almost forgot how to speak. She stared at him for a few seconds as he stood in the middle of the room, hands shoved into the pockets of his jeans as he looked around.

"Wow," he said, turning in a circle, taking it all in. "This place hasn't changed a bit."

"So everyone keeps saying." Everly hadn't meant to sound so derisive, so she followed her comment with a soft laugh.

Rose made to stand, heaving herself forward so she could get up. "I should probably go."

Everly was immediately at war with herself. She thought about the kiss she and Jonathan had shared at the bar, how utterly panty-melting it had been, but Rose leaving was the last thing Everly wanted. They had more to discuss. Her flight out of Splendid left the next day. There was an urgent need inside her to figure out what the hell was going on.

"Oh, Rose." Jonathan held out a hand, passing a glance Everly's way. "Please don't leave on my account. I just came over to hang out."

The war raged on inside Everly's mind. Having sex with Jonathan on the yellow couch, the exact spot where he'd taken her virginity a million years ago, was a thought that made her pulse pound. But the notebook. Nathan. Roots and Wings.

Everly patted the cushion next to her, motioning for Jonathan to sit. "Yeah, Rose, stay. Let's talk old times." Her conscience had won out over her libido. Maybe if they talked long enough, Jonathan would get bored and leave.

Rose sank back into the bean bag, beans snapping as she readjusted, while Jonathan sat next to Everly, closer than necessary, the side of his thigh touching the side of hers. She had to fight the urge to reach over and hold his hand, which rested casually on his leg, fingers tapping, almost as if he were also thinking about what the couch had meant to them.

The three of them sat, talking for almost half an hour. Jonathan had *ooh*ed and *ahh*ed over the old records, digging through the pile to find his favorite: Depeche Mode's Music for the Masses. The record played while they talked and laughed.

Everly hadn't felt this light, this carefree, since landing in Splendid. It was nice to enjoy old friends without feeling self-conscious. Rose avoided the topics that had led them to stop talking—Red Manor, nightmares, Everly's obsessions—instead bringing up old teachers and peripheral friends—those people they'd gone to school with but weren't in their immediate circle.

After talking about Ms. Moore, everyone's favorite teacher at Splendid High, and how she was now a retiree with an award-winning garden, Rose slapped her knees. "Okay, you two. Now, I'm leaving for real. It's almost ten, and I haven't eaten anything since breakfast." She scooted forward to stand. "I think I'm getting too old for the bean bag."

"No chance." Everly stood. "I'll walk you down." She needed the chance to talk more about what had happened, to ask Rose if she should cancel her flight and stay another couple of days to see what more they could uncover.

Before she even made it around the crate, the door flew

open, and Leigh stumbled into the room.

"What the fuck?" Rose was startled, a hand flying to her chest.

Leigh held the side of her neck, a dazed look on her face. "I came back to ..." She trailed off, toppled forward.

Jonathan jumped to his feet, catching her before she fell.

"Leigh!" Rose shouted, rushing over to where Jonathan had her cradled. "Call 911, Ever."

Everly fumbled with her phone.

"I had to tell you ..." Leigh started again. She pulled her hand from her neck. There was blood on the tips of her fingers. Leigh gasped, then sighed, Rose holding her head, Jonathan cradling her body. Leigh shuddered, then was still.

"Leigh! Lay her down, Jonathan."

He did, Rose pushing him out of the way. She crouched over Leigh to begin compressions.

Everly screamed into the phone that they needed an ambulance.

Rose was crying so hard that Everly was sure she would throw up. Rose's cries had become heaves as she sat, crumpled forward on the front porch. Elsie sat in her wheelchair behind Rose, bent at the waist as she leaned forward as far as she could, rubbing Rose's back as she cried.

Everly stood beside Jonathan, his arm around her, so in shock, she didn't feel much of anything. The pain was there, the same pain she'd felt at Nathan's loss, but everything had happened so fast, so blindingly fast, her brain hadn't caught up to her heart.

Blue and red lights flashed over the pavement, over the house, over them, as the paramedics loaded the zipped-up black bag into the back of the ambulance. Leigh was inside that bag. Rose had administered compressions for the four minutes it took them to arrive. Once they took over, they gave her bursts of oxygen, continuing compressions for several more minutes. In the end, they couldn't revive her.

Rose, too distraught to speak coherently, had clung to

Everly's arm as she did her best to explain, first to the paramedics and then to the police, what had happened in the crow's nest. She pointed out the wound in Leigh's neck, a wound that looked like a puncture mark before their friend was zipped into the grim black bag.

For some reason, everyone who'd come to the house looked at Everly like she was a criminal, like the one who'd hurt Leigh.

The ambulance doors slammed shut, and Rose's heaves became wails.

Everly was starting to feel it now, starting to feel her own cries building in her diaphragm, the back of her throat tight and painful. Leigh was gone. First Nathan, now Leigh. Sweet, innocent, soft-spoken Leigh. Leigh had once scooped up a spider in the crow's nest and walked it all the way downstairs to set it on the grass. Leigh had saved that spider from Everly, who'd tried to smash it with her shoe. That was Leigh. The tears spilled out of Everly's eyes as she wrapped both arms around Jonathan's middle. He pulled her in tight.

A car door slammed, and feet ran up the brick walk. "What the hell happened to her?" Fletcher was screaming at no one and everyone.

Then he was screaming at Everly. "What did you do?" He reached out a hand to grab Everly's arm, wrenching it off Jonathan.

"Woah, man." Jonathan pushed Everly behind him, her arm singing with pain as he tore it from Fletcher's grasp. "Everly didn't do anything. Leigh came to see us. We were all up in the crow's nest."

"Fuck the crow's nest and fuck her."

Everly peered around Jonathan, Fletcher pointing at her. "This is her fault, and everyone here knows it." Tears flowed down Fletcher's face—a mask of utter despair, red, puffy, and frightening. Fletcher stooped down and wrenched a brick from the walkway. He stood, throwing the brick with all his might, in a perfect arc, like Nathan would have, toward the house's front window. Glass shattered. Rose jumped to her feet to cover Elsie's body, but there was no need. No one was hurt.

Fletcher's eyes glowed with fire as he glared at them all, the blue and red lights making him look like a demon. "We're through. I'm done with all of you." He spit out the words, spittle dripping down his chin. He opened the back door of the ambulance, ignoring the protests of the paramedics, and disappeared inside.

The scene was cleared as quickly as it materialized, leaving the four of them stunned and silent in the calm night.

PART FOUR
Revelation

CHAPTER TWENTY-ONE

The steam from the shower floated in the air like smoke. Smoke would have been more apropos, as the lives of Everly and her friends went up in flames.

The shower tile pattern, cold and wet under her bare backside, was probably permanently branded into her flesh. She'd been sitting on that shower floor for a good hour, long after the water had gone cold and been shut off. All Everly could do was sit there, shivering—although the room was still warm—naked, and broken.

After the scene with Fletcher, after the ambulance had left with Leigh's dead body inside, Jonathan had wrapped Everly up in his arms, softly murmuring in her ear that he would stay the night and do anything she needed. Part of her wanted him to stay, but that other part, the one that had been alone for so long, craved solitude. Only in solitude could she think, could she plan. Everly had had every intention of packing, of throwing herself into the shitty rental car and driving the long way back to New Orleans. There was no solace to be had in Splendid. She'd known this for longer than anyone, and there was no solace in her. She'd done enough, hadn't she? Maybe Fletcher was right. Maybe this had all been her fault, and if she split town and left them all to their seemingly perfect lives, maybe the cards would stop falling.

But she hadn't left. Either she'd been too tired, or she was too stubborn. Either way, Everly had asked Jonathan to take Rose home, then she'd hugged her mom, climbed the stairs to her old bedroom on the second floor, stripped off her clothes, and taken the world's longest shower. She'd had every intention of washing but slumped onto the floor, crying out every bit of moisture her body contained.

Now, all she could do was stare at the drain, the glass of the shower door, and the blue of the tile.

It must have been close to three in the morning by the time Everly dragged herself out of the bathroom, still naked but long dry, and into the soft bed. Her childhood room was not as unchanged as the crow's nest. The four-poster bed was the same, but the Beetlejuice comforter had been replaced by a maroon duvet. The Teen Beat posters were also gone. Now there were a couple of dull landscapes, most of the white walls bare. A faint scent of Exclamation perfume and Aqua Net still clung to the air. These products, sprayed about a hundred times a day, year after year, had probably been absorbed into the paint.

She covered herself, stared at the ceiling, and tried to form coherent thoughts. What should she do now? Leave today as planned? That seemed the best option. But what about Jonathan? What about Rose? What about her mom? There seemed to be people who needed her now, which felt strange. No one had ever needed her, not once in her life.

She rolled her head to the side. Nathan's notebook sat on the bedside table, right where she'd left it when she'd gone to shower. The last thing her heart wanted was to pick it up and thumb through it. Too bad Everly was ruled more by her head than her heart. She flipped on the lamp, pulled the book toward her, and sat up in bed. The bedside clock, the ancient brick-sized alarm clock she'd had since fifth grade, read 3:13 a.m. She should be sleeping, but how could she when Leigh was in the morgue? Leigh, who, less than five hours ago, had been living and breathing, telling her and Rose to grab kitchen knives for protection.

What had Leigh come back to tell them? Had she thought of something important related to Nathan, or had she forgotten to say goodbye before Everly left again?

Everly swallowed down the hard lump in the back of her throat. Whatever it was, Leigh would never be able to tell them now. Everly was convinced Leigh had been murdered. She'd told the paramedics, the police, her mom, all the same thing. When Leigh stumbled into the crow's nest, she had a puncture wound in her neck. Rose and Jonathan corroborated this, giving the same explanation for what happened as she did.

The paramedics had exchanged a look Everly was familiar with, a look that meant they thought they were dealing with the unhinged, then they explained that the puncture wound had been a bee sting. They even showed her the wound. It was small, the size of a pinprick, red and swollen around the center, just like the bee sting she'd gotten in the third grade. They'd explained that Leigh had been deathly allergic to bee stings, that she carried a card, which they showed her, and an EpiPen in the center console of her car.

Rose asked about the blood on Leigh's fingertips, and they'd even explained that away by saying that sometimes a particularly large hornet's sting could draw blood.

The logic had been hard to argue with, even if Everly didn't remember Leigh being allergic to bee stings when they were kids. There were always bees buzzing around the roses, nestled in the long stems of lavender that grew in abundance in the front yard, so the chances of one getting Leigh on her way up the walk were pretty high. But if she was so deathly allergic, why didn't she carry the EpiPen in her pocket or her purse? How would the lifesaving elixir help her from so far away, were she ever to need it? It hadn't saved her tonight. And why had Rose seemed so bewildered by the explanation? Because she hadn't known. How could

Rose, someone who had been so close to Leigh, not only in childhood but also adulthood, not know about something so important?

To Everly, the answer was simple. Rose didn't know because the excuse was bullshit.

She opened the notebook, picking up where she'd previously left off. There wasn't much else to discover within the pages except for one ambiguous page toward the back, penned in Nathan's handwriting. That page listed four dates. *May 1910, December 1910, April 1911, and September 1911.*

September 1911 was the date of the axe murders on Dale Street. The last known murders to occur in Splendid. What the other dates signified, Everly had no idea.

Curiosity was eating her up inside. Were Leigh's and Nathan's deaths connected to Roots and Wings, or was this another case of her overactive imagination? And if they were connected, then why? The notebook didn't seem that damning, as Rose had already pointed out. Yes, there were some names listed, but so what? There was no way to tie the society to anything that had happened.

Everly ran a finger over the dates. Her flight didn't leave until three p.m. The library opened at seven.

She got up, dressed, and then pulled out her suitcase. As soon as the sun dawned, she'd toss her belongings in the rental car, spend the morning in the stacks at the Splendid Public Library, and swing back by to say goodbye to her mom, who seemed to sleep late these days. Everly had to come to terms with the fact that she may never get the answers she wanted, but she could at least continue to try until the minute she had to be at the airport.

The others, Rose especially, would be furious with her for leaving before Leigh's funeral, but there was no way she could stay in Splendid for one second longer. She had to compartmentalize her pain over Leigh and tuck it away to be dealt with later. If her mom needed care, she'd have to move to New Orleans and live with Everly. Maybe she could get Jonathan to come, too. This town had taken enough from her.

CHAPTER TWENTY-TWO

Splendid's Public Library, built in the same neo-classical style as the museum, the post office, and the original City Hall, sat on a quiet side street off the beaten path of downtown. The Corinthian columns, the soaring ceilings, and the marble flooring made the place feel more like a palace than a library, but the inside was always warm, the sun streaming in from the massive windows, creating sunlit spots where you wanted to curl up and sleep like a cat. Parking was plentiful, both in the mostly empty lot and on the street, the same type of massive, ancient oak trees that lined every other street in Splendid, shading the sprawling grounds dotted with benches and sculptures from local artists, much like the museum.

The library had been one of Everly's favorite places growing up. The reading room with its colorful posters and cushy floor pillows, where her mom took her as a child every Saturday morning for story time, was her favorite. Later, when she was lonely and scared, the quiet stacks were a refuge, a place where she could hunker down in a corner with a sandwich and a book, where no one would bother her.

The second Everly walked through the front doors, the

smell of paper and old bindings washing over her, she was spotted by a librarian, her bun low at the nape of her neck, a few loose tendrils brushing the frames of her glasses. A bit of a stereotype, except that she was young and pretty, her skinny jeans and tank top more fitting for a night at the club than a morning in the stacks. It was possible this girl, like Everly, hadn't been to bed.

"Can I help you?" she asked, her smile as warm as the surroundings.

Drawing attention to herself and what she was looking for was the last thing Everly wanted. Splendid had made her a paranoid person, and she imagined there were enough eyes on her as it was.

"Just looking for a new romance. I know where to go, thank you." Everly walked right past the pretty librarian, heading for the area that used to be the fiction section. She hoped it still was.

The librarian said something about finding her if she needed help, so Everly tossed a quick *thanks* over her shoulder.

Once she was inside the library proper, she dashed between a couple of stacks to get her bearings. The library was largely empty at that time of the morning. There appeared to be no one else except the staff around.

If memory served, the microfiche was in the basement. The area was self-serve once upon a time, but who knew how much things had changed in twenty years? For all Everly knew, microfiche was a thing of the past, and everything was online now.

There was only one way to find out. She made her way toward the staircase by meandering, stack by stack, in a zig-zag fashion, stopping now and then to run a finger along some of the spines and pulling out a random book to peruse. There was no way to know if she was being watched or if there were cameras trained on her.

Halfway to the stairs, she ran into another librarian, this one far older, her sweater unraveling a bit at the sleeves.

"Can I help you find something?" she asked, her watery eyes blinking too many times.

Everly pulled a book from the shelf. "Nope. I'm good, thanks."

The lady with the watery eyes lingered for a moment before moving on. Everly shoved the book back, peering over her shoulder to ensure she wasn't being observed from between the open metal shelving. The lady was nowhere in sight.

The stairs were five feet away. Everly walked as lightly as possible over the marble floor, her eyes shifting from left to right. She tried to keep her head even. The last thing she wanted to do was look like she was trying to sneak around.

It wasn't until she'd gotten halfway down the stairs without incident that she began to feel stupid. She had every right to research whatever she wanted. What she was doing wasn't illegal, even in Splendid. Everly almost chuckled to herself, imagining what Rose would say if she knew Everly was sneaking around the library because she wanted to look at some microfiche. The paranoia was reigning supreme, and Everly knew it.

The lights were on in the basement, and yet still, the room at the back, the room which used to house the microfiche, seemed dark. Dark and cold. All Everly wanted to do was run back upstairs. All she had on, besides her usual jeans, was a short-sleeved concert tee, this one from a Better than Ezra show at the House of Blues in New Orleans. She shivered, goosebumps rising like anthills over her upper body.

She hugged herself, rubbing her hands up and down her arms as she looked around. The room was exactly as she remembered it. The sole fluorescent, at least as old as she was, flickered and zinged overhead. The linoleum floor, grimy and sticky, was the color of puke, and the rows of filing cabinets were gray and dented. There was an unmistakable scent of body odor and stale food, which made sense, as there were no windows or what looked to be any ventilation. This was not an area of the library that was much cared for. That was obvious.

Everly went to work. She was looking for articles from the local paper, *The Splendid Sentinel*. The less time she had to spend down there, the better.

The first filing cabinet was empty. Not helpful. The second was full of articles from the paper, all on microfiche. Eureka. Not only that, but the contents were also ordered by date. Everly thumbed through the '90s, then back to the '40s. She moved on.

The next filing cabinet had microfiche from the '30s back to the 1850s. A moment of giddiness filled her head, dispelling the cold and the foul odors. She pulled articles from May 1910. That was the first date in the notebook, which seemed a great place to start.

The microfiche machine was freezing to the touch. Despite this, Everly popped in the film and moved her face toward the viewer. She squinted through the lenses.

The Splendid Sentinel was a daily paper, so there was a lot to get through. Starting on May first, she turned the knob repeatedly until she reached the final day of the month, May 31st. Everly began to wonder if she'd missed something or if there wasn't anything to find when she found what she'd been looking for on the final turn. The article should have been front-page news, but for some reason, it had been buried on the second-to-last page of the paper.

Local Woman Found with Throat Slashed

Bertha May Ballard, 21, was found yesterday morning, the victim of a possible homicide. Ms. Ballard lived alone in a boarding house on the corner of Platte and Cascade Avenues. Edna Howe, the property's proprietor, discovered her in the early morning hours. Ms. Howe did not see anyone enter or leave Ms. Ballard's room but did find it odd that Ms. Ballard was stretched out on her bed, a single red rose placed over her chest. No suspects have been named at this time. Ms. Ballard will be laid to rest next week at Everwood Cemetery. Details will be forthcoming.

Everly didn't know what to make of this. The date coincided with the date inside Nathan's notebook, but there weren't enough details to draw any conclusions. Unless there was a suspect named in later articles.

Everly slid her phone from her back pocket and snapped a picture of the article before moving on. She returned the microfiche to the filing cabinet, grabbing the file for June 1910. Perhaps she could find a follow-up. Certainly, a young woman found with her throat slashed, and a single red rose placed on her corpse, warranted more information for the public.

There was nothing to be found in the June or July articles. Everly decided to skip to December before she froze to death in the basement. That date was in the notebook, after all.

Again, she flipped through the entire month of December before coming to an article of interest from the 31st, also on the second-to-last page of the newspaper.

Tourist Found Dead on Train Tracks
Anna Kane, 23, was found on the train tracks at the depot yesterday evening. Ms. Kane was in Splendid to attend the wedding of her cousin, Katherine Kane, now Katherine Stratton of N. Tejon Street. Mrs. Stratton had not seen her cousin since the wedding day, assuming that she had traveled back to her home in Kansas after the ceremony. Ms. Kane was found face down on the tracks, dead from a single knife wound to the throat. According to an unnamed source, a single red rose had been placed on her back. No suspects have been named at this time.

As if these deaths weren't chilling enough, the detail about the single-stemmed rose left Everly shaken. The MOs and the rose connected both murders. Not only that, but both women were young and seemingly single. The name Stratton was also intriguing. Katherine Stratton must have been an ancestor of Nathan's. Possibly his grandmother or great-grandmother.

Everly skipped forward to April 1911. If her instincts were correct, a suspect in these crimes was never named.

On the final day of April, April 31, 1911, Everly found what she was looking for.

Woman Found Stabbed to Death with Gardening Shears

Mary Ashburn, 27, was found yesterday morning, stabbed to death in her greenhouse. Ms. Ashburn was killed with her gardening shears and stabbed multiple times in the neck. As at previous crime scenes, a single red rose was found next to the body. Ms. Ashburn was a long-time resident of Splendid and a much-beloved teacher at Splendid Primary School. A memorial will take place at Everwood Cemetery. Details forthcoming. No suspects have been named at this time.

Almost a year after the first Red Rose murder, there still wasn't a suspect.

The notebook, open to the dates, sat by her elbow. She looked down at the creamy white page. The next date was September 1911, the month and year of the infamous axe murders. Was there a connection between the famous, final murders to take place in Splendid and the other unsolved crimes?

With only one way to find out, Everly plugged in the next microfiche. She didn't even bother with much of a look at any of the previous days, rolling right through to the last day of the month, the 31st. It wasn't much of a shock to find the axe murders had taken place on the last day of September, as the other murders had taken place on the final day of their respective months.

Shocking Quadruple Murder in Downtown Splendid

The town of Splendid was rocked last night after the discovery of four grisly murders at the residence of Thomas and Sadie Matthews. A neighbor discovered the Matthews after the family failed to attend a planned neighborhood party. The bodies of Mr. and Mrs. Matthews were found in their living room, while the two young Matthews children, 8 and 11, were discovered in a bedroom. All of the victims had been killed with the same axe, an axe that belonged to Mr. Matthews and was found lying in the yard. As with previous disturbing murders that have taken place in Splendid within the last year and a half, a single red rose was left on Mrs. Matthews's lap. Authorities believe these killings, as well as the killings of Bertha May Ballard, Anna Kane, and Mary Ashburn, were all the work of the same killer. According to Splendid Police, a man whose name has not been released has been taken into custody in Sacramento, California. This man has confessed to several similar murders throughout the country. The police have assured us there is no further threat to the community. The Matthews were well known in the community of Splendid. Mr. Matthews worked as a chauffeur for Edward Palmer, grandson of our founder, Eli Palmer, and Mrs. Matthews worked as the personal secretary of Mrs. Rachel Palmer. The couple and their children will be interred at Everwood Cemetery. Details will be forthcoming. The Palmers ask that in place of flowers, those who wish may donate to the Children's Charity League in the Matthews's name.

Everly leaned back in the hard plastic chair, staring at the screen. Her stomach had dropped somewhere in the region of her feet when she'd seen the Palmer name. Her family was associated with the victims of the axe murders. How was this not common knowledge? How had her mother never shared this information? Way back during senior year, Mom knew that Everly was working on an article about the axe murders for the paper. But that article, the article Everly ended up writing between class periods because she'd run out of time, had been copied down from memory, from bits and pieces she'd heard here and there. She'd written about the Matthews, about how they were killed, how they were found, how a suspect was arrested in California, how they'd been killed with their axe. She'd even written about the empty lot where their house used to be. The murders had been so heinous that the city had torn down the little Victorian cottage, and no one had built on the property since. But at the time, because she'd been up against a deadline and her friends were being less than helpful, seventeen-year-old her hadn't thought to come to the library and do actual, honest to god research. Everly wanted nothing more than the ability to reach back in time and slap herself.

As she sat there in the frigid cold, her fingers almost numb, she thought about that corner lot, that bit of land that was empty for so long. Someone had to own it, but who? If the city owned the property, it would have no doubt built on it long ago. The lot wasn't massive, but there was enough space for an office building or a small apartment complex.

She leaned forward, rereading the article. The name of Palmer was mentioned a lot, a lot more than was comfortable.

A thought jolted through Everly's mind. The Matthews worked for her great-grandparents. In her mind, she saw the portrait by the back door of her house. In the picture, Edward Palmer stood looking somber, a single rose on his lapel. The picture was in black and white, so discerning the color hadn't been entirely possible, but what if the rose was red? Did that mean anything? It also stood to reason that if the Matthews worked for her family, then perhaps the house and the lot were a Palmer property. The Palmers owned several properties around town. Not only did her mother own the house they lived in, a home built by Eli Palmer for his daughter, but they also owned Eli Palmer's original property, the stone castle he'd built for himself closer to the mountains. The castle was a museum now, dedicated almost entirely to Eli, run by volunteers. There was also the Long Building and the Paget Building, both downtown. So, it wasn't out of the question to think her mom held the deed on that little corner lot.

Her phone pinged on the table. Before reading the text, Everly snapped a picture of the article. Where did she even begin with all of this? Time was running out on her trip to

Splendid. It wasn't even eight a.m., but her flight would leave at three that afternoon, and she wanted to be on it.

She looked at her phone. The text was from Jonathan. Guilt pinched in her gut. She should be with him or with Rose, sharing in their grief, not stuck in that ice locker of a basement, flipping through old microfiche, researching murders that occurred over a hundred years ago.

Jonathan: *How are you holding up? I didn't text you sooner because I had hoped you were getting some sleep. Rose was a wreck when I dropped her off. I offered to stay with her, but she said she would take an Ambien and go to bed. Please call me when you get a chance. I'd love to hear your voice.*

Everly stared at the screen for two whole minutes, thinking of what to say. Dragging a response from her vacant insides seemed nearly impossible. She wanted to hear his voice, too, but what good would that do? She could not stay in Splendid one second longer than necessary.

Everly: *I'm okay. Didn't sleep a wink, but I imagine none of us did, even Rose with her Ambien. I'm heading over to her place now to check on her. I'll call in a bit. I'd love to see you one more time before my flight.*

Her finger hovered above the blue-and-white arrow. Jonathan wasn't aware she was leaving today. It occurred to her that she'd never told him. But when would she have had the time? The minutes and hours she'd spent in Splendid were like a whirlwind. It felt like she'd been there for hours rather than days.

A hand, icy as death, touched her already cold bare arm. Everly jumped so far out of the cracked, plastic seat that she fumbled with her phone before dropping it on the cement floor. "Shit," she said.

"Oh, dear. I'm so sorry." The pretty, young librarian stood in front of her. "I didn't mean to startle you. I cleared my throat when I entered the room, but you must not have heard me."

Everly channeled Rose's stare of death. She'd never wanted laser beam eyes more than at that moment. There was no way the librarian had cleared her throat. Everly may have been older, but she wasn't *that* old. She would have heard someone clear their throat in the empty room, as the sound would have echoed all over the place.

"Right," Everly said as she crouched for her phone. The phone had fallen face down, and the screen had shattered. "Damn it."

"Yikes. You'd better take that to the We Fix It shop. They'll pop a new screen on there, lickety-split."

Everly slid a gaze toward the librarian. Who, under the age of seventy, still said things like lickety-split?

"Did you need some help finding something down here? Or did you already find what you were looking for?"

Everly held her phone gingerly in one hand. "I found what I needed. Thanks."

She'd found more than she'd needed to prove that Nathan was investigating some seriously weird shit. The problem was that the pictures of the articles were on her now-shattered phone, which did her zero good. She huffed an annoyed sigh, closing the notebook and slipping it into her back pocket. She then moved past the librarian, who hadn't budged.

"Did you need help putting this microfiche away?" the librarian asked behind Everly in a voice her mom used often when she was young. Her voice said *I think you left your mess behind.*

Since Everly was annoyed over her phone and wanted to go check on Rose, she shot a look over her shoulder. "Nope. Have a great day." Leaving her mess behind was petty, but something about it felt good. Everly was tired of walking on eggshells in that town.

The day had warmed up even more than usual when she slipped inside the rental car. The windshield had been pointing east, soaking up all the rays as the sun shone, so when Everly shut herself inside, the heat surrounded her like a warm blanket. After how cold the library basement had been, she wondered if she'd ever feel warm again.

She scowled down at her broken phone before setting it on the passenger seat. There was no way to know whether Jonathan had received her text. She didn't think she'd hit *Send*, but maybe the impact with the floor sent the text flying through the ether. She hoped not. He deserved to see her face to face, to get a verbal explanation for why she had to leave and get out of Splendid once again.

As she sat in the warm car, soaking the heat into her bones, her heart felt heavy. Why couldn't they go with her? Rose and Jonathan? They could all start over together somewhere new. It didn't have to be New Orleans, as long as it wasn't Splendid. Rose could write from anywhere, and bars were a staple from east to west, north to south. If only she could convince them that Splendid was rotten to its core, that bad things happened there. But how? She didn't have much more than Nathan had had.

Before the information she'd learned could leave her brain, Everly pulled a pen marked *Holiday Inn Denver* from the center console and took the notebook from her pocket. She opened the page with the no longer mysterious dates, writing down as much as she could remember about each murder underneath each date. She may not have pictures of the actual articles, but maybe if she showed this new information to Rose, it would turn the tide in her favor. Rose could continue down the rabbit hole with her, or Everly could go alone. It wouldn't be the first time.

CHAPTER TWENTY-THREE

The Ambien haze would not wear off, no matter what she did. The cold shower hadn't helped clear the fog from her mind—the only thing the icy water had done was probably give her pneumonia. The first cup of coffee had helped, but not enough, so it was on to a second cup of steaming dark Colombian roast.

Rose sat in her nook, a usually safe space, Pancake sunning herself in a warm spot on the seat next to her. There was no trying to make sense of what had happened. Rose had tried the previous night. Once Jonathan had dropped her at her door, offering to come in and sit with her, her face sore and wet from the heavy sobbing, all she could do was shake her head no and mumble about taking a pill. She couldn't fully speak, her throat painfully sore and tight.

She'd dragged her weary, heartsick self inside the front door, then up every single stair until she reached the second floor, her legs as heavy as her heart.

The whole thing was so unbelievable. How could Leigh be gone? The odd surrealness of it all hit her in the same way Nathan's death had. How could someone be so vibrant and alive one second and then dead and gone the next? Was life really so fragile? Leigh had been frail in the last six months, but her cancer was gone, her treatments were over, and she was getting strong again. She'd been given a second chance at life, just to what? Have it all taken away by the sting of a single bee? Nothing made sense.

If Leigh had had a life-threatening allergy, Rose would have known about it. Hell, Rose probably would have been trained on how to use the EpiPen to save her life. The excuse seemed like exactly what it was, an excuse.

Rose wasn't stupid. She knew that a lot wasn't adding up, beginning with her encounter with old Mayor Hart all those years ago. But in that moment of sheer grief, all she'd wanted to do was pop a pill and fall into oblivion. What did any of it matter if Leigh was dead?

Now, as Rose sat guzzling her third mug of strong coffee, she didn't want to think about the previous night. She didn't want to think about anything as she contemplated taking another pill and returning to bed.

She groaned when the doorbell rang. The last thing she wanted to do was deal with an actual human person, whether a Girl Scout selling cookies or Fletcher coming to scream again.

Her stomach lurched as she got up from the table. Too much coffee on a queasy and empty stomach was not a good combination. The thought of Fletcher and his intense pain made the back of her throat swell and her eyes swim. He may have been a dick sometimes, but he and Leigh hadn't spent a single night apart since their wedding twenty-two years ago. His was another death on the horizon; there was no way he'd survive this.

The face framed in the glazing of the door, watery and distorted though it was, did not belong to Fletcher.

Rose opened the door to Ever, tears running down her cheeks. Rose stepped aside, holding the door wide so Ever could step inside.

Ever took the door handle, pulling it out of Rose's hand to close it. Ever's face screwed up, like she was in physical pain, her bottom lip sucked inside her mouth. "Rose," she said, then her voice cracked. Instead of continuing, she sucked her lip back into her mouth, tugging Rose toward her.

Rose opened her arms. She couldn't remember the last time she'd hugged Ever, the last time she'd hugged anyone. The closeness felt so good that Rose allowed herself to melt into Ever's arms, their chests pressed tight against each other. They cried, both of them, Ever softly, Rose violently. There was a lot of pent-up pain there—forty-six years' worth.

"Why is this happening?" Rose asked, her voice so hoarse she didn't recognize herself.

Ever's head shook against her shoulder. "I'm not sure, but we need to talk." Ever released her. "Is that coffee I smell?"

Rose wiped her nose on the back of her hand as she nodded toward the kitchen. "Help yourself. Mugs are in the middle cabinet." Rose was too tired, too hazy, still, from the Ambien to help. She crossed in front of Ever, leading the way through the living room with its greige paint color, neutral furnishings, and gold accents, past the dining room with the giant antique table and chairs, into the kitchen, her favorite room in the house.

"Everything is so beautiful, Rose." Ever opened the middle cabinet. "Not surprising. You've done very well for yourself."

"Thanks," Rose said as she resettled alongside Pancake. At that moment, she felt like the least successful person in town. Wasn't happiness supposed to come with success? With Nathan and now Leigh gone, she wasn't sure she'd ever feel that emotion again. "What do you want to talk about, Ever? I don't know how much bandwidth I have. Someone has to check on Fletcher at some point today, and that's either going to have to be me or Jonathan."

Ever glanced at Rose while she poured herself a cup of coffee. There was a look in Ever's eye that told Rose she was there to talk about her least favorite subject.

Before Ever could begin, Rose held up a hand. "Let me stop you before you even get going, Ever. I can't keep going down this road with you. Secrets, societies, and, according to you, the murders of our friends. I just can't right now. All I can do is sit with this grief."

"I feel the pain of losing Leigh, too, Rose. But I found something out today, something I need to explore further."

"You always have something to explore further, Ever, and nothing ever comes of it." Rose rubbed her eyes. "Why does nothing ever come of your explorations? Let me tell you, because there is nothing to discover. There is no grand conspiracy. What we have here is a bunch of weird coincidences. Tragic coincidences. And not only that," Rose braced her hands on the edges of the breakfast table. "How the hell can you stand there, pouring coffee, talking more of your bullshit, while Leigh is in the morgue? Ever, read the fucking room."

"I'm as upset about Leigh as you are, Rose." Ever stood behind the kitchen island, her shoulders relaxed, her hands cupping the mug.

Rose scoffed, which sounded more like a laugh. "You're as cold as ever. Look at you." Rose waved her hands. "Ready to go off on another fact-finding mission. Only there aren't any facts to find. And even if there were, what good would it do?" Rose's voice was rising now, her throat still raw, but she didn't care.

Everly turned the mug on the marble countertop, her gaze downward. "I'm only trying to get at the truth, to find out what happened to me, what's happening now."

"And that right there was always your problem, Ever. You always thought you were the only one with issues. You still think your messes are special. Newsflash, Ever, we're all damaged goods, every one of us. All our lives have been shitty. You know about mine, about how I grew up, you know Leigh was sick, deathly sick, but you don't know about Nathan, about how he struggled with depression, with anxiety. Part of me believes the heart attack scenario just because of that."

Ever's eyes snapped fire as she stared at Rose. "Don't do that."

"What?"

"Rationalize. That's what led to our downfall before. You kept things from me and just rationalized everything away." Ever's face was hard, her jaw popping as she clenched. "You're doing it again. You're a smart woman, Rose, you know this place is wrong."

Rose slammed a hand down on the table, startling Pancake into moving farther away. "I like Splendid, Ever. We all do. There's nowhere else I'd rather live, and my rationality didn't lead to our downfall. But you wouldn't know that because you wouldn't talk to me. You just shut down."

"Shut down," Ever practically yelled. "You stopped talking to me, Rose. If it wasn't all this." Ever waved her hand around. "What was it? The time I fooled around with Fletcher? Did you and Leigh hate me for that? There was a time I thought you did."

Rose scoffed so sharply that the cat jumped off the bench. "Get over yourself, girl. No one cares that you made out with Fletcher once. He thought of you as a sister. Don't be such an idiot. He was never in love or lust with you. That night was a stupid, Boone's Farm-fueled mistake, one he always said he regretted because that wasn't you. We were more than that, all of us. You did shut down, Ever. Maybe you remember a slightly different version of events than I do, but I remember trying to talk to you at prom, and you ignored me. And something else you probably don't know. I went to your house the morning after graduation. I missed you so damn much, and we'd wasted the last four months of school not talking. Leigh encouraged me to go see you, so I did, and what did I find? Not you. You were gone, Ever, just like that." Rose's throat burned like she'd taken four too many shots of Fireball, but she didn't stop. She couldn't stop now. "That was when I wrote you off, Ever. All through those long four months, I held out hope we'd talk again, that the specter of this town would fade away and we could return to being us."

Ever pushed the coffee cup away, a scowl marring her brow. "The specter of this town. You believe all this shit as much as I do."

"Of course, I do, Ever, and I'm sure we're not the only ones. I knew something was wrong back then, and I was scared for us both. Now I'm terrified." Rose leaned back, her hand reaching out to coax Pancake back.

"And all you want to do is go back to your comfortable life, the comfortable life Splendid has afforded you."

Rose crossed her legs, dizzy fury buzzing in her ears. "My life has never been comfortable, Ever, make no mistake. All I want to do right now is mourn another friend, a friend who never so much as swatted at a fly. I have things to do because people rely on me and need me to be strong. I was strong for Lily even though she was the big sister. I was strong for Charlie and Nathan's family, and now I have to be strong for Fletcher. I don't have time for anything else, and you're leaving anyway, aren't you?"

"I'm leaving anyway."

Rose wanted to stop Ever from going, she did, but she was too exhausted, body and soul. She watched Ever storm out of the kitchen, her Converse thudding over the floorboards, the sound getting softer and softer until Rose heard the front door open and close. As swiftly as she'd re-entered her life, Everly Palmer was making her exit.

CHAPTER TWENTY-FOUR

1994

The meetings were not giving her what she needed. *Haunted Happenings,* the informal club, and the newspaper column were not yielding the results she'd hoped for. When Everly had formed this nugget of an idea, the goal had been to investigate more about Red Manor, about why she felt so tied to the place. But Rose seemed to thwart her at every turn regarding that topic. She wanted to explore other stories from the area that were little known.

Today, Everly had had it. After yet another argument with Rose, who seemed to be ignoring her more and more, Everly had decided to take matters into her own hands. She didn't need anyone else to help her. So, on a sunny Saturday morning, before the clock struck six a.m., she was dressed and slipping out the front door.

Everly had gotten her driver's license six months earlier, but there was no need to make all the noise required to bring the car out of the garage. She could walk the six blocks, and why wouldn't she want to? The day, early though it was, was already starting to warm up, even though they were now at the beginning of December. Everly knew this kind of weather was not normal. All she needed was a light jacket over her sweater, and she was perfectly snug.

There wasn't a plan, not really. The idea was to knock on the front door of Red Manor. No one but the staff would be there this early. She'd say her dad had left his wallet in one of the rooms, and he'd sent her to fetch it. Would they go for it and let her in? Absolutely not, and Everly knew it. But she was counting on the fact that if she said her dad was Mr. Edward Stratton, Nathan's dad, they'd ask her to wait at the door while they went to look about. She would stand dutifully on the threshold, then slip inside once the staff member bustled off.

From there, she planned on going right up the stairs where she'd seen the phantom dog standing on the staircase. Something was up there, there had to be. Why else would the dog have been standing there, staring at her with such intensity?

The thought of walking into Red Manor, the place where she'd experienced such terror, where she'd been so afraid she'd knocked herself unconscious, filled her with an unwieldy amount of dread. But she refused to let this deter her—there were answers to be found inside Red Manor, and she knew it. She wouldn't have been able to say why she felt so sure of this fact, but sure she was and had been since the day after that terrible night.

Her hands shook as she walked, so she shoved them into her jacket pockets. A chill ran up and down her spine despite the sun's warmth as it rose to her left. Feeling the fear was fine, she could be afraid. As long as she saw this through to the end, that was all that mattered.

Everly walked five blocks, her hands still shaking. She slowed when she rounded the last corner, the somber façade of Red Manor looming in front of her. The building had an unmistakable air of exclusivity. The windows had a refractive film over them, impossible to see through. The walk up to the front door was covered with a green awning, the kind Everly had seen in movies set in New York City.

The landscaping was almost as beautiful as the grounds surrounding the Museum of the Founders. Roses seemed to be in bloom year-round, the grass a neatly trimmed emerald green.

She pulled her hands from her pockets, wiping the sweat off on the back of her jeans. This was the moment. She'd already have to answer to her mom about what she was doing so early, so she might as well make it count.

Her pulse raced in her ears all the way to the front door. She swallowed down as much terror as she could and rang the bell.

The giant, solid oak door opened so fast she barely had time to breathe. She concentrated on the man in front of her, doing everything in her power not to look down at the foyer floor she'd once lain on after knocking herself out.

The man, dressed in a tuxedo that looked ridiculous in the early morning, held the door with one hand as he blocked the entrance with his hulking body. "Can I help you?" If he had looked down his nose at her any more, he would have been cross-eyed.

Everly held up her chin like she'd seen her mom do a hundred times.

"Yes." *Maintain eye contact.* "My dad, Mr. Stratton, left his wallet here in one of the rooms. He couldn't remember which, but he asked me to get it for him on my way to school."

"Mr. Stratton?"

Everly felt like she'd been doused in ice water. Most kids weren't so formal with their dads.

She laughed, trying to sound like she was in on the joke. "I mean, Edward Stratton. Do you know him?" She was spiraling, and she knew it.

"I know him." The man in the tuxedo stared her down for another couple of seconds. Everly did everything she could to keep the smile plastered on her face.

"Wait here, please."

Finally, a moment to breathe. The man had left the door

ajar, just as Everly had imagined he would. Maybe this would go her way after all. She nudged the door open with the tip of a finger, peering inside without stepping over the threshold. Before she could get both feet inside, a hand wrapped around her bicep.

Everly's breath caught in her throat. She was already walking and was so startled by the cold touch of whoever was behind her that she faltered, her brain unsure if she was moving forward or stepping back. She almost tripped, but the hand closed tighter on her arm, pulling her back onto the porch. She'd been near her goal. The staircase she'd intended to ascend was so close that had she had another five seconds, she would have been upstairs.

She found her footing and, heaving an exasperated sigh, turned to face her new roadblock. Everly had half expected to see Rose hovering over her, that mixed-up look of worry and annoyance that had become Rose's dominant expression as of late.

Only it wasn't Rose. If Everly had felt doused in cold water after her slip-up with the staff member, now she felt as if she were trapped under a sheet of ice, desperately looking for a way to escape drowning.

Mayor Hart still had hold of her arm. Something in his eyes told Everly he wouldn't be letting go anytime soon. She shrank away from him, but there was nowhere to go. Her back up against the porch railing, all she could do was shrink away, make herself as small as possible.

"What are you doing here, Miss. Palmer?" His voice was cold with an edge of irritation she'd grown used to hearing in the voices of her friends.

Everly shook her head. She didn't have a single plausible excuse for her presence at Red Manor. Instead of grasping for a lie that sounded like what it was, she decided to say something so ridiculous it just might be true. "I'm not sure. I thought I would come by to apologize for that night, when Rose and I broke in. I feel awful about it." Everly tried to make her face do what Leigh's did when she tried to sweet-talk Fletcher. Leigh's version of a puppy dog face, only cuter with a pouty lip.

Mayor Hart didn't look like he was buying her subterfuge. His grip tightened on her arm, causing Everly to squirm. She tried to pull away, but his hand was like a vise.

"You're hurting me, sir," she said, her heart racing, her stomach feeling sick. There was something about the utterly calm and almost psychotic look in his eye that brought her to the edge of panic. This was how she imagined someone like Ted Bundy looking at you before they plunged the knife. His eyes were glazed over, his face blank, like he wasn't inside himself at the moment.

The cold clamminess of his hand and the way he held her, combined with this sociopathic gleam, sent her into the dream world of her nightmares. The nightmares were always the same, a man holding her bicep in a tight grasp, the touch frigid and wet as if the person were perspiring slightly, then a pain in the soft part of her arm, inside the elbow, a searing agony that made her scream.

Everly thought her heart would beat out of her chest. She felt the panic rise within her, cold sweat under her arms, and dripping down her back. She yelled, "Let go of me!"

"Everly, calm down."

Everly, calm down.

She'd heard those words before, those exact words in Mayor Hart's exact voice. She began to hyperventilate, her breath coming fast and shallow.

She opened her mouth to scream, but right before she could, the mayor let her go. He dropped her arm, stepping back to allow her to pass, and pass she did. Everly ran down the walk, under the fancy green awning, and didn't stop until she tripped up the steps to her house.

Everly pushed open the door, stumbling over the threshold. Her mom, on the phone in the hallway, one hand on the long, brown cord, spun toward her.

"Everly, what on earth?" she sputtered, setting the

phone on the receiver without caring who was on the other end.

Tears streamed down Everly's face, as they had been since the second her feet began pounding the pavement. She heaved deep breaths, winded from her five-block sprint. The wood paneling of the foyer felt good against her back—hard and steadying—as she collapsed against it. She needed to feel steady. She pressed a hand to her chest, breathing until she felt calm enough to speak.

"Tell me what happened to me at Red Manor, Mother."

Her mom folded her arms across her chest, a hip leaning against the hall table. "When you and Rose broke in and you knocked yourself out? Don't you already know what happened that night?"

Everly shook her head, still a bit out of breath. "Before that. Stop lying to me, Mom. I know something happened to me there. I can feel it."

Mom laughed one quick, fast chuckle, then covered her mouth, wiping away her amusement. "You can feel it? Good grief, Everly. Maybe it is time you see a therapist; your dramatics are getting out of hand. The nightmares, the obsession with Red Manor, and now your friends."

"What about my friends?"

"I believe they, too, are getting rather tired of all the theatrics. I'm telling you this as your mother because I love you. You're going to lose them if you don't stop."

Everly felt like the mayor's vise grip on her arm had moved to her heart. "They would never abandon me." Even as Everly said the words, she knew they were a lie. The group had already begun to fall away, everyone but Jonathan. Even Rose, her soul friend, and Nathan, her best friend, hadn't wanted to hang out much.

Mom didn't say anything. She stared at Everly as if challenging her to prove her wrong. Everly couldn't.

The blue edges of her sadness caught fire the longer her mom stared her down. Anger took over. "I know you're hiding something from me, Mom. One day, I'm going to find out what."

Everly turned on her heel, slamming the front door closed behind her in much the same manner as she'd slammed it open. She should have been on her way to school. She was going to be late as it was, but she couldn't bear the thought of facing anyone else, so she turned toward the park instead.

AD BRAZEAU

CHAPTER TWENTY-FIVE

Everly sat inside the horrible rental car—the smell, stale and rank—outside of Rose's house. She wasn't sad, not about Rose, but she was angry. How could everyone in Splendid turn a blind eye when there was so much that seemed so obvious? Had they all been so brainwashed that even after two mysterious deaths, they were content to continue as if nothing had happened?

Rose could order her life in any way she saw fit, but Everly had to know the truth once and for all. She had to know if her family owned the plot of land where the axe murders had occurred. She had to know more about this connection. The final article mentioned a serial killer in Sacramento who'd been blamed for the Splendid killings, but something about that didn't sit well with Everly. Why wasn't the man named? Everly smelled a cover-up.

Sitting and mourning wouldn't serve Leigh or Nathan. If their deaths had been foul play, then Everly owed it to them to find out the truth. She had to say goodbye to her mom anyway, so the next logical stop was home, and while she was there, she could ask her mom about the ownership of the property.

The front porch of their historic home was Elsie's favorite place to sit. This had been a fact throughout Everly's childhood and seemed just as true now.

The day already felt like a long one, even though it wasn't past nine o'clock in the morning. Warm rays of the morning sun warmed Everly's back as she walked through the wrought iron gates of her mother's home, the brick pathway rough underneath the worn soles of her favorite sneakers.

The sun touched everything before her, casting a golden glow over the house from the copper roof, glinting in the light, to the Doric columns that held up the white eaves of the porch. The home, the home that had been built by her ancestor, Eli Palmer, although he had never lived in it, could have been featured in *Architectural Digest* any day of the week. She was proud of the home when she was younger, proud to have lived in such a magnificent place, but now, as she stalked over the brick emblazoned with the symbol of Roots and Wings, she felt nothing but dread, a deep, sickening sense of wrongness.

Elsie sat in her chair on the north side of the porch, facing the sun, dressed in a chic pair of matching beige-colored sweats. Behind her, the broken window looked like a gaping wound. She held her book in her hands, her gaze trained on the pages, but Everly knew she wasn't reading. She was staring, no doubt still in shock from Leigh's sudden and horrific death. That death had happened inside Elsie's home, and Everly had no idea how this would affect her mother going forward.

When Elsie saw Everly approaching, she dropped her book in her lap, folding her hands over the cover. She tried to smile, but the effort seemed too much, so she dropped the pretense and stared at Everly with sad eyes.

Everly pulled over the rocking chair, the black paint weathered and cracking.

"I was afraid you weren't coming back," Elsie said, gazing forward toward the gate that was as old as the house.

"I wouldn't have left without saying goodbye, Mom."

Everly wanted to say more, like, D*o you think I'm such a horrible daughter that I wouldn't say goodbye to my mother?* Or *Do you think I'm so devoid of feeling that I wouldn't check on you before I left?* But she didn't say any of those things, she just dropped her head back against the chair's hardwood. "Are you okay, Mom?"

Elsie looked down at her lap, readjusting the book, plucking a fuzz off her pant leg. "Not really, no. Leigh was a good girl. I always liked her. She died in my house, Everly."

"I know, Mom. I'm so sorry that happened. I'm sorry for Leigh. I'm sorry that you have to live with that memory. I'm even sorry for Fletch. I don't think he's been separated from Leigh for a single day since high school." Everly would forever, for the rest of her life, see Fletcher's face, twisted with pain, red and blue lights washing over him, coloring his tears as they streamed down his cheeks. No matter how she felt about Fletcher, he didn't deserve that.

"Don't speak ill of Fletcher. He's done a lot of good for this town in recent years."

"I didn't speak ill of him, Mom." Everly rolled her head toward her mother, who was still staring down at her lap, fidgeting with her clothes. "What do you mean Fletcher's done a lot for this town? How?"

The fidgeting stopped, her mom clasping her hands together. A slight tremor in her hands tugged on Everly's heartstrings.

"Well, he joined the club last year. The club needed some new blood, as you can imagine. The younger generation, your generation, what do you call yourselves, Generation X? They don't seem as interested in keeping to old traditions, but Fletcher gets it."

Everly tried to make sense of what her mom was saying, but came up short. Gets what? "What does he get, Mom?"

Elsie shrugged. Everly noticed for the first time that Elsie's hands had gone white from the tightness of her clasp. "He's made a lot of money, you know, from his video games. I don't like to talk about money, but he has made many donations to the town in recent years. Donations to the schools, to the hospital. He even funded new plumbing and wiring for Red Manor."

Something inside Everly went cold. A chill swept her arms despite sitting in the full sun. Mom said that Fletcher was a member of the club. That in itself didn't mean much. Her mom was also a member, but Roots and Wings, the secret society within the mainstream society of Red Manor, would have had seven members. Was it possible that Fletcher was a member of Roots and Wings? Was it possible that was why he'd been so adamant about her leaving town, leaving the others alone?

Everly rubbed a hand over her throat.

Don't jump to conclusions. That always gets you into trouble.

Her mother wouldn't know about Roots and Wings. Everly was sure that membership was based on gender, as regular membership to the club at Red Manor was back in the day. There were other questions she had for her mom. "Mom, do you know that empty lot over on the corner of Dale Street?"

Everly studied her mother for any tell. Elsie looked at her, her brows pinched together, her eyes blinking more than what should have been normal. "Do you mean the location where those horrible murders took place?"

Everly nodded. "Yeah. I was wondering if that lot is part of the Palmer portfolio. The family who lived there worked for your grandparents."

The look on Elsie's brow went from one of bewilderment to one of surprise. "What?"

"Mom, do we own that lot?" Everly's time in Splendid was running short, and she was running out of patience.

Her mom blinked a few more times. She shifted in her chair, putting herself closer to Everly. "I'm not sure. It's possible, I suppose. We hold the deeds on more than twenty properties around town."

They owned more Splendid property than Everly

realized. "How can I find out? Is there a stack of deeds somewhere in the house?"

"Yes." Elsie seemed to briefly chew on the inside of her lip. "They're in the safe, in the office. But why is this important? There's nothing on that lot now but dirt and dead grass."

Everly shook her head. "I'm not sure why it's important. Maybe it isn't, but I'd like to check."

Elsie waved a hand. "Go ahead. The code for the safe is your birthday, 090676."

"Thanks, Mom." Everly pushed out of the rocking chair, then did something she hadn't done in a very long time. She bent down to kiss her mom on the cheek.

Mom grinned up at her. Everly had another thought, a question that always sat unasked between them. She sat back down. "Mom, who's my dad?"

Elsie went still, her stare suddenly hard. "You know your father was nothing more than a sperm donor, Everly."

Everly licked her bottom lip, studying her mom's face. "Was Mr. Stratton my dad?"

"What?" Elsie jerked in her chair. "Don't be ridiculous, Everly. Edward Stratton was a kind gentleman. Mary Stratton was a good friend. Shame on you for asking such a thing."

"Okay, but he was someone else, someone you knew." Everly's gaze raked her mother's face. "Your eye twitched when you said *your father*." Everly was bluffing. Elsie hadn't twitched; even if she had, the involuntary spasm would have meant nothing. Everly was working on a hunch she'd had as a kid. There was no sperm bank in Splendid, a fact Nathan had shared with her during their freshman year of high school. After that revelation, they'd taken turns imagining who her dad could be, each suggestion more outlandish than the last, with famous actors and hall-of-fame football players making the list. The time for the truth had come. "Who was he, Mom? Is he still alive? I have a right to know. DNA tests are easy to come by these days."

They were easy to come by, but the extra one hundred dollars had never been in Everly's budget.

Elsie looked down at her hands, massaging the palm of her left hand with her right thumb. "No, he isn't alive. I'm afraid he died in a horrific accident with his horrible wife, a wife he was finally ready to divorce because their children were grown."

Shock bloomed in Everly's chest. Her neck flushed with heat, the inside of her mouth going dry. "Are you telling me that Rose is my half-sister?"

Elsie continued massaging her hands, her gaze on the lawn, the book in her lap, anywhere but on Everly. "I am."

Sharp pains stabbed her stomach, her chest, thoughts tumbling through her mind as astronauts tumbled through space. Everly swallowed, a lump in the back of her throat large enough to choke her. She took a breath.

"Does Rose know?"

Her mom looked at her, the hardness behind her eyes. "Of course not. Paul was a good man, Everly, trapped in a loveless marriage with a woman he claimed had the devil in her. He always planned to leave, but not until the girls were out of the house."

"He was a good man who stood aside while his wife abused their daughters, you mean."

"Everly." Elsie's eyes snapped fire. "The conversation is closed. Don't you have something else to do?"

Everly stared at her mom for another half a second, then shot up from the rocking chair.

The office was another time capsule in a house and a town full of them. The deep green wallpaper, embossed and masculine, looked a little dusty but hadn't yet begun to peel. The room was furnished in heavy oak with a large desk and bookcases that lined every wall.

Everly shut the door behind her in a state of shock.

Rose is my sister.

The whole artificial insemination story had always

seemed exactly what it was, a story. Over the years, Everly had begun to suspect that Edward Stratton was her dad. The two families had always been so close, so finding out Paul Hibbard was her father wasn't much more of a stretch.

How could their parents keep such a secret from them? This information was so vital that Everly felt a shift inside her. Of course Rose was her literal sister. Their bond had been intense from the jump, like something in their DNA had called out to the other. Everly wasn't sure if she wanted to go back over there, not after their latest fight, but she would make sure Rose knew before she got on that plane.

Everly pulled a painting of a hunting scene off the wall. This was where the safe was. She'd never been given the code before and was almost a little amazed that her mother had given it to her now. But Everly suspected, given her mother's condition, that her mom was beginning to think toward a future when Everly would be the last Palmer. Everly would inherit it all.

The last thing Everly wanted was to be responsible for the upkeep of the Palmer legacy. She wondered what the town would think if she put it all up for sale, every last stick of furniture, every last one of the properties. Like Rose, who didn't want to live in a house that reminded her of her mother, Everly didn't want to be responsible for the history of a town she loathed.

She punched in the code, and the safe door opened with a click.

The contents were a bit of a surprise upon first inspection. There were large stacks of cash, like the kind you see in movies about bank heists. Nestled among the cash were boxes of various sizes. Everly opened one to find a ruby necklace. She remembered that necklace. Her mom had worn it once when Everly was a child to an anniversary party celebrating Splendid. The necklace had belonged to Queenie Palmer. Everly didn't doubt that the enormous, deep red gems were priceless. She put the necklace back in its place. Money and jewels were not of interest to her.

Toward the back of the large wall safe was a stack of papers, folders, and envelopes. Everly pulled these out, plopping them down on the worn green blotter on top of Eli Palmer's carved mahogany desk. Everly took a seat. There was a lot to go through, so she would have to stay focused on her goal: the deed to the lot on Dale Street.

Everly put her hands on the stack, then gazed back toward the still-open safe. The painting she'd taken down sat on the floor, leaning against the bottom of a bookcase lined with leather-bound books. She'd never really looked at it before, as she'd never spent much time in this room. But now she could tell the man in the portrait, the man in knee-high leather boots, a rifle in his hands, pointing down at the ground, was her ancestor. Portraits of both Eli and Queenie hung all over the house, so this wasn't a revelation. What gave Everly a start was the dog standing alongside Eli, a giant dog, his black, woolly fur muddied around the legs, his dark, fathomless eyes staring out of the portrait straight at Everly.

She froze in the chair as she stared at the dog. He looked exactly like the apparition she saw at Red Manor the night she and Rose were caught by the mayor. Was Eli Palmer's dog the hellhound?

With a renewed sense of urgency, Everly tackled the pile of paperwork before her. Halfway through, she came to a folder containing everything she'd been looking for. Within the covers of the tan legal folder were the deeds to every property her family owned, including the lot on Dale Street.

Everly gazed down at the deed in her hands, the dog, who may or may not be the hellhound, staring at her from the floor.

She looked from the dog to the deed, then back again. "The murdered family worked for the Palmers, the Palmers owned the home and the land where they were murdered. You," she said to the dog, "appeared before the axe murders. I wonder if you showed up before any of the other Red Rose murders. And why? Why did you appear to me and Rose at Red Manor? A threat? You're my entity, aren't you? The one who attached to me after that night." Staring at the dog, she chewed on her lip. "No, not a threat. There were two apparitions yesterday: one attacked me, and one saved me. Were you the savior? If so, you warned me of danger at Red Manor that night. Maybe you were warning the neighborhood before the axe murders, protecting people against the threat of the real hellhound."

Everly thought back to the articles. There had never been much written about suspects for these crimes. A normal community would have been up in arms, demanding that the police keep its citizens safe by keeping them aware. But, of course, Splendid's police force hadn't done that. Not until the axe murders, when a man was caught in another state by some miracle. The murders had stopped after that, but perhaps the killer had just changed his MO.

"Was it a Palmer?" Everly continued her musing out loud. "Was a Palmer responsible for the murders?"

She picked up another folder from the stack, papers from inside slipping out and onto the desk. They had jagged edges and strange words written on them, like *conjuring* and *cauldron*. The missing ritual pages from the notebook. "What the hell?"

Everly heard a floorboard creak behind her half a second before a hand reached around her, clamping a damp cloth to her mouth. Everly pushed the chair backward, straining forward in an attempt to twist away. But the hand on her face was so tight, and the arm around her waist was like a vise. She tried to fight, tried not to breathe, but she could only hold out so long before the sharp tang of vapor hit her lungs.

CHAPTER TWENTY-SIX

There was a dank smell reminiscent of moldy basements, a briny scent that was not as bright as ocean water, but putrid, like standing water.

Nausea bubbled in Everly's stomach, her head pounding at the temples. A sick taste sat at the back of her throat like she'd recently thrown up. Her hair had fallen over her face and was stuck in the sheen of sweat covering her from head to toe. She tried to reach up to brush the hair away, but couldn't move her arms.

Her mind was fuzzy, like she'd been electrocuted or … drugged. She forced her eyes open when all they wanted to do was stay closed. Even if her hair had not been in her face, she still wouldn't have been able to see, as her vision was blurry around the edges. She blinked over and over until her eyes adjusted. She flicked her head to the side to move her hair to take in the room.

Dim light flickered from a handful of candles set around the edges of the circular room. The walls were such a dark stone, they appeared to be painted black. There was a heavy, closed door in front of her. She tried to move her arms again and, again, then realized they were bound. A hollow, whooshing sound came from a dark opening to her left. The tunnel.

All the fog cleared from her mind in one moment. Realizing that she was in real trouble hit her like a bucket of ice water to the nervous system. She was in a chair, something that reminded her of an antique dental chair with a reclining back and headrest. Black leather thongs strapped her arms to the chrome armrests.

There was no one else in the damp room. She craned her neck around to try and see behind her, but she couldn't make out anything except the dark stone walls bathed in soft candlelight. The symbol of Roots and Wings was painted red on each wall. At least, she hoped it was paint. A faint sound of dripping water could be heard.

Panic swelled through her. Pulling her arms free of the leather straps felt impossible as, with each tug, the raw edges bit into her flesh. Her right arm was positioned so that the fleshy underside was turned up, as it is in the doctor's office when they draw blood.

"It wasn't a dream," she said to herself. This was the room, the chair, and the way she was bound in the nightmares of her youth.

She may have felt some smug satisfaction at being right if she hadn't been in such an obvious state of danger.

Freeing herself was the important thing. Everything else could come later.

Everly bent forward as far as she could, pulling her arm upward as much as possible. She opened her mouth, attempting to snatch at the ends of the leather fob with her teeth, straining her muscles, stretching her skin and bones as far as they would go. She managed to take hold of enough of the fob to loosen the strap, but only slightly. She tried again, this time getting more of the leather in her mouth, thrashing her head from side to side. The leather released a little more.

There was a sound of metal on metal, hinges giving way. Everly stopped what she was doing, panic swelling in her breast. A void seemed to open against the wall about thirty feet before her. The sound of footsteps echoed around the room as a figure emerged from the dark hole ahead. The figure was wearing a cloak, much like the ones described by Rose the night of the break-in.

The tall figure walked forward, his hands clasped in front of him. Everly wrenched her arm up, pulling with all her might to free herself from the chair. She was helpless in that position. If only she could stand her ground and have a fighting chance.

The figure stopped beside her feet, raised his hands, and pulled back his hood. Everly wasn't shocked to see Richard Hart, the mayor of Splendid and her old high school principal.

"I didn't know you were into BDSM, Mr. Hart. If you were, all you had to do was ask."

Hart cracked a sad sort of grin, the kind you give someone when they tell you they've been diagnosed with a terminal illness but are going to live their best life until the end.

Hart re-clasped his hands. "I can't tell you how very sorry I am that things have gotten to this point, Ms. Palmer. You should have been the one to usher us into a new age. Instead, you left the nest. It was your meddling that led to the death of your friend, you know. Poor little Leigh. It's a shame she was caught in the crossfire. Poor Fletcher, our newest member." Hart waved a hand as he began a stroll around the room. "As I think you already know, he's quite distraught. I hope that this unfortunate event doesn't make him want to tie up his purse strings."

Everly's brain still hurt from the chloroform. She tried to make sense of what Hart had just said. "This is all about money? Fletcher's money? Is that why you killed Leigh? She was going to tell us, wasn't she?"

Hart, behind her now as he walked in a slow circle, laughed like a cartoon villain. "Don't be silly, Everly. I believed that Leigh was going to tell you something she shouldn't, but what's more, Leigh was always so soft. She had to go before she warned you away. You were never leaving, Everly. Not this time. We need you here to not only continue to feed the town, Elsie is growing weaker after all, but we also need you here to settle down and carry on the Palmer line. We couldn't let Leigh interfere. Anyway, you need tougher skin when dealing with a wayward Palmer, and Fletcher isn't the only rich person in Splendid. No, this isn't about money. This is about blood."

At the mention of blood, Everly's mind went to her nightmares. This chair, the blood dripping from her arm. She tried to wrench her arm free again. The half-sitting, half-prone position she was in became more uncomfortable by the second, but she couldn't relax. She had to try to get free of the chair. "I don't understand," she said as she felt the strap give way. "What do you mean, this is about blood?"

Hart was still walking around her, his back to her now. Everly twisted her hand to hold on to the strap so it wouldn't fall to the ground, alerting him that she was partially free.

Hart came to a stop, again near her feet. "You haven't figured it out, Everly? I thought surely, with all the running around you've been doing, that you would have figured it out by now. Have your friends been too much of a distraction?" He eyed her with a disbelieving look.

"I've figured out that your little secret society killed Nathan, and I knew that Leigh, too, didn't die a natural death. Did Fletcher kill her? That's what I'm guessing, and I'm sure he was the one who attacked me at the house. I know that something happened to me here when I was little, that Roots and Wings are tied to everything in this city. That the Palmers are tied to a serial murderer and that the ghost of Eli Palmer's dog appears as some warning, but only concerning a Palmer descendant. I don't know anything about the hellhound." Everly felt stupid the second the words were out of her mouth. Her bulleted list of indictments would never hold up in a court of law or even the court of public opinion. She had no real evidence of any wrongdoing, and the more crazy shit she uncovered, the more she thought that maybe she was as insane as everyone seemed to believe.

Hart smiled, not the earlier sad grin, but a smile that reached his eyes. With his eyes full of joy, he looked more like the thirty-year-old man he was twenty years ago. "You have so many threads, Everly. So many loose threads."

Emphasis on the loose.

She didn't respond, hoping he would tie up those loose ends for her right before she freed herself to kick him in the balls.

His joyful smile turned smug. "Let's start from the beginning, shall we? I'm waiting on a couple more people, so there's no harm in wrapping up the mystery. You won't be talking to anyone ever again."

A stone dropped in Everly's empty gut. Stomach acid churned in a stomach that hadn't seen a real meal in days, bile backing up on her until she tasted it in the back of her throat. She was going to die in the cellar of Red Manor. Confirmation of where she was wasn't needed; she knew. All roads led back to Red Manor, after all. Whoever had kidnapped her had tied her up and taken her down to her basement. The entrance was probably easily opened with a sledgehammer. With Mom on the porch, she might not even have heard, and probably thought Everly was still inside the house. Even if Everly could free herself from the chair, how far would she get? Could she get back down the length of the tunnel in time, or was she sealed in that tomb with a man ten years her senior and twice her size? She had no weapons; she wasn't even trained in self-defense. All she could do was bide her time.

Everly tried to steady her breathing. She'd gone from being the end-all-be-all to expendable in three days. She had to keep Hart talking.

"From the beginning," she prompted. As much as she wanted to live, she also wanted to know the truth. All of it.

Hart inclined his head as he continued his walk around

her chair. "It all begins with the founding of Splendid, but we needn't spend much time there. Roots and Wings was founded with the town. Not only was Eli Palmer the founder of Splendid, but he was also the founding member of Roots. Roots was founded as a rather benign society. Rich, older gentlemen who kept an eye on the town, conducting under-the-table business with Splendid's growth in mind. Fast forward to 1910, the year of the first Red Rose murder. The identity of the murderer was never a secret, not really. Not to us, the members of the club, and certainly members of Roots knew exactly who the murderer was—your great-grandfather, and Eli's son. But it sounds like you were on track to figuring this out. There was talk among the members of Roots as to how to bring his madness to an end, for mad he was. A sociopath is what he would be called today. Reasoning with the man didn't work, and he couldn't be arrested, but he also couldn't be allowed to continue slashing the fair women of Splendid. The idea of an arrest was too unseemly, so the members of Roots came up with another idea. My grandfather was a student of the occult. He believed that by sacrificing your great-grandfather, by consuming his blood, the members of the society would gain certain powers. My grandfather had amassed quite a collection of rituals that the society had begun to perform with some success."

"Wait, what? You sick fucks ate my great-grandfather instead of turning him in?"

Hart huffed a laugh. "They didn't eat him, dear, they drank his blood. Almost all of it. When they had finished the ceremony, they took the rest of his blood and poured it out in strategic places all over Splendid, and do you know what?"

Everly choked on a gasp. She sputtered as she coughed, spittle on her chin that she couldn't wipe away.

Hart laughed again. "Come on, Everly. You tell me what happened."

Hallucinogenics had never been Everly's drug of choice.

But she imagined if she'd ever dared to let a tab of acid dissolve on her tongue, this was the sort of surreal nightmare she'd have. She swallowed, her eyes closing for the briefest moment just to absorb what she heard and what she believed. "I'm guessing the town came alive." For Everly, a lightbulb went off, blood rushing in her ears. "That's what's wrong with Splendid."

"I wouldn't say wrong, Everly. I would say right. Splendid is a living, breathing entity that takes care of us as long as we take care of her."

"But you only fed the town once."

"Wrong. We have continued to feed our town ever since."

The stone in Everly's stomach turned into sludge. "Palmer blood."

"Precisely. We need Palmer blood to survive. Your mother has always been a willing participant, as all the Palmers since your great-grandfather have been. But you, you had to be difficult. During your first bloodletting, you made such a fuss, not only then but for years afterward, that your mother had to contrive a story about a botched blood draw at the doctor's office. After that, we had to drug you to get your blood. Your mother was good enough to visit you in New Orleans when it was time for more. Hers is weakening as she ages, but luckily, it doesn't take a lot. A few drops a year, left to absorb in strategic places around town. I'm sure you've seen the symbol at different locations, all areas sacred to our history. She was a little squeamish when it came to drawing your blood, but a small pill crushed into her famous spaghetti sauce and a slim hypodermic made the job easier."

Everly nearly gagged on acid burning the back of her throat. "Mom was part of this?"

"Of course, she was, Everly. She's indeed weaker now, unable to provide as she once did, so we needed to keep you here, but Elsie continues to reap the benefits of our sacrifice."

"You mean our sacrifice, not yours."

"True, the sacrifice is yours alone. The town doesn't seem interested in blood from any other bloodline. We have to give the town what it wants, Everly. Anyone would be happy to provide a few vials of blood to continue living in such a blessed place."

"So, you need me?"

"We needed you, Everly, but that time has passed. Like your great-grandfather, you've become too much of a loose cannon, albeit in a different way. We took precautions, years ago, of freezing your mother's eggs. It isn't ideal, but if we drain you and store your blood, that should keep us until the child is old enough to begin the ritual bloodletting. Splendid is degrading. People are getting sick, the first sign of things to come. Splendid will always give up the people before itself."

"Telling me you stored my mom's eggs is gross enough, but now you're telling me that you plan to kill me and then grow my sibling with the sole intent of taking its blood for the rest of its life?"

"Exactly. I always knew you were as smart as your friends, maybe even smarter."

"Why do I only have this one scar? If you took my blood so many times, there would be more scars."

"A simple spell crafted by my grandfather. Once the ritual is over, your arm is healed quite easily."

"Easy for you." Dizziness began to wash over her, lingering vapors from the chloroform reinvading her lungs. Everly bit her lip to keep herself awake. She wasn't done yet. "Did you send an animal to attack me?"

"What do you mean?"

"Two hellhounds, one that belonged to Eli Palmer?" Everly began pulling her left hand from the strap.

"I don't know what you're on about, Everly, but magic has been another gift from Splendid to its people. If someone conjured a hellhound to attack you, it wasn't me."

Eli's dog was protecting me, then. Maybe if I stall a little more, he'll show up again.

Footsteps echoed far off, the soles of shoes hitting the stone with rapid steps.

"Ah." Hart raised a hand into the air. "My right hand has arrived."

Fresh terror flooded Everly's senses. She heard a whooshing in her ears as if she had pressed a conch shell to the side of her head. Her heart rate spiked, adrenaline coursing through her, causing her extremities to shake.

She could only think about one thing through all the fear and instability she felt in every molecule of her body. "Does my mom know you're going to kill me?"

Hart had been looking over his shoulder at the void from which he had earlier appeared. When she spoke, he glanced back in her direction. "Poor Everly. Of course she knows."

She took the news like a slap to the face, her head lolling back as she stared at the ceiling. "What about Rose?"

"Rose Hibbard is fast becoming Splendid's new figurehead. All she knows is what you've told her, but Rose is good at looking away when it suits her. Elsie will tell her you ran back to New Orleans, she'll take our word for it, and Rose will never be the wiser because Rose won't bother to seek out the truth. She's enjoying her life of fame and fortune as anyone would."

Everly lowered her head, fixing Hart in Rose's famous death stare. "Rose is a lot deeper than you give her credit for. She'll figure it out. The five of us were special for our minds, and Rose's might be the sharpest. I always thought Nathan was the smartest of us, but now I'm pretty sure it's always been Rose."

Hart laughed, waving her off like he thought she was the dumbest woman alive. "It hardly matters now. I'll be able to handle Rose. You should be more concerned about what comes next."

The footsteps, Everly realized, had been bounding down the stairs. Now, they were at the mouth of the void. A figure was coming into view, but the cavernous, dimly lit cellar made it hard to discern whom she was looking at.

"Fletcher?" she asked, narrowing her eyes to get a better look at the face underneath the heavy, black hood. The figure was tall, like Fletcher, with a similar body type and bearing. He blamed her for Leigh's death, so why wouldn't he come to help kill her?

But when the figure moved up alongside Hart, hands sweeping up to the hood to push it back, Everly leaned over the arm of the chair she was strapped to and vomited on the floor. There was no more holding on to the hot bile that burned her throat. She saw stars as she heaved a second time, bringing up nothing but hot, choking air. She took deep, labored breaths, a line of spittle slipping off her lip.

"You could have had it all, Everly. You were to inherit all the Palmer glory, the money, the properties, and you and clueless Jonathan Hunt would have produced beautiful children. It is sad. But now, this man and I"—he clapped Nathan Stratton on the shoulder—"this man and I have to clean up your mess."

Everly had to do everything she could not to pull her free hand up to wipe her mouth. That one free hand was the only advantage she had. Instead, she let the sick fester in the corner of her mouth as she stared at Nathan, his face pale, his eyes on the floor. "This is not how I imagined our reunion. I guess this day couldn't get any worse, could it? And you let everyone think you're dead. Does your family know you're alive?" Everly was happy about one thing—all the trauma from the past couple of days had left her partially numb inside. While her heartbeat raged and her stomach was sick, this new revelation didn't add much more to the panic beating a drum in her brain.

Hart chuckled. "Oh, don't be stupid, dear. This day is about to get much worse." He turned away from them, Everly half-reclined, her stomach muscles burning, Nathan still staring at the ground.

"My mom and sister don't know." Nathan looked at her then, the strangeness of hearing his bass-like voice after so many years hitting Everly like a slap to the face. This was Nathan, the best friend of her childhood. The boy who'd wiped her tears when she fell off her bike and broke her arm, holding it up for her while he helped her home. The boy who'd come out to her in the eighth grade, whispering as they lay on the expanse of lawn between their homes, gazing up at the night sky. This same boy, now a man, stood in front of her after deceiving everyone they'd loved, knowing full well she was going to die.

He seemed to sense her thoughts. Although she remained silent, he looked at her with pain in his eyes. "I did my best, weirdo. My death was meant to draw you back, but once you were here, I tried to chase you away. Charlie was to make sure Rose knew he wanted things from my office. I knew you would find the note in my window and go with her, at least I hoped. If you're anything like the Everly of old, you still have the same questions burning inside you. I couldn't make it too easy. I didn't want Hart to catch on. Once I unleashed the hellhound and scared you and Rose at my house, I thought for sure you would leave."

"You ransacked your own room? So, Hart knew nothing about your notebook?" Everly's mind was having trouble keeping up.

"He knew nothing. He tried to keep you out of my office simply because he thought you'd find evidence that I was still alive."

"That's enough," Hart said, his eyes narrowed at Nathan. "I'll deal with your betrayal later."

"I always want what's best for Splendid, Richard. This time, I was torn. I know now we're at the point of no return."

"You're really going to let this happen?" Everly croaked at him.

When he didn't so much as flinch, she knew he was useless.

Everly kept her gaze on Nathan but clocked Hart with her peripheral. He looked to be heading toward a metal table, sitting against the wall. The bloodletting was about to happen.

The options available were few. She knew her chances against Hart had been slim, but now there were two men in the room, one of whom was Nathan. He was still at peak physicality. The only thing Everly could think of, which would give her any sort of chance, was to grab whatever instrument Hart had, slash him, preferably in the throat, slash Nathan when he inevitably lunged at her, then free herself and run. She almost laughed at the astronomically low odds. Who was it who said, *Never tell me the odds?*

All she could do was try. All she could do was go down fighting. She refused to lie there like a limp fish and let them kill her. If they wanted her dead, they'd have to work for it, perhaps losing some of their blood in the process.

Focusing was not easy. Her body was shaking from the cold and the fear, her heart raged dangerously in her chest, and her breath was shallow, but along with the fear, she was angry. There was no more room for anger at Rose and the others. Fletcher aside, Jonathan, Leigh, and Rose didn't know the extent of the Splendid madness. No, she was no longer angry at them. She was angry at her mother, Hart, and mostly, Nathan. She was still shocked to see him standing in front of her in the same robe the others wore. Maybe she should have guessed, his ancestor's name was on the original list of Roots members, but so had all their ancestors been. She wanted to say something to him, wanted to know how he could deceive her like that. Had it all been bullshit? The entirety of their close friendship?

But there wasn't time to spew any diatribe his way. Hart pushed the metal table over, the caster wheels squealing as they turned over the rough concrete floor.

"We're not wasting any more time waiting for the doctor. You and I will put Everly out of her misery without him." Hart spoke to Nathan over the screeching of the metal table.

A mist materialized in the far corner between the tunnel

opening and the door that led to Red Manor's first floor. Eli Palmer's dog stood, mute and gray, in the corner, staring at her with his sad eyes. She stared at him, willing him to go after Hart, but all he did was stand, his half-embodied form waving back and forth like a flag in the wind.

"Do something," she said to him.

Nathan winced. He thought she'd been talking to him, but he didn't move beyond that. The dog didn't move either. Maybe she would have been more surprised to see Nathan if she hadn't seen ghost dogs. Everly supposed it made sense that Eli's dog couldn't attack the living, only the conjured hellhound. When that realization hit her, she almost gave up.

Hart pushed the table to within a few inches of her free hand, a hand no one but her knew was free. There were scalpels, tubes, a bucket, and the antique fleam, iodized and rusted. Picking up a syringe, he flicked the tube to pop the air bubbles, then glanced down at Everly. "We're not monsters. I'll put you right to sleep. You won't feel a thing."

He stepped around the table, his goal to plunge that needle into her upper arm. He leaned over her, grabbing hold of her shoulder. Everly knew this was the only chance she'd ever get. Pulling her arm out of the loosened strap, she lunged to the side, her left arm still bound, grabbing for a scalpel. She twisted around, plunging the scalpel into Hart's neck as he leaned over her. It all happened so fast, Everly couldn't believe she'd actually done it. She hesitated for a second in her shock, staring at Hart as he screamed. He dropped the syringe, staggering backward, his hand flying to his neck where the scalpel was still lodged.

"Don't pull it out," Nathan yelled. He ran by the table, knocking it out of the way so Everly couldn't grab another weapon, then ran to where Hart had slumped against the wall.

Everly went to work. With her free hand, she unstrapped her left arm, then moved to the strap that held both her legs down. She fumbled a bit, her hands sweaty, wiped them on her jeans, then pulled her legs free.

She swung her feet to the ground, standing as she glanced behind her. Nathan was bent over Hart, now sitting on the cement floor, blood pouring over the hand at his neck. Hart had gone ghost white, his eyes staring straight ahead.

Everly turned to run for the tunnel, Eli Palmer's dog standing at attention alongside the opening, but didn't consider that she'd be wobbly from the drugs, the vomiting, and the general fear of death that had permeated her senses for the last half hour. Her legs, shaky and exhausted, failed as she tried to step forward, and she went down, hard, on both knees. She grabbed onto the side of the chair to pull herself back up. That's when she locked eyes with Nathan. Hart had slumped to the side, both of his hands down at his sides. Nathan let him go, and he fell over, dead.

There was no time to feel anything about this. Nathan was on his feet.

A new wave of panic-driven adrenaline hit her nervous system. Everly lurched to her feet, running toward the void, her arms flailing to keep her balance. Nathan's footsteps, pounding concrete, were gaining.

She felt something like fingertips swipe at her back. She planned to keep going, throwing herself into the void. Maybe there was a door she could slam on his arm. But before she reached the opening, another figure emerged.

This one was not clad in a ritualistic robe, this one wore a stylish, no doubt expensive, pantsuit, a gun held in an outstretched hand.

"Get behind me," Rose yelled one second before firing the gun.

CHAPTER TWENTY-SEVEN

The morning had been hell. Rose thought she knew hellish mornings, but she had been naïve. Fighting through an Ambien-induced migraine that no amount of caffeine seemed able to alleviate, dealing with the fresh feelings of loss compounding the grief she'd already been living with, then fighting with Ever had given her a new definition of *the seventh layer of hell.*

After Ever had left her house in a blaze of misfit glory, Rose had dressed and taken another half a bottle of pain relievers. When she felt somewhat able to face the day, she'd left the house with zero intention of ever seeing Ever again. But the bitch's wallet had slipped out of her back pocket, fallen onto Rose's dining room floor, and Rose wanted to make sure there was no way Ever could miss her flight. Why Ever couldn't carry a purse like everyone else was annoying enough.

She had intended to leave her car running outside the Palmer house, run up to the porch, and drop the wallet there. Instead, what she saw made her question whether she should ever take a sleep aid again. As she idled a couple of houses down, at war with herself as to whether or not she should take the wallet up to the house after all or chuck it out the window, she saw Nathan, she was sure it was Nathan, pull down the long drive to park behind the house. Shock moved through her system like jolts of electricity. Her instinct to run to him and jump into his massive arms almost won out. But she didn't do that. Instead, she crept from her car up the sidewalk, where for another five minutes, she watched as Nathan spoke to Elsie on the porch in a hushed voice. When Elsie said through tears that Ever was in the office and to be as gentle with her as possible, Rose swore to herself, returned to her car, and went home to collect a handgun that was accumulating dust on the top shelf of her giant walk-in closet. She'd purchased the gun for protection while living in San Francisco during college, had never once fired it, and had no idea if the thing even worked.

Apparently, it did.

When she returned to Ever's house, she walked right through the front door, giving Elsie, who was now in the living room, a fright. Rose demanded to know where Ever was, and Elsie had said to find the tunnel in the basement and to hurry. "*Please hurry*," she'd said, her eyes pleading with Rose.

Nathan didn't die. He wasn't even that injured, all things considered. Having never fired a gun before, Rose wasn't the best shot. She hit him in his upper arm, enough to knock him off balance so they could run.

Outside, they were met by police and EMTs. Nathan was patched up before being taken into custody. One of the officers wanted to arrest Ever for killing the mayor, but when the chief of police arrived, he merely shooed the officer away. Chief Penrose took Ever and Rose aside to get a full account of what happened.

"Nice pin you've got there," Rose said, pointing to the small, golden infinity symbol with the rooty tree in one loop and the wing in the other.

The chief shifted uncomfortably in the grass. The press had gathered on the sidewalk, a reporter from the local news station preparing herself to go on air.

Rose had one arm around Ever, who shook against her, her other hand on her hip. "I guess that most people in town don't know about your little Rosemary's Baby club, but they do now." The chief looked over his shoulder at the female reporter. Rose continued, "That's right. We went to school with Anya. I made a quick call to her right before I shot that spineless jellyfish in the arm. This story is about to blow up. So, here's what's going to happen. With the mayor out, that leaves an opening. It won't be hard to convince the city council to name me interim mayor. Ever here will be taking over Elsie's spot in the club. It's time for a new generation to take control of this city." Rose now had to deal with a different pain, the pain of knowing Nathan's death had been an act. She wasn't sure what hurt more—the initial horror of his sudden demise or the sudden reveal that it had all been a lie.

"That isn't all." Ever clung to Rose's side like she was in danger of drowning. "There won't be any more Palmer bloodletting. We will no longer be feeding the town."

"What?" Rose whispered in her ear.

The chief placed a hand on his gun belt, leaning in so close Rose could smell the coffee on his breath. "You can't do that. We have no idea what will happen if we cut off the supply."

"Splendid was a normal city once. I guess that things will go back to the way they were. The weather will normalize, and crime will return. These are things we'll have to face like everyone else. I will no longer supply this society with my blood, and I'll be damned if future generations of Palmers will be used in this way ever again."

"I have no idea what she's talking about, but I'm with her." Rose tightened her grip on Ever's shoulder. "This society will come into the light. We will partner with the town to improve this city. Work in the shadows will cease."

Three Months Later

The breakfast nook had become Everly's favorite place. After three months of living with Rose, Pancake had finally come out of her hidey hole and had very nearly let Everly pet her twice. Sunning herself in a ray of sun on the gleaming wood floor, Pancake lounged while Everly sipped her coffee.

To the right of her hand, sitting face up on the table, her phone buzzed. Elsie's name appeared on the screen, another day, another text. Elsie had tried to either call or text Everly every day since Everly had been attacked and kidnapped at her mother's behest. The texts and voicemails all revealed the same general sentiment: *I'm sorry. Please let me explain. I told Rose where to find you.* Or some variation. Everly had no interest in making nice with Elsie. In a majority vote, she'd taken Elsie's spot in Roots and Wings. Everly had been wrong about her mom not being a member. Eli Palmer had originally been Draco, but that had changed once the bloodletting began. The Palmer member then became known as Andromedus, the chained lady. Come to find out, only four people in the society performed the ritual of the blood: Elsie, the mayor, Doctor Sprague and his descendants, and Nathan. The other three members knew but were not directly involved. These four, and their ancestors, had played the biggest roles in the feeding of the town. The mayor, who had always been a Hart since the founding of Splendid, was always the ritual leader. A Sprague made sure the bloodlettings were safe. A Stratton, in this case, Nathan, was always the henchman, and there was always a Palmer whose blood was freely given to the cause.

Nathan was now on the hook for faking his death and killing Leigh. He was in hotter water than he probably imagined.

Well, Rose was the interim mayor now. The city council

was easy to convince. She already had such intense support that a win during the general election was guaranteed. Once everything had calmed down and Everly could spill, she'd revealed everything to Rose, including the fact that they were sisters.

"Well, duh," was Rose's response. Then, "I guess your mom is worse than mine was, huh?"

"I didn't think it was a contest," Everly had said.

"Well," Rose responded. "If it were, you'd win."

The doorbell rang as Everly took another swig of coffee. Pancake's head perked up, languid eyes looking to Everly.

"Same, Pancake. I don't want to deal with anyone either." Everly got up from the nook, her gray sweats warm from sitting in the sun. She hadn't left the house much in the last three months. While Rose was taking control of the city, kissing babies, and creating new policies, Everly was hiding from the light like Nosferatu, typing away on Rose's old laptop. Writing about what had happened was therapeutic, and the idea had come to Everly to turn her ordeal into a book. She needed to make money somehow.

The doorbell rang a second time as Everly stepped into the foyer. "Coming," she called. She pushed herself against the door, checking the peephole. The last thing she wanted was to open the door to her mother. Jonathan was procuring small-batch whiskey from a distillery on the Western Slope, so she knew it wasn't him. He'd wanted her to join him on the trip, but she wasn't quite ready to be out in public. Being away from him was hard. Jonathan had been with her every second that he didn't have to be at his bar, and they planned on being together every second they could from then on out.

Fletcher stood on the porch, hands shoved into the pockets of tan slacks.

"Shit," Everly whispered. The second-to-last person she wanted to see was Fletcher. She hadn't seen him since the night of Leigh's death. As far as she knew, no one had. Rose had gone to the Decomposition House several times, and he had never opened the door to her. Rose had become so worried at one point that she called for a welfare check. Even Jonathan, one of his best friends, couldn't get him on the phone.

She watched through the peephole as Fletcher made a face. "I know you're here, Everly. Rose sent me over. I just saw her at City Hall. I want to talk to you about a few things. You're safe with me, I promise. I don't see any loose bricks around." He passed a hand over his face. "That was a bad joke."

Everly stepped away from the door, her stomach going a little wobbly. She opened the door. "Hey."

"Hey," he said, pointing off to the side. "Let's sit out here. I think this is the last nice day we'll have for a while."

It was true. The forecast called for a blustery few days ahead. After the warm, stable weather of the last hundred years or so, the residents of Splendid were in a near panic. Rose and Anya had gone on air to discuss how to keep warm, shovel snow, and keep pipes from freezing. Without the Palmer blood supply, the residents of Splendid were about to experience their first winter. Everly wondered if her mom would try to work around them, but it seemed she hadn't.

She stepped out onto the porch. There was already a chill in the air, a cold breeze blowing leaves around the yard in little swirling tornadoes. But the sun was still warm, cutting through the cold in the air, warming her bare toes as she stood in a patch of sun. She leaned against the white porch railing, her hands behind her, braced for support.

Fletcher sat in Rose's favorite rocking chair, a black spindle-back antique. He leaned forward, his elbows on his thighs, his hands folded together. He stared at the grass. "I guess I'll start with an apology."

"You don't—" Everly started.

Fletcher cut her off. "I do. I've been unfair to you since high school, Everly." He leaned back in the chair, the old spindles creaking slightly as he sat against them. "Rose told me everything, like everything. It's honestly hard for me to fathom how much of what she said could be true, but the weather is changing, and I guess, according to Rose, there was a carjacking last week. There's never been so much as a bar fight in Splendid. I'm not going to pretend I understand how your family's blood made the town so perfect, I don't, and maybe I don't even care. I'm still dealing with my problems." He glanced off to the side. "Anyway, I just wanted to apologize. None of this was your fault. You were a victim as much as Leigh. This whole Nathan thing is so nuts." He roughly rubbed his eyes. "I also need you to know that I was just the money. I knew about the society and was technically a member, but I had no idea they'd been siphoning your blood."

Everly remained silent, which is what she did when she had no idea what to say. She was tired of crying, so instead of letting any emotion take hold, she bit her lip. All she could think to say was, "How are your kids?"

Fletcher shook his head as he stared off. "Not great. Thank god for our parents. They've helped me immensely, shouldering most of my parental responsibilities for now." Fletcher's gaze darted to Everly's face. "I think I know why Leigh went back to your house the night she died."

Shock hit Everly's system like a live wire. She and Rose had speculated endlessly about what Leigh had returned to tell them. She desperately wanted to know what had gotten her friend killed, but didn't want Fletcher to sit with this pain. "It's okay, Fletch," she said. "We don't have to talk about this anymore."

"This will be the last time, trust that." He fixed her with a stare she couldn't quite decipher. "I'm pretty sure she found out Hart was involved in all this."

"How?"

"She received a text right before she went back to your house. According to Rose, Hart had been monitoring our texts. The text was from Leigh's cousin, who works at the bank. The text was nothing but gossip, but apparently,

Nathan wasn't as well off as we all thought. Bad investments. He was about to lose the family home when a corporation swooped in last minute to save him. The corporation was called Hart Industries."

Everly crossed her arms. She was starting to feel the chill of the air through her sweats. "You should pass this information on to the DA. Let them take it from here. I just can't reconcile the Nathan we knew with Nathan the killer."

"Tell me about it. Makes me never want to leave my house, and I've already told the DA. It's so hard to believe that Nathan, my best friend for over forty years, could have hurt my wife, could have hurt you." Fletcher closed his eyes, his head lolling against the back of the rocking chair.

"I know. My mom was involved in all this, too. The insanity was deep."

"Yeah, no shit." Fletcher sighed, then opened his eyes to look at Everly. "I haven't held Leigh's funeral yet."

She nodded. "Rose and I were wondering about that."

"I couldn't face the idea of saying goodbye for good. I had her cremated per her wishes, and she was interred in her family's crypt. If you wanted to go and visit her, that's where she is. Maybe I can have a memorial one day, but I'm just not there yet."

"I get it. Saying goodbye is hard."

Fletcher stood up, the chair rocking behind him. "Don't be a stranger, Everly."

Everly thought he might hug her, but instead, he smiled, a half sort of smile, before walking away.

She had no plans to ever be a stranger again. She and Rose had had several long discussions about changing the town's legacy. Splendid was her town, but more importantly, now that Roots and Wings had ceased its secret operations, Splendid was everyone's town. If Fletcher could survive, if she and Rose could survive, then maybe there was still hope to be found in the little mountain town of Splendid, Colorado.

The hero didn't die after all, not literally, anyway.

ACKNOWLEDGEMENTS

Thank you so much to Melissa Keir at Inkspell Publishing for continuing to support my writing endeavors. Thank you to Elizabeth Quinlan for always reading my first drafts and providing such important feedback. I can't thank my friends and family enough for their endless love and support. Finally, thank you to Emily's World of Design for the beautiful cover and Yezanira Venecia for the insightful edits.

DON'T MISS ANOTHER FABULOUS SUPERNATURAL SERIES BY AD BRAZEAU- AVAILABLE NOW IN EBOOK AND PRINT!

Deepest Midnight

True love never dies.

For Millicent, a once French noblewoman turned immortal vampire, forever is a long time to live in despair. The love of her life is murdered the night she becomes immortal. Over two hundred years later, she locks eyes with an English actor, who happens to look exactly like her long-dead love.

Sadness turns to happiness as Millicent and Jack find

passion in each other's arms. Their fling quickly turns serious as Millicent finds joy once again—and possibly her one true love.

Their relationship becomes complicated by her own uncertainty and Jack's mortality. The other man in Millicent's life, her sire, Alexandre, isn't making the situation any easier. When Alexandre puts his foot down, Millicent must decide if she's going to continue to be led by others or take the reins and drive the outcome of her life.

Deepest Midnight is set in modern-day Savannah, Ga, with occasional glimpses back to 18t- century France. This is the first book in The Immortal Kindred Series.

EXCERPT

I reach into my clutch to take out my phone. Someone may as well get lucky tonight. Before I can begin my text, Alexandre is next to me. Being psychically linked to him stinks sometimes. Ok, all the time. If I wasn't so lazy, I would learn how to shield my thoughts.

I put my phone away. He says, "You know I hate texting."

"Why are you whispering? Who could possibly hear us?" I ask, in my sweetest southern belle accent. Irritating him is what I do best, although he doesn't always take the bait.

"Do you see her?" He pauses, looking around. "There she is in the back, next to the man with the copper hair. Don't you have a thing for gingers, Mills?" He tugs on my arm, pointing with his other hand, as I look up.

Alexandre starts explaining how he is going to approach her. I roll my eyes. He thinks he can just walk up to a world-famous movie star, throw up an eyebrow, and she'll be stripping naked. The annoying thing is, she probably will. On the last half of my eye roll, I lock eyes with a man who was murdered over two hundred years ago. All the breath leaves my body.

Rebel Heart

Always and Forever

Annie is a Culper Spy captured by Hessian soldiers. Powerful and mysterious Captain Thayer Emmerich takes mercy and releases her. Annie is inexplicably drawn to the handsome German, but she hates the feeling of powerlessness the enemy has left her with. Annie would give anything to be stronger.

One evening at the famous Green Dragon Tavern, Annie befriends the ethereal Millicent. Soon after meeting Millicent, Annie discovers her secret--her new friend isn't human. Millicent introduces Annie to her maker, Alexandre, and Annie joins their preternatural family.

Annie finally has the strength and freedom she needs to aid the revolution and see Thayer, once again. The two discover a passion neither has known before. But, too many complications exist for the pair to find happily ever after. Not only are they fighting on opposite sides of the war, the evil Emilia Romanov has plans for Thayer that do not include a love affair.

Rebel Heart is set in 18th century Boston and Savannah, as well as modern day Germany and France. This is the second book in The Immortal Kindred Series.

EXCERPT

Captain Emmerich took one brisk look to each side, then walked with an air of confident command toward the edge of the camp. It was dark with only a few lanterns lit and very few people about. This helped ease my anxiety. I tried walking with the same confidence, which was more difficult with my head down. The absurd cap threatened to fall off any minute, which would send a cascade of auburn curls falling around my shoulders.

Just as we were nearing the tree line, and I was beginning to relax, a soldier came running around the corner of a tent, right into the captain. The soldier snapped to attention, saluting. Captain Emmerich did the same, saying something in German. The young man relaxed, moving away.

As he walked by me, he looked me dead in the face, stopping in his tracks. I immediately put my head back down, but it was too late. It was obvious I was a woman in a man's uniform. There was no hiding this fact. The young man looked back at Captain Emmerich, turning as if he was about to run. The captain grabbed him by the neck with one hand. A sickening crunch reached my ears, right before the man crumpled into the mud.

"That was unfortunate," was all he said. The coldness of his voice shook me more than what he had just done.

I tried to hide my shock but knew I wasn't succeeding. "Why are you doing this for me? To kill your own man, it doesn't make sense," I said, still staring down at the young soldier.

"I'm beginning to wonder," he said as he grabbed my arm, yanking me into the dark woods. The trees looked ominous, and I hesitated just for a moment. Captain Emmerich took a handful of my uniform, at my shoulder this time, hauling me stumbling alongside him.

The King of Kings

Love has no limits...

Alexandre has retreated from the world. He has no one to love, nowhere to call home. While licking his wounds in the middle of nowhere, Alexandre is approached by Irish lass, Bria. She has a proposal for him; to follow her to Ireland and fight demons.

Alexandre finds this amusing, but intriguing. More than anything, he is curious to see the individual who sent Bria, someone from his ancient past.

In Ireland, Alexandre confronts a dilemma greater than fighting demons. He must face down fiends of all kinds, deciding once and for all who he really is. Sparks fly between Bria and Alexandre, adding to the already complicated situation. Can a bad boy vampire really change?

The King of Kings is set in southern Ireland with a glimpse back to Ancient Egypt.

EXCERPT

The finely decorated lobby was full of posh men and

women, all wearing their best designer clothes and bespoke suits. Bria wasn't fazed in the least by her surroundings as she devoured a granola bar, crumbs falling to the marble floor. She was wildly out of place here and I kind of loved it. Her flaming hair was enough to draw attention. Her clothing, which screamed survivalist, made her that much more conspicuous.

I moved up behind her. "You deserve a spanking for the ruckus in the hallway."

"The man who spanks me is suicidal," she said in a loud voice, drawing even more looks from the guests and staff. Bria began walking toward the glittering revolving door, not bothering to see if I followed.

We took the train to the coast, making it just in time. Bria chided me the entire way for "sleeping in". I couldn't wait until we were on the boat with what I hoped was a roaring motor.

Goddess of the Moon

An impossible attraction. An apocalyptic threat.
After vanquishing a Celtic death demon, Selene should

be kicking back and enjoying some free time. However, her life is anything but relaxed. She must travel to Romania, the last place she'd ever thought she'd be, facing another demon threat. Just another day at the office for the daughter of Cleopatra.

The situation soon escalates. The simple problem Selene thought she was facing, becomes intense--FAST. The dilemma is much greater than she initially feared. Throw in a sexy witch she doesn't want to be attracted to, and her life really gets complicated.

Overconfidence leads Selene to make a mistake which could cost everything. Can she unravel the mystery before it's too late? Or will her latest nemesis be the death of her and those she loves?

Goddess of the Moon *is the fourth book of The Immortal Kindred Series and is set primarily in Brasov, Romania.*

EXCERPT

Before I could pick up the first trunk, I heard it. The dull sound of cloven feet pawing at the soft grass. Not a tone a mortal could hear, but for me, the scraping was as clear as a bell. The sound barely preceded the smell. Demons typically had some sort of pungent, unpleasant odor. This guy was no different. He smelled of days' old refuse rotting in the sun.

I scrunched up my nose, releasing my tote which contained my laptop, letting it fall without grace to the earth. It was a good thing I paid extra for the durable case. If I was reading the situation correctly, the creature had me in its sights and would charge at any moment.

I knew what it was before I saw it, but this was not one of the creatures I had been hired to vanquish. The martolea were deceptive shapeshifters who could change their form at will. This one chose the form of a medium-size hound, as they most often did. Their diminutive size would lead one to believe they couldn't possibly be much of a threat. But, as with a vicious dog, these guys were deadly and strong.

Dark Star

The compelling final story in the enchanting series which began with Deepest Midnight....

The Immortal Kindred gather together as chaos erupts. Two of their own have gone missing, sucked back in time. Vampire demigod Selene messed with the wrong goddess of death. Now they're all in danger.

Millicent and Annie come face to face with the distant past. No longer immortal, they must draw on their inner strength to see them through travails long thought dead and buried.

Tash, the witch, draws on every spell he knows to bring the women home as he taps into the power of the dark star. Will it be enough to grant the immortals their happily ever after? Will the goddess, Nephthys, put an end to everything they know and love?

Dark Star is an epic adventure that will take you all over the globe and through time itself.

EXCERPT

After losing track of how far I'd gone, the path gave way to a clearing. At the center of the clearing was the cabin, as it was the night I came here in desperation. The assault on my senses was profound. It was like moving from one moment of déjà vu to another. I closed my eyes, my feet swaying a bit underneath me.

The small, rounded door swung wide. There he was. My breath all but stopped. Alexandre, dressed as a peasant in a loose white tunic over beige pants, stood with one hand on the open door and the other stretched out toward me. Here he was, the Jupiter from my dreams who became my maker, my friend, my lover, and almost my killer.

I admit, I wanted to run to him, to allow him to take me in his arms as he did the night my world turned upside down. I knew he would hold me tight, keep away everything that scared me. But I resisted. This me knew better than to trust him so blindly.

AVAILABLE IN EBOOK AND PRINT WHERE BOOKS ARE SOLD

ABOUT THE AUTHOR

A.D. Brazeau is an award-winning author who writes what she loves. From dark and fantastical fairytale retellings to quirky romance and everything in between, she loves nothing more than to immerse herself in new worlds. A.D. Brazeau is a book-obsessed wife, mother, and dog lover who grew up surrounded by stories. Not much has changed. A.D. is from Colorado Springs, CO.

www.ingramcontent.com/pod-product-compliance
Lightning Source LLC
Chambersburg PA
CBHW020051180626
46812CB00006B/2285